BLOOD STREET

CARL ALVES

BLOOD STREET

CARL ALVES

Paul,

Never go against the family.

Weaving Dreams Publishing
Watseka, IL

True Grit Publishing

(an imprint of Weaving Dreams Publishing)

Copyright © 2012 by Carl Alves

ISBN # 978-1-937148-18-8

Library of Congress Control Number
2012908104

www.truegritpublishing.com

Cover Art by Jason Williams

Printed in the United States of America
10 9 8 7 6 5 4 3 2

Dedication

I would like to dedicate my novel *Blood Street* to my awesome
boys, Max and Alex, and my loving wife, Michelle, without
whom this wouldn't be possible.

Acknowledgments

I would like to thank all of the people who made this novel possible.

Special thanks go to Benjamin Kane Ethridge and JG Faherty for their keen insight in helping me whip this novel into shape.

I would like to thank the great community of writers who supported me. Although this is a large list, I would like to specifically acknowledge Tim Marquitz, Ronald Malfi, Adam Cesare, Christopher Payne, Cyn Vespia, Brad Carpenter, Deborah Leblanc, Angel Leigh McCoy, Martel Sardina, Mara Hodges, Scott Nicholson, and the late Michael Louis Calvillo.

Also, my thanks go to Jason Williams for the fantastic piece of artwork for the cover of *Blood Street*.

Finally, I would like to thank my family and friends for all of the support over the years, in particular Michelle, Max, and Alex.

Chapter I

The Goat was worried, though he tried not to show it. He checked his watch again for the fifth time in so many minutes. *Never let them see any weakness.* But inside there was no hiding how he was feeling. He had been waiting an hour for Johnny Gunns inside the restaurant. Johnny was never late. He didn't always have the money, but he always showed.

Where the hell was Johnny? They met here at Frankie's Steaks every Tuesday night at nine, with Johnny always arriving first.

Something must have happened. The Goat checked his cell for messages. Nothing. He dialed Johnny's cell, but there was no answer. Then he paged Johnny. Doing his best to keep his cool, he finished sucking down his soda. He took a bite of his greasy cheesesteak, but his anxiety only grew like a three-alarm fire.

Frankie Angiolini, the owner of the joint, came over to The Goat's booth, putting a hand on his shoulder. "Everything okay?"

"Yeah, no problem, Frankie," The Goat said.

In his late fifties, Frankie made payments to the organization The Goat worked for in exchange for protection and other favors. The Goat was also Frankie's bookie. So far he hadn't had to hurt Frankie, which was good because the cheesesteaks at his joint were off the hook. That's why the place was always packed even though it was a wreck with peeling wall paper and cracked tiles on the floor.

"No sign of Johnny?" Frankie asked.

The Goat shrugged. "He had to take care of something. Just running late. Should be here soon."

Frankie smiled. "That's good."

The Goat had to find Johnny. Besides his concern for his friend's well being, there was the matter of the four grand he owed. The Goat was responsible for the book from Delaware Avenue to Oregon Avenue. Johnny Gunns worked for him and had to pay him four thousand every month, part of which went to The Goat's superiors. If Johnny was short with the money, things could get ugly. His boss didn't tolerate his workers coming up short.

Enough sitting around. It was time to do something. He left without paying as usual; he was a bundle of nervous energy. Something was going down. He could feel it.

The Goat got into his BMW and drove the city streets toward Pattison Avenue. Johnny frequented a strip joint called the *Cat House*. He was a big spender and a favorite among the dancers. Besides cash, he provided them with clothes, furniture and the occasional cosmetic surgery.

He walked into the gentleman's club and found Joe Senneca, the owner of the joint. Joe also worked for The Goat's boss.

"Yo. How ya doin, Goat?"

"Not bad. Not bad." The Goat didn't want Senneca to think he was feeling a bit jumpy. "So, ya seen my boy Johnny Gunns lately?"

"Of course I seen him," Senneca responded. "Like he ain't in here all the time."

"Yeah, I know that. I mean, ya seen him today?"

Senneca's brow furrowed. "I think so. Hey, Sam, Johnny Gunns in here earlier?"

A dancer at the club, Sam was a classy gal, studying part time at LaSalle and majoring in Psychology. Petite and small breasted, she was different from the other dancers. Sam possessed a genuine innocence to her that was atypical of most dancers The Goat knew. Her school girl good looks made her popular with the customers. She turned down The Goat flat, making her all the more desirable.

"Sure," Samantha replied. "He left with Tina a few hours ago."

Tina, Johnny's favorite dancer, had serious issues with booze and pills. Rumor had it Johnny was the father of her illegitimate child.

If Johnny left with her, that meant he could be in a number of places. The most likely place was Tina's row home in South Philly.

The Goat drove to her house. Johnny better have a damn good explanation, or there would be hell to pay. He may be a muscle head, but that wouldn't stop The Goat from kicking his ass.

He rang the bell to Tina's row home, and her freaky massage therapist roommate invited him in. Glancing around at the house, he felt uneasy as he told her he was looking for Johnny, but she wasn't much help, telling him she had not seen him all day.

Damn. He wanted to take care of business soon, so he could go home to see his girlfriend Karen. They had a huge shouting match last night, and this morning she sent a text that read "go to hell". Hopefully, that meant they could make up. If not, he could always go to the *Cat House* and find a replacement for her for the night.

He drove to Johnny's brother's house. Johnny sometimes took his lady friends there. When he got to the house on Westin Street, he couldn't find any open parking spots, so he double-parked someone. Screw 'em. If they didn't like it, they could kiss his ass.

The Goat searched for Johnny's car and spotted his bright red Mustang on the street. He walked up to the house and was about to ring the doorbell when he noticed the door was ajar. Something was definitely wrong.

Pulling out his Smith and Wesson, he stepped into the

house, immediately catching the rusty scent of blood in the air.

He walked into the sparsely furnished living room. Johnny's brother was a bouncer at a night club. He was an uncultured brute who had no appreciation for the finer things, like a cool *Goodfellas* poster here and there. The sofa in the living room was plaid, old and filled with holes. Next to it was an overturned and shattered lamp. It was dark and he could barely see, but he didn't want to turn on the lights and alert an intruder of his presence.

Stepping past the lamp, he made sure not to kick or step onto the broken ceramic. He held the gun with two hands close to his face and walked through the door leading from the living room. No signs of Johnny, Tina, or anyone else. He went down the hallway, peeked inside the bathroom, but found nothing.

Footsteps came from behind. He turned and aimed his Smith and Wesson, but found nothing but an empty hallway.

The Goat walked up the steps after searching the kitchen and dining room, cursing under his breath as the stairs creaked. This place had too many loose boards. He could wake up the dead, let alone alert an intruder of his presence with all the noise.

After reaching the top of the stairs, he stepped into the master bedroom. All the furnishings inside herse were dark. Mirrors covered the ceiling above the bed. No sign of disturbances here, so he kept moving.

He stepped toward the other bedroom. The smell of blood was more pronounced.

This was no time to get weak. Despite what he told himself, he felt unnerved. Just who the hell was he up against?

The Goat walked into the bedroom and gasped. Draped across the bed lying in a pool of blood was the deceased body of his former associate, Johnny Gunns. He wore no clothes and had a large, gaping puncture wound in his chest that spread to his stomach. Bites and scratches covered his arms and neck. His entrails had spilled onto the floor. *What the hell did this?* He expected to see a couple of bullets in Johnny's head, not this. This was ... uncivilized.

He looked around the room. It appeared that there had been a violent struggle, one which Johnny lost. Johnny had shards of glass in his forehead from the cracked window.

The Goat's heart continued to beat in rapid fire fashion. Blood was splattered everywhere. It was like a heart transplant surgery gone wrong. He grabbed a sock lying on the floor and walked to the closet. With one hand he held the Smith and Wesson. With the other he used the sock to open the closet door. He would get rid of the sock when he left to avoid leaving prints.

He opened the door and let out a short scream when the mangled body of Tina Monterulo fell toward him. Her body was a mess. He tried to avoid it, but wasn't fast enough. Tina's corpse landed on him, knocking him over and splattering him with blood. He landed inches away from his business partner's corpse.

"Motherfucker!" He had never seen anyone get wacked like this. He was a gambling man and was willing to bet that this was no mob hit.

He pushed away Tina. In the process, he leaned against Johnny's body, making his skin crawl. He had seen his share of death, but this was too much for him.

Scrambling to his feet as he held the pistol, he backed out of the room as fast as he could. As he passed the door, he turned to shut it. An icy hand gripped his neck and choked him. The hand clutching him was like steel. Whoever this was attacking him was impossibly strong.

He took a good look at his attacker. His skin was pale, his face ghostly. He had long strawberry blond hair and cold blue eyes. He had no facial hair and wore a sly smile, like he didn't even care that The Goat held a gun.

Blood rushed to his face. Consciousness started to ebb.

His mind got hazy. This was it. He was going to die. There was so much he had to do in life, and this inhuman bastard was going to end it all.

Before panic set in, he raised his gun to abdominal level, since that was all he had the strength for. His mind wavered, and he pleaded with his brain to keep it together. With his remaining strength, The Goat pulled the trigger. A shot tore through the man's waist, sending him flying back as he released his death grip.

The Goat crumpled to the floor and sucked in air, near asphyxiation. He looked up. To his horror, the man he just shot was back on his feet as if the bullet was a mere inconvenience. He tried to catch his breath. "What the … who the fuck are you?"

The blond smiled. He wasn't bleeding, and the bullet wound had already closed. "I am your bringer of death."

"Bullshit." He shot the lunatic again.

The blond staggered back and hit the floor, but got right back up with no visible wound.

"No. Can't be, asshole." He fired three more shots, missing one. Damn, this guy really was a bringer of death. This was how it would end. Not in some gangland shooting or a mob hit, but by the undead. "Sweet mother of mercy."

The man got to his feet and smiled, revealing a set of sharp fangs. The Goat did not want to say it, for to acknowledge such a thing would drive him crazy, but he knew what this thing was.

The attacker stalked The Goat, his cold blue eyes boring into him. He wondered if his demise would be as bad as Johnny's.

The attacker stopped at the sound of a siren. The sirens got louder, and he hesitated. The Goat met his stare, filled with newfound courage. His Sicilian heritage took over and wouldn't allow this thing to win a battle of wills. If he had to die, then so be it, but he wouldn't give him the satisfaction of knowing that The Goat was terrified of this monster.

The man smiled. "You shall live for now, but I'll come back for you."

The Goat gritted his teeth. "Not if I kill you first, motherfucker."

A strong swoosh passed through the air, and he disappeared.

The Goat couldn't believe his eyes. The police would be here any second, and there were two dead bodies. He had to get the hell out of here.

Chapter II

Enzo Salerno put his head on his desk. It felt like it was going to spontaneously combust. When he started building his empire, he knew it would be no picnic being the boss, but that didn't make days like today any easier.

Enzo called in Sophie Koch, his consigliere, into his office. It was odd for women to take part in organized crime families at such a high level, but Enzo was unlike any boss this city had ever known. Times had changed and he thought it reasonable to have a woman at the highest level of his organization. In fact, Sophie was the most valuable member of his syndicate. She was bright and energetic, having graduated near the top of her class at Penn Law School. Like Enzo, she hadn't found any satisfaction in the "legitimate" business world.

Sophie entered his spacious office in Old City. Although he had a nice view of the skyline, he kept the Venetian blinds closed to keep away prying eyes.

Enzo lifted his head from his desk. He felt like crap, but Sophie appeared alert and attentive. As always, she maintained a professional appearance and could pass for a partner at a prominent law office in the city. The difference was she had a soul, unlike most of those blood-sucking leeches.

"What's the matter, Enzo? You don't look well."

"Thanks. You know just what to say to make a guy feel good."

Sophie gave him a dazzling smile. "You know I don't mean it like that. I'm just wondering if you're sick. Have you been getting much sleep?"

"Hardly. I got a splitting headache. My head's going to explode. You ever have one of those days?"

"I've had a few. You're too tense. There's this full service spa I go to out in Wayne that would do wonders for you."

Enzo frowned. "Full service spa? I'm not a fucking fag, okay."

"You don't have to be a homosexual to go to a spa," Sophie said. "There are plenty of men who go there and they enjoy it immensely."

"And they're not gay?"

Sophie crossed her arms. "No. And I know this first hand, in case you're wondering."

"What you do at these spas is your own business. You date a lot of these guys?"

Sophie grinned. "I'll plead the fifth."

"Do you have any friggin' Advil?" he asked.

"Sure. In my desk. I'll bring you some."

"Great."

"So what's bugging you?" Sophie asked.

"That prick, cock-sucker O'Leary," he replied, referring to Philadelphia councilman Stephen O'Leary. "That land deal on Delaware Ave. is fizzling, and he isn't coming through."

"Why don't we attack this another way? We can squeeze them on the Convention Center. If the council won't go along with this deal, we'll give them labor problems they can't afford."

Enzo had a controlling influence on the city labor unions. Unlike other parts of the country, labor unions were still prominent in Philadelphia. No work could be done in the city's Convention Center without going through the unions. Since Enzo could manipulate these unions, he could prevent them from working at the Convention Center. With several large and lucrative conventions coming up, lack of participation from the unions could force the city to cancel them.

Enzo sighed. "There's some merit there, but it could cause law enforcement to squeeze us. I'll have to look into it."

Sophie left the room, then returned with the Advil and a glass of water.

"Thanks. What else do I have on the agenda today?"

"Paulie wants to speak to you about uncollected debt he's concerned about, and Mr. Scrambolgni would like to speak to you on behalf of his associate Pat Adesso."

"The Goat?" Enzo asked.

"Yes. He's here with The Goat."

Enzo thought for a moment. "Bring Fat Paulie in first."

Sophie left the room, and moments later Fat Paulie Randazzo entered. Fat Paulie stood at five feet eleven inches and weighed over three hundred pounds. He had short wavy black hair and a dark complexion. His main business within Salerno's enterprise was loan sharking. He sought low risk clients in need of fast cash and charged them obscene interest rates. Enzo instructed Fat Paulie to avoid loans with a high risk of default. When necessary they used extreme violence or extortion to get their money back, but he preferred avoiding violence whenever possible in order to keep his organization under the radar.

"I got all kinds of motherfuckin' problems," Fat Paulie said, after he had been admitted in.

"What's wrong?" Enzo used the calm and professional demeanor he tried to maintain with his associates.

"It's this fucking recession. It's getting harder and harder to collect. It's always business is tough, money's slow; can't pay right now. I had to give an order to break Desouza's hand with a hammer. Motherfucker just wouldn't pay."

Enzo sighed. "My daughter plays soccer with his kid."

Fat Paulie shrugged. "This son of a bitch recession's killing me. Businesses are going belly up."

"Listen Paulie, these things are cyclical."

Fat Paulie frowned. "What are you talkin' about, boss?"

Sometimes it was hard for him to deal with his less educated underlings. "Recessions are cyclical, meaning the economy will perform well for some time, and then there'll be a cooling off period where unemployment is higher and profits are lower. This will kill off some firms, but the ones who survive the shakeout will come out stronger."

Fat Paulie folded his arms. "So what's this got to do with us, boss?"

Trying to contain his frustration, Enzo put his palm to his head. "It means these small companies will perform better when the economy is doing better. Then we'll have a valuable firm we control. If not, we can still liquidate them and sell off their assets. The main thing is we control the company if they can't pay. Got it?"

Fat Paulie's eyes narrowed and he nodded slowly. "Sure thing, boss."

"So the rules stay the same. Keep away from the losers who don't look like they can pay back and target those that have businesses or personal assets we can seize."

"And if they don't agree?" Fat Paulie asked.

"You know what to do, but make it discreet."

"Okay, boss. Will do."

"And for God's sake, lay off Desouza. He's got assets. I'll work out a deal with him."

After Fat Paulie left, Tony Scrambolgni and The Goat entered. The Goat had this almost crazed look on his face, like he had just gone face to face with the Devil. He looked much older than twenty-nine. Tony, on the other hand, looked like a parent who had been called in to school because his child was misbehaving. Enzo leaned back in his chair, his curiosity piqued.

The Goat was a strong earner, running the books well in his section of South Philadelphia. He had the potential to be an excellent earner, but he was a hothead with a vicious temper. Not to mention, Enzo heard rumors about a possible heroin habit. His top guys had to be clean. That was non-negotiable.

After exchanging greetings, Tony said, "Enzo, I don't know why I'm here. This son of a bitch is talking crazy shit. I don't know. He's like seeing ghosts."

"It wasn't a ghost," The Goat yelled.

Scrambolgni glared at him. "Anyway, I don't know what the kid's got going on in that soft head of his, but he's been telling me some wild shit. I told him he's fucked up, but he insisted I take him to see you." Tony shrugged. "What can I say? The kid's persistent."

Enzo gave a comforting smile. "Tell me what you have come here to say. You look distressed. What's going on?"

"Mr. Salerno, I know this is gonna sound fucked up, but I swear it's true."

"Call me Enzo. Now relax and tell me your story."

"Enzo, what I'm gonna tell you is gonna sound crazy. Believe me, I'd think it's crazy too if I didn't just go through it. But it's all fucking true. You gotta believe me."

"Just tell me what happened," Enzo said in his soothing voice. "I'll judge if it's crazy."

The Goat went through his entire outlandish story starting from when he was in Frankie's Steaks to his trip to the strip joint and then to Tina Monterulo's apartment. He finished with the discovery of two corpses and his near death experience with an inhuman invader.

Enzo's face went white when he heard about Johnny Gunns. "My God." He put his hands to his face and turned to Tony. "Is this true? Is Johnny dead?"

Tony made the sign of the cross. "I checked with a source inside the coroner's office. Both he and his lady friend Tina were DOA."

Enzo shook his head. "My God." His throat constricted. "My father and his uncle were good friends. They used to go on fishing trips to Cape May." Rage smoldered inside of Enzo, sucking out his grief. "Someone clipped Johnny

Gunns, and you come here with some bullshit story about a fucking vampire. What do you think, I'm fucking stupid or something?" He smashed his closed fist against his desk. "You have some kind of balls and you'll be lucky if I don't string you up by them before this is over. Johnny's dead, and you're telling me it's a vampire. Tell me, do you think I'm dumb enough to believe this shit?"

The Goat leaned over the desk. His face showed sincerity. "Look Enzo, you gotta believe me. I saw this thing with my own two eyes and he wasn't fucking human. He was ... "

"Enough with this shit. You say that again, and God help me, I'll cut your fucking throat."

The Goat wouldn't give up. "Enzo, think about it. If what I'm telling you turns out to be complete bullshit, then I'm a dead man. I got absolutely nothing to gain by this. Come on, you're a smart guy, and I'm not just saying that. You're smarter than anyone around here by a fucking mile. No offense, Tony, but you are. So why would I come in here with a bullshit story? I'm telling you this because it's true. What I saw scared the shit out of me."

Enzo quelled his rising anger. Although the story was complete lunacy, The Goat had a compelling point. If it were not true, then his career — if not his life — would be rendered meaningless. Enzo stared at him. He wasn't drunk or high, and he looked dead serious.

Enzo didn't live in a world where the undead walked. In his world, people got whacked for financial and territorial reasons, or even personal reasons. Someone you knew might flip and become an FBI informant, or an employee might kill you for personal gain. That was the risk of doing business. What The Goat told him was storybook fantasy stuff.

Enzo pondered this while Tony and The Goat remained silent. "Although I put no credence in your story, you'd have to be insane to make it up, and you don't strike me as being crazy. Therefore, Johnny's death, may God rest his soul, will be investigated, and we'll find who killed him. He was a good man, and rest assured, someone will pay."

Scrambolgni stared at Enzo wide-eyed, while The Goat took a long breath.

"Tony, you'll oversee this matter. Contact our guys on the force and find out everything you can. Also, call Johnny's mother and tell her we're going to get to the bottom of this. This is going to kill her. What a sweet lady."

Tony nodded. "I'll get right to it, boss."

"Thank you, Enzo." The Goat extended his hand, and Enzo shook it. "Thank you. You'll find out that what I'm saying is true. I wish this shit was all in my fucking head, believe me."

They left Enzo's office. With all Enzo had to worry over, adding this worsened his headache. He considered taking more Advil, but decided against it. Instead he opted for a walk in the late spring air. If Sophie was available, she could accompany him. There was much they needed to discuss, but for now he would not tell her about The Goat's story. He would wait to hear what Tony had to say before making any decisions.

Chapter III

Tony "the Wop" Scrambolgni wasn't thrilled about his assignment. What was he suppose to do, confirm Johnny Gunns got wacked by a vampire? Maybe the others were right about Enzo being a little soft or crazy. But Enzo was the boss, and Tony would do what he was told.

Tony waited inside Nunzio's Pastry Shop for Detective Brown from Homicide. Brown asked to meet at Nunzio's because of his fondness for cannolis. The fat pig couldn't get enough of them. Even though it was obvious he despised Enzo's "family", calling them greaseballs and worse, he didn't have a problem being on Enzo's payroll.

Detective Brown came late for his meeting with Tony, like he was too good for him. He scanned the pastries before seeking Tony's table. He sat down and put an envelope in front of him. "I don't know what's wrong with you fucking people."

"What are you talking about?" Tony asked.

Brown's face tightened. "What kind of fucking hit was that? Whoever did this was a sick fuck. I've seen crazy shit, but this was over the top."

Tony glared at him. "What the fuck are you talking about?"

"The fucking bodies you asked me about. I ain't never seen a crime scene like it. There was blood everywhere. I saw their bodies at the morgue. Both had massive punctures in their throats. Their chests were caved in. That chick, Tina, her lungs collapsed. Johnny's liver and heart were removed from the body. They had scratch and bite marks all over. The girl's flesh was torn all the way down her stomach. See the pictures for yourself."

Tony sat in stunned silence. What kind of psycho was he dealing with? His heart thumped. He didn't want to look at the pictures, but he had to see them. Brown's assessment didn't do it justice. Even for a hardened career criminal like Tony, they were tough to see. "My God." He didn't make it to the end.

"So which one of you animals did this shit?" Spit shot out of Brown's mouth.

Tony went face to face with Brown. "That was no hit. I've seen some pretty fancy hits, but that ain't one of them. That's … " Tony struggled for the right word. " … inhuman."

"Whadaya mean inhuman? This is South Philly. You think we got wolves and tigers and shit running around here? Of course one of you guys did it."

Tony leaned over the table. "Listen to me. Nobody gets clipped like that. I don't know who or what did this, but that was no hit. Now you better watch your mouth, because my patience is running thin."

"You and your fucking Guinea friends are all the same."

Blood rushed to Tony's face. The information wasn't worth the aggravation. "I think it's time for you to leave."

"Fine." Brown took the envelope and grabbed four cannolis for the road.

Tony thought about the pictures and The Goat's story. If he were inclined to believe that vampires existed, which he was not, then maybe this creature could have killed Johnny and Tina. There had to be another explanation. Maybe a cult doing human sacrifices, or just some nut job.

He needed more information. He had another inside guy that could get him the coroner's report. Meanwhile, he would find out if Johnny Gunns had any enemies deranged enough to tear him apart like that.

The first place he went was the murder scene, the row home of Johnny's brother, Jim Debenedeto. He walked up and down the block. Earlier, The Goat told him the guy who killed them vanished, but people can't vanish. Maybe he just made a quick getaway.

Tony studied the house and its positioning within the street. There were some younger kids at play, and some older ones acting like they were hot shit. The smell of home-made gravy wafted through the air. Typical of most sections in South Philadelphia, row homes lined this block of Westin Street.

The man must have exited through the front of the house to Seventh Street. One of the neighbors would have noticed the stranger. Sure, the cops interviewed the neighbors, but they wouldn't say squat to them. They would be more receptive to talking to his people.

He rang the front doorbell. It took a few rings before Jim Debenedeto answered. He looked like shit. His answers to Tony's questions were slurred and jumbled. He could barely understand any of it and left without any better idea about what happened.

Tony drove to the *Cat House*. A dancer was gyrating around the pole on the main stage, but she did it with little enthusiasm. The guys sitting at the tables near the stage sat back in their chairs and didn't issue the normal round of catcalls. Even Joe Senneca, the manager of the club who always could get you rolling with a good joke, seemed depressed. Tina Monterulo's death had cast a shadow on the club.

He followed Joe into his office. Joe sat behind his desk and took out a case of Cubans. He gave one to Tony, took one for himself, and lit them both.

"It's a tragedy what happened to Johnny and that girl," Tony said.

Joe waved his cigar. "Tina was real troubled, but she was a sensational dancer. The guys went crazy for her, especially

Johnny. She was his favorite. And Johnny ... well I can't say enough about him. He was a good earner and had a big heart. Real generous, too. He bought the girls fancy gifts, bracelets and coats, the occasional plastic surgery."

Tony took a puff of his Cuban. "He was one of the good ones. Fucked up way to die, I'll tell you. Their bodies were torn to pieces. Had to be a real sicko to carry out that job."

"You think it was a hit?"

Tony shrugged. "Who can tell?"

"It's a fucked up world we live in."

"So which one of the girls was Tina close with?"

Senneca put down his cigar. "That's easy. Sam. Real smart girl. Cute as a button with a nice ass, let me tell you."

"She around?"

"Sure."

Tony followed Senneca out of his office. Two dancers were on stage showing their stuff. They went backstage to the quiet dressing room. Samantha sat in the corner reading a textbook.

Senneca put his hand on her shoulder. The girls seemed to like him even though he was touchy feely, probably because he protected them.

She looked up at them.

"Sam, this is my associate, Mr. Scrambolgni. He wants to ask some questions about Tina. Mr. Scrambolgni is a very important man, so please cooperate with him."

Sam gave a half smile. "Sure."

"This won't be long, honey," Tony said. "I just had some questions about Tina and Johnny. I understand the two of you were close."

"Myself and Tina, or Johnny?" she asked.

"Tina, of course. Joe tells me the two of you's spent a lot of time together."

"We talked. She had her share of problems. We went out for drinks. Sometimes I would baby-sit her son." Sam put her hand to her face and sobbed.

"It's okay." Tony didn't get why women were so emotional. "Take your time."

"I'm sorry." Sam wiped tears from her eyes. "Why would someone kill her?"

"That's what I'm trying to find out," Tony said.

He gave her time to regain her composure.

Sam choked back tears. "Tina was finally getting her life together."

"Her and Johnny spent a lot of time together. Do you know if they were into anything weird? You know, some satanic bullshit, maybe the occult."

Sam frowned and shrank back. "She wasn't into anything like that."

"Did Tina have a drug problem?"

Samantha hesitated. "Yes. She did heroin, cocaine, all kinds of pills. But she was getting clean. I helped her enroll in a rehab center."

Tony nodded. "What about Johnny?"

"I'm not sure. He supplied her."

A drug deal gone bad? Not if Johnny was her supplier. If Johnny had trouble with dealers, Tony would have heard. He had spent most of the day questioning people who would know such things. Johnny didn't owe drug money, and the different factions of dealers in the area would never kill someone in such a nasty fashion, especially someone with Johnny's connections.

Samantha didn't have any helpful answers. He was moved by her gentle nature. "You know this is no lifestyle for a girl like you. You're too smart to be stripping."

Sam shrugged. "I need to do it to put myself through school."

"I got a friend who's looking for someone to do some secretarial work. It pays good cash, but it ain't exactly a legal business if you see what I'm saying." Tony wrote down a number on a slip of paper and handed it to her.

"Yeah? Maybe I'll look into it."

"Good." Tony stared at the dancer. Even though Samantha was young enough to be his daughter, he wouldn't mind having a little romp with her.

Tony didn't know what to tell Enzo. He had to talk to the neighbors and pray they could give him some leads.

About the only upside to this whole deal for The Goat was his girlfriend Karen showing him great sympathy since the incident. She told him it was a blessing from God that he escaped death, and she was determined to make the most out of their time together. Normally they had a bi-polar relationship, always fighting and yelling at each other followed by hot sex and affection, but the past twenty four hours had been pure bliss.

Karen had convinced him to tell Enzo Salerno about everything. She was the only one who believed him. She was a great girl, working at a beauty salon at Fourth and Shunk where she was the afternoon manager. They had been together for four years. She drove him crazy, and sometimes he treated her like crap, but the good times were real good.

When he entered their apartment, she hugged him for dear life. "So how did it go? What did he say?"

The Goat raised his brows. "They're gonna look into it."

"I told you," Karen said. "I knew he'd believe you."

He frowned. "I'm not so sure about that. I thought he was going to rip my fucking throat out until I convinced him there had to be something to what I said."

"That's great, Patrick." Karen hugged him again. "I still can't believe you were almost killed by the undead. It's a miracle, I tell ya."

"Relax with that miracle shit, okay." She had been acting like a holy roller ever since that night. "The only reason I'm still alive is 'cause that vampire heard the sirens and thought it would be a good idea to bust his ass out of there."

Recalling that night still gave him chills. That monster's

strength was unlike anything he ever felt.

"So who's looking into it?" Karen asked.

"Tony."

Karen's face tightened. According to her, Tony hit on her all the time. She was probably overreacting, and even if she wasn't, what could he do about it?

"Tony's not going to find out shit. That guy can't zip his fly by himself."

"Tony'll take care of things."

"Why don't you do your own investigation?" Karen asked.

"'Cause Enzo trusts Tony, that's why. So Tony's gonna check things out and he'll see I was telling the truth, 'cause there ain't no other way to see it."

"I hope you're right."

"Of course I'm right, baby." The Goat drew her in and kissed her. Since yesterday they had been going at it non stop, and it was wearing him out.

Suddenly she pulled away from him. "Let's get married, Patrick."

"You know the time ain't right just now."

"When will it be?" Karen asked.

"Soon. When it happens, this wedding will blow your mind. First class all the way."

He smiled. If he could deal with the Grim Reaper, he could deal with marriage.

Chapter IV

"What else would you like me to pick up?" Federal Bureau of Investigations Special Agent Mark Andrews glanced at the grisly photos on his desk as he spoke to his wife on the phone. "Okay, chicken breast. Should I pick up some rolls? Sure... I'll probably be home around six. How's Sarah? Tell her daddy says hi... Okay. I'll see you later. Love you."

He stared once more at the shots of the butchered bodies of John Debenedetto and Tina Monterullo. Butchered wasn't quite right. It was more like bitten and torn apart. The Philadelphia police officers present called him in to view the murder scene because they believed the deceased was a member of Enzo Salerno's crime regime. Mark confirmed the identity of John Debenedetto, also known as Johnny Gunns.

It was the most bizarre mob death he had ever seen. Scratches, bite marks and wide punctures covered the bodies. There were no usual gunshots, stab wounds or other markings normally found on a murder victim.

His superiors weren't interested in this murder. Mark understood the FBI had shifted priorities in recent years. Some of his agents had been pulled in order to combat terrorism. Other departments of the FBI, including his own, had weakened as a result.

Mark made his bones by tackling organized crime in Philadelphia. For over a decade, he worked to bring the mob to its knees. The bureau had rewarded and highly decorated him for his efforts, but in recent years he had come away empty handed and frustrated. Part of the problem was his reduced budget, and the other was Enzo Salerno.

Mark couldn't pin anything on the bastard. The mobster kept a low profile. Since Salerno and his regime did not exist in the public's eye, Mark's superiors didn't make it a high priority to bring him to justice. He was intelligent and cultured and operated his empire like a business, albeit one that used violence and extortion. He was also as slippery as a fish.

On several occasions, Mark thought the bureau would pull him and his team off the assignment. If that happened, then who would stop Salerno? Salerno had gotten too big and powerful, controlling many areas of commerce and politics. If Mark could get some solid, concrete evidence, perhaps he could indict the mob boss.

He looked at the photographs for the hundredth time, trying to piece together how the victims were killed and who did it. The investigating officers spoke to Jim Debenedetto's neighbors. One lady told the officers she saw a suspicious character leaving the house at the time of the murders. It's not like these bites could have belonged to an animal. The bite patterns were distinctly human.

Mark put away the pictures. His sources on the street had not provided any useful information. Maybe he could arrange a sit down with Salerno. The two had met before at neutral territories. He may be able to convince Salerno that they could help each other in this matter.

Mark took a deep breath. He had to pick up the groceries and make it home by six. Unfortunately, his wife and kids were used to him working late hours.

His marriage had undergone trying times, mostly when he took his work home with him. His wife Victoria was an intelligent woman with an even temperament that contrasted with his fiery temper. He loved his two kids even though he didn't always show them affection. Spending so much time away from home, it was hard to get involved in their lives.

After dealing with the worst element of society, he sometimes found it hard to separate his work mindset from his home mindset.

Working with local officials, he systematically dismantled the Philadelphia mafia. When the Italian mafia weakened, they targeted the Russian and the Jamaican mobs and brought them down. The other ethnic crime factions were easier to defeat. They lacked the political connections of the Italian mafia. The only thing holding Mark's career back was that he often voiced his opinion when he disagreed with the brass. He knew he should hold these opinions to himself if he wanted to advance in his career, but his temper got in the way of good judgment.

Mark made a few more phone calls. The first was to see if an identification had been made on the torn skin found near the two bodies. The second was to a neighbor who saw a man entering the house shortly before the police arrived.

The call to the lab turned out to be a dead end. The skin belonged to Debenedetto and Monterullo, apparently torn off in the struggle. How could the perp not have left fingerprints or hair fibers at the crime scene? It was like he was dealing with a phantom.

His second call was no better. The lady who saw a man entering the house was not home. He sighed and got ready to leave. Why was he wasting time and energy on this case? It probably didn't involve mafia activity. The locals could handle an animal attack or some other strange killing. Perhaps it was the bizarre nature of the murder that attracted him. Maybe he just wanted to see Salerno's reaction.

He put on his coat and closed his briefcase when his boss, Special Agent Rick Carroll, entered the office. Rick was heavyset, in his late fifties with graying hair and a thick mustache. Rick would look much better if he trimmed his hair and mustache.

His boss's face looked worn. "Hope you weren't planning on going anywhere."

"Yeah, home," Mark said.

"Better tell your wife you might be a while."

Mark frowned. "What's going on?"

"We had another one. Just like your friend Johnny Gunns."

Mark put his briefcase down. "Where?"

"Near Kensington. A young Vietnamese woman in her early twenties. Her body wasn't mutilated like Johnny or this girl, but the bite marks are the same."

"Was she missing a lot of blood?" The most glaring thing he read in Debenedetto and Monterullo's autopsy reports was that the killer had nearly drained both bodies of blood.

"I don't know," Rick responded. "Let's take a look. I'll drive."

"Okay. Let me call Victoria." He hoped she would understand, because he had a feeling that this was going to be a long night.

Chapter V

Tony Scrambolgni sat at a private table at the rear of Stephano's Restaurant drinking a cognac and smoking a cigar, waiting for Enzo to arrive. Stephano's made the best veal in the city. Their gnocchi and Sunday gravy wasn't shabby either.

He had been antsy of late. He puffed on the cigar, trying to stay calm. Enzo would ask about Johnny tonight, and he didn't have any answers. He hoped Enzo wouldn't show, but that was wishful thinking. The boss was always punctual.

Earlier, he and a member of his crew had spoken to Jim Debenedetto's neighbors, asking if they had seen anyone peculiar at the time in question. Several of them had seen someone that matched The Goat's description. He was tall with strawberry blonde hair, icy blue eyes and no facial hair. His shirt had been covered with blood. Each person said he looked like a vampire.

Tony tried to steer them away from this characterization. Perhaps the man was Eastern European, which could account for his pale skin tone. Or maybe the lighting was poor, and that's why his skin looked pale. The blood could have been makeup or a gravy stain. No matter how much he tried to guide their story, they insisted he looked like a vampire.

So what to do? No way he would tell Enzo a vampire killed Johnny.

Enzo arrived alone. The hostess took his coat and led him to their table. Tony greeted him with a hug and offered him a cigar.

Enzo held out his hand. "No thanks. Trying to cut back."

Their waiter brought Enzo a glass of red wine. After Enzo's broiled flounder arrived and he still had not brought up the murder of Johnny Gunns, Tony figured maybe Enzo forgot about it. Half way through the meal, Enzo said, "So what can you tell me about our friend Johnny? His funeral is Tuesday at Saint Cecilia's."

Tony nodded. "I spoke to his mother this morning. She's handling it like any mother would. She was absolutely hysterical. I mean, in our line of work, you never know when you're gonna buy your ticket, but it's always toughest on the mothers. Her other son's a drunken moron, which doesn't make things any easier."

Enzo pursed his lips. "I sent flowers today. So what about the investigation?"

Tony drained his glass of Chianti. He wished he had a shot of whiskey instead. He took a deep breath and searched for their waiter, hoping he could stall by ordering another drink. "Well, the pictures of Johnny and his girl were ... real fucked up. They were torn apart. I ain't never seen nothin' like it. That dickhead Brown showed them to me. I was about to strangle that son of a bitch."

Enzo shrugged. "He may be an asshole, but he's useful."

"If you say so, boss. I also looked at the coroner's report."

"Good work," Enzo said.

"Yeah, um, that was all fucked up too."

Enzo's brows arched. "How so?"

"Well ya see, both Johnny and the girl were missing about eighty percent of their blood."

Enzo chuckled. "Sounds like the work of our vampire."

Blood drained from Tony's face. He eyed the exit, wishing he could leave. "I don't know what to say, other than it was all fucked up. Some of their organs were missing too."

"Could somebody have killed them to harvest their organs?" Enzo asked.

Tony shrugged. "I thought maybe an animal did this, but the coroner said the bites were human. You wouldn't think that could happen in South Philly, but who knows."

Enzo continued eating.

"And there's one more thing. Several neighbors saw a guy leaving the apartment. Guy had some blood on him, you know, near his mouth and on his shirt collar. And, um, this guy fit The Goat's description pretty good."

"Ah, our fearless vampire."

"Hey you said it, not me."

Enzo finished his flounder. "So, tell me what you think."

"I don't know, boss. I mean, it was probably some sick fuck with a hard on for Johnny. The whole blood and organs thing, well who knows?"

"What about The Goat's story?"

"Given the circumstances, I would say that maybe it wasn't crazy for him to jump to his conclusion, but I don't believe in that shit."

Enzo signaled the waiter and ordered an Espresso. Tony got another drink. Halfway through the Espresso Enzo stared at him. "I'll tell you want you're going to do. You're going to get this sick bastard and find out why he killed Johnny. Then you're going to kill him. Got it."

"This guy's gonna pay, boss. No doubt about that."

The Goat waited in his BMW for Fat Paulie to leave his house. He wasn't crazy about this assignment, but was in no position to complain. Tony thought it would be good for him to tag along with Fat Paulie in addition to his regular duties. Tony wanted him to learn about other aspects of the business besides the bookmaking operations he ran.

This was a sign of respect. He had been doing a good job, and Tony rewarded him. If this worked out, he could rise in Enzo's regime. The drawback was working with Fat Paulie. He was a rude bastard with bad hygiene. When they worked together, Paulie insisted he do shit work like pick up his dry cleaning or wash his car. Just this morning, he told The Goat to trim his hedges. *What do I look like, his bitch?*

His mood was already foul after Tony told him the police recovered a bullet lodged in the wall of Jim Debenedetto's house. This bullet had come from his gun when he shot at the vampire. He already discretely disposed of the gun. They could not pin the murder on him since neither Johnny nor Tina had any bullet wounds, but it would look bad if they found out the bullets came from his gun.

To make matters worse, Karen kept getting on him about Tony's investigation. She always got pissy whenever he brought up the subject. She told him Tony would make him look bad. This led to several shouting matches between him and Karen. He trusted Tony, and more importantly Enzo Salerno trusted him. In the end, Tony would confirm what he said, *'cause there's no other way to see it.*

The Goat waited outside Fat Paulie's house with his car running. He lit a cigarette. *If he was going to take so long, he could have at least invited me inside.* Paulie had told him to wait a minute so he could get a bundle of cash for the next job. Eight minutes later, he was still waiting.

Finally Fat Paulie waddled out from the front door. He'd done more than just get cash, as evidenced by the marinara sauce smeared on his chin. Paulie opened up the passenger side door of the BMW and plopped himself inside.

"It's about time. I think I used a half tank of gas while the car was idling. What, did you grab a side of macaroni while you were in there?"

Fat Paulie looked at his reflection in the vanity mirror and used his sleeve to wipe the stain on his face. "Shut up and drive."

"Where we goin'?" The Goat asked.

"I told you, we're gonna see some Russian dude in Gray's Ferry. Vladimir something. If you don't have any other questions, why don't you just fucking drive."

"I thought you said he was Ukrainian?"

"Ukrainian, Russian, what's the difference? It's all one big, fucking cesspool anyway."

The Goat frowned. "So what's this guy's deal?"

"This Russian bastard owes money. I was going to put the screws to him, and he tells me he's got a plan to get all the money he owes with interest, lots of it. So I'm a businessman. If he can make money, I'd like to hear it. Says besides what he owes, he'd like some start up cash. Probably just to get some coke or move out of that shithole he lives in. Anyway, we'll talk to him. If I don't like what I hear, then we send him a message."

The Goat nodded. He didn't need any further explanation.

As The Goat drove, Fat Paulie took out a comb and fixed his hair. "It's a shame about Johnny. I heard he went down in a bad way."

Blood drained from The Goat's face. "Yeah, I guess so."

"He was all messed up. So what do you know about it?"

"What do you mean by that? I had nothin' to do with it."

"I mean the two of you were friends," Paulie said. "What's your problem?"

"I ain't got a problem. I don't know anything about it. Just what I heard on the street."

"What time's the funeral?" Fat Paulie asked.

"Eleven."

They barely spoke the rest of the way. The Goat kept glancing back in the rear view mirror as he drove. He pulled up to a run down apartment building in the Gray's Ferry section of Philadelphia. A young black kid stood by the stop sign on the street corner near The Goat's car. The boy lingered, staring at the BMW. The Goat glared at him. "What are you lookin' at? Beat it."

The boy shuffled away.

Fat Paulie put on his coat. "You gotta watch out with the people in this neighborhood. Bunch of animals."

They walked through the front entrance of the apartment

building and up two flights of steps. By the end, Fat Paulie needed a rest.

"You all right there?"

Fat Paulie put his hands on his legs. "Yeah, I'm fine. Let's go."

The Goat walked to apartment 328 and knocked on the door. The building smelled like stale food and laundry detergent.

A young Russian girl with short brown hair opened the door. She was no older than nineteen with pale skin, long legs and exotic features. She wore a light blue robe and had smoky brown eyes that mesmerized The Goat.

"Is, um, Vladimir here?" The Goat asked.

The woman walked into the apartment and motioned for them to follow.

Empty take out boxes and half-full bottles of vodka littered the chaotic apartment. The air was dense and stuffy. Feeling claustrophobic, The Goat wanted to open a few windows and get fresh air.

"Cozy place, huh?" Fat Paulie asked.

The Goat did not respond. He wanted to get this meeting over with.

The unshaven Ukrainian emerged from the bedroom. He towered over his two visitors, standing at six and a half feet tall. He was long and lanky, with groggy eyes that suggested he had just awoken. "Welcome to my apartment, gentlemen. Please take seat."

The Goat eyed the filthy sofa. "I'll stand."

"This is Vladimir Usa … us … " Fat Paulie began.

"Vladimir Ustanov." His accent was as thick as mud.

They all shook hands. The Goat could tell right away that this guy was sharp. He had an air about him that he could hold his own with the college professors at Drexel.

"Right, right. This is my associate Pat Adesso. We call him The Goat."

"Oh, because of beard," Vladimir said. "I understand. Can

I offer you drink?"

Fat Paulie said, "Yeah, give me one of those strong ones you guys make."

Vladimir fixed a Screwdriver for his guest.

"So Vlade, we'd like to hear about this operation you plan on starting," The Goat said.

He handed Paulie the beverage. "In Ukraine, I was biologist. I come to this country seeking opportunity and I find none, so I make own opportunity."

Fat Paulie nodded. "Don't we all."

Vladimir sprawled himself on his checkered, hole-filled sofa. The Goat felt ill thinking about the critters that occupied it.

Vladimir started typing on his laptop and brought up a company website. "You see this company. They sell picture frames, knick knacks, shit like that."

Fat Paulie shrugged. "Why the fuck do I care about that?"

The Goat said, "Pay attention. This guy's onto something."

Vladimir waved his hands. "Not very exciting company. I know. But people buy their shit. They're Internet security is not so good. So I break into website, change code to divert payment for products from their accounts into dummy accounts I create. Sound good, yah?"

"Slow down, Ruskie," Fat Paulie said. "I don't understand all this Internet shit."

Vladimir instructed The Goat to create an account and buy products off the website to demonstrate how it worked.

"That's fucking brilliant," Fat Paulie said. "Then you can loot their dough. I like it."

"So you see I give you money you need. I need five thousand dollars start up cash."

The Goat looked at this rat's nest. Vlade didn't need start up cash. He recognized a user when he saw one. As long as Vlade made money, he didn't give a shit.

"Well, that deal's off the table," Fat Paulie said. "I have a better one. I'll forgive what you owe and I'll give you the five G's, but instead of interest, we'll take a cut. Thirty percent."

Vladimir scowled. "Nyet. That is not what we talk about."

"That deal's off the table. You'll take our new deal."

"I don't think it's in your best interest to reject this offer, Vlade," The Goat said. "Be glad we're not taking a bigger cut."

Fat Paulie took out his bundle of cash. He counted out $5000 and gave it to the lanky Ukrainian. Vladimir glared at him before taking the money.

After shaking hands with their new business associate, Fat Paulie and The Goat left the apartment building and got in the BMW.

Fat Paulie grinned. "We took that Ruskie by surprise. Wait 'til Enzo hears about this. He's gonna be impressed by my attraprenuerialism."

The Goat nodded, glad to be out of the apartment. Something about it was eerily similar to the feeling the vampire gave him that night he attacked him.

Chapter VI

Nikki Staretz sat on the sofa in her Front Street apartment drinking a Margarita. She glanced out the window yearning to get a glimpse of the man she met last night. She never wore dresses, but she had one on tonight, hoping he would like it. This was reckless. Before leaving, he told her he would come to her apartment tonight. Her senses told her to say no, to tell the man she wasn't available, but she had no resistance around him.

Nikki met the dashing stranger the previous evening at the Rock Lobster on Delaware Avenue where she had been out with two friends from work. It was odd for her to even go out. She was normally a homebody. A small town girl, in college she would stay at the computer lab late at night while her friends went out to party it up.

The last thing she had wanted last night was to meet a man. After all, she was engaged. After leaving her friends to get drinks at the bar, she spotted him. She gazed at his cold, blue eyes from across the room as if in a trance, forgetting about the drinks and her friends. The only thing that mattered was her mystery man. His stare pulled her toward him as if he was so full of magnetism.

She headed toward him. An inner voice told her this was a bad idea. Nothing good could come of it, but she quieted these voices.

When she reached the man, it seemed as if everyone else at the club disappeared. She introduced herself. Despite the loud music in the background, she heard everything he said with clarity. It was like his voice echoed inside her head.

His name was Alexei. By his looks and accent, Nikki concluded he was Eastern European. His complexion was fair — no, pale was more like it. His face was enchanting. He was an older guy, probably in his late thirties. Neither age or anything else mattered. When she held his hands, she felt amazing strength. When they touched, her entire body tingled.

They spoke for a half hour. She was completely at ease with him, telling him intimate details of her life. She confided in him about her childhood, her hopes and fears, things she wouldn't even tell a close friend.

When she spotted her friends, Alexei suggested they meet again tomorrow at ten. She agreed and gave him her address. When speaking with her friends later, she made up a story about how Alexei was an old friend from school. She wasn't sure why she had done that. Maybe she had been embarrassed since they all new she was engaged to Rico.

Back in her apartment, she closed her eyes, still not believing this was real. Nikki had never approached a guy and invited him to her apartment, even before she was engaged. She was getting married in seven months. If Rico found out, not only would he call off the wedding, he would want to hurt Alexei. Rico had a fiery temper. He was a foreman at a construction company. Most of her friends thought they made an odd couple because of the disparity in their education level and family backgrounds, but Nikki loved him. Yet her desire for Alexei overshadowed her feelings toward Rico at the moment.

She watched the clock tick. It was almost ten. She breathed hard. What if he didn't show? If she didn't see him, she would rip apart at the seams.

She walked toward the window, looking out at the street. There was no sign of Alexei. It was stupid to think such a beautiful man would keep his commitment. She turned around. Alexei stood ten feet away. Her heart fluttered. She didn't put more than a second of thought to how he entered her locked apartment so silently.

"We meet again," Alexei said.

"I was ... I was afraid you wouldn't show."

Alexei seemed to float toward her. "I wouldn't do that to you." He inhaled deeply. "Your scent is intoxicating."

He put his hand on the small of her back, and she felt the same electricity she had experienced last night. Alexei was so different than anybody she ever met. He made Rico seem insignificant. She closed her eyes and leaned toward him. His embrace left her dizzy.

He brushed his lips against her neck. She swayed to the music in her mind. If she died now, she would be happy.

"Take me, Alexei," she whispered, and kissed him. Excitement coursed through her body. "Please."

"You're so inviting, so filled with vitality." Alexei took her off her feet and held her as if she were a small child. "Will you give yourself to me?"

"Oh, God yes."

He carried her to her bed and lay her down gently. "I can give you a gift. It will be the greatest thing you'll ever experience. I give this freely and ask for nothing in return. Is this what you want? Think, my child."

"I don't want to think. I just want you." She drew Alexei toward her quivering body.

"Then I will give you what you want."

He lowered himself and opened his mouth, exposing sharp fangs. Nikki did not feel any fear, nor did she make a move to escape. She savored the moment with Alexei.

"Uhh. Ohhh," she whimpered as he sunk his teeth into her neck.

Her warm blood spilled into his mouth. Savoring the taste, he drank her blood. He had opened a small gash to prolong the experience.

"Don't stop." She grabbed his head and pushed it in

toward her neck.

Alexei obliged and continued to feed. As the intensity of the experience increased, he bit deeper into her neck. He could feel her life slip away and her heart beat slow. It would not be long before it stopped beating, and that was what he relished most. He thought about stopping before her life expired, but could not. The feeling was too overpowering. Why should he deprive himself of this? After all, she was perfectly willing to give her life to him.

Nikki moaned as she clung to him. The beating of her heart echoed inside his head. It got fainter as each moment passed. Her voice choked as the end came near.

He was on such a high he could not stop. With razor sharp nails, he tore into her abdomen, slicing cleanly from below her breast bone to her mid section. He lowered his face into her exposed abdominal cavity and feasted on her organs.

This was not something his kind did. It was almost unheard of. Alexei's "family" knew nothing about his fascination with consuming organs. But now that he had started, he could not stop.

When he finished, he was covered in blood. He went to the bathroom and cleaned himself up, not wanting to attract any unnecessary attention as he walked the streets of Philadelphia.

He looked in the mirror. He was a ghastly sight. He stared at his ageless face. It had to be depressing for mortals to deal with the aging process. Some of his kind spoke of their desire to become one with humans and walk in the bright sunlight once more, but he had no such desire. He enjoyed them, especially the exquisite ones like Nikki Staretz, but their lives were tedious and boring. It had been so long since he was one of them he scarcely remembered what it was like.

Unlike Magnus, who preferred to stay home and be with his own kind, Alexei always left the house after dusk to be among the mortals. He went to bars, nightclubs, and movie theaters. For the special ones like Nikki, he gave them his intimate gift.

After exiting the bathroom he stared at the huddled figure lying on the bed. She was at peace. He felt no remorse or guilt. This was what she wanted. Even when they didn't ask for it, like the couple he visited earlier that week, he was still willing to give his gift.

The phone rang. It would be prudent to leave. Still, he lingered. He wanted to be near Nikki so soon after her death. He did not want her to be alone. After an hour, he opened the window of her apartment and scanned the surrounding area. It was empty of prying eyes, so he made his exit.

Magnus' rage built inside of him like a pit of lava ready to burst as he read the lead story on the front cover of the *Philadelphia Inquirer*. When he finished, he slammed the newspaper on the solid oak table. He gritted his teeth.

Unfortunately in the summer it became dark too late in the evening. By the time he woke from his sleep, the newspaper was old and the local television stations showed meaningless sitcoms and nauseating reality television shows. He had to wait a couple hours to watch the ten o' clock news.

With the advent of modern technology and the information age, he'd become dependent on media outlets. He craved information about the world around him. He even learned how to use a computer. Surfing the Internet was a modern marvel. Now he had to find out what they were saying about this string of brutal "murders" plaguing the city.

When he read the article, especially the part about how the corpse had been torn apart and was missing organs, he knew the culprit. Alexei might not realize that Magnus was on to him, but Magnus was fully aware of his vile habit. His patience with Alexei was gone. Magnus warned him numerous times to use discretion, but his words fell on deaf ears. He had to do something drastic to capture Alexei's attention.

He and Alexei were the oldest vampires in the brood. Alexei was rebelling because the others saw Magnus as their leader. Traditionally, the oldest and most powerful vampire was the leader. The brood sought Magnus for advice and guidance. He made the important decisions. This clearly bothered Alexei.

Having recently arrived in the United States, in the city of Philadelphia, Magnus did not want to leave so soon, but with the media and the local law enforcement investigating these crimes, it would be difficult to stay.

Magnus spun around when he heard faint breathing that would be undetectable to human ears. Standing silently in the corner was his precious Gabriella.

They had been together for over three hundred years. From the moment he first saw her on a beach near Cadiz in Spain, he knew he had to have her. She was one of the few of their kind that he was responsible for making.

Gabriella had captivated his heart. He still remembered those days with her as if they happened a year ago. After courting her for a few months, he had revealed his true identity.

On a beach in Cadiz over three hundred years ago, he said to Gabriella, "Please join me. Make no mistake, I won't force this upon you. You must make your own decision. If you say no, I will leave heartbroken, but I won't bother you again. I will give you a week to make your decision."

Gabriella gazed into his eyes. "I don't need a week. I will let you know tonight." She had come from a large, prominent family from the southern coast of Spain and wanted to say goodbye to them forever.

Magnus waited for Gabriella.

She had tears in her eyes when she returned. "It hurts so much to know that I won't see my family again, but they would never accept me like this. And I have to be with you.

Every moment that I am gone from you I ache so much with longing."

Magnus held her close to him. "I understand your pain. This is a difficult decision, but my kind are the only family you will ever need."

At night on the empty beach, she willingly submitted to him and he turned her into a creature of the night. For most of that century Magnus and Gabriella traveled together throughout the world. He showed her spectacular sights of natural beauty. They took in concerts and plays and lived a life of splendor. Gabriella was the only companion he needed.

In time she became lonely and felt isolated, wanting to be with others of their kind. Because of this, he started his brood, collecting creatures of the night along the way. Their numbers had fluctuated over the years. Currently there were twenty-two living in the mansion he had purchased in Gladwyne, an affluent Philadelphia suburb. He wanted a large group so Gabriella would never again experience loneliness.

"I sense some unpleasantness." Gabriella moved with such stealth that most people could not detect her. Sometimes she even surprised Magnus, despite his keen senses.

He handed her the newspaper, and she scanned the article.

"Who do you suspect?" Gabriella asked.

"Please don't feign ignorance, my sweet. We both know this could only be Alexei."

Gabriella shrugged. "Our friend has extravagant tastes, always experimenting."

Magnus rubbed his temples. His life would be so much easier if it were still only he and Gabriella. "Alexei's a fool. He knows the rules of the house, yet openly violates them. He had to realize we would discover this."

"At times he gets carried away," Gabriella said.

"Why do you persist in defending him? He's been nothing but trouble over the past couple decades. If he's going to feed openly, he'll have to do it on his own. I'm tired of dealing with him. I'm going to give him an ultimatum. He follows the rules, or he leaves."

Gabriella slithered toward Magnus. She rested her head against his chest and looked into his strong, blue eyes. "Let me speak to him. Don't worry yourself over this. The others need your leadership, especially the young ones. Internal strife isn't good for them. We have an entire world of humans who would kill us if they knew about our existence. We have to be united."

"That's precisely what's wrong with the way Alexei feeds. He has no regard for our need for secrecy. He's reckless. And that's why..."

Gabriella put her index finger to his lips. "I'll talk to Alexei. Stop worrying about this. When was the last time you were out? Can you even remember?"

Magnus shook his head.

"It's not about sustenance. It's about your spirit. Have you fed even once since our arrival to the City of Brotherly Love?"

Magnus grinned. "I'm so old that I no longer have to feed."

"Then take the young ones and show them how to do it right."

Magnus shrugged.

"Do it for me. It will be good for your soul."

Magnus gave her his most charming smile. "If it will make you happy, then I'll do it." As he left the room, he thought of the taste of fresh blood. Maybe it was what he needed.

Chapter VII

Magnus breathed in the warm summer air, staring at the full moon as it lit up the night sky. Gabriella was right. He had been living in Philadelphia for six months and barely knew the city. Mostly he stayed in the mansion in Gladwynne and read books, played an instrument, or worked on the computer. At times he felt like he had seen and experienced everything. Even for someone who had lived for half a millennium, that was a foolish notion.

Tonight he brought two younger members of his brood, Kristoff and Ursula, with him.

Kristoff had been part of his brood for twenty years. Alexei had turned him while the brood had been in Dusseldorf where Kristoff was a track athlete trying out for the German Olympic team. His specialty was the javelin. Alexei, a regular at a bar near a training facility, befriended many of the athletes, but was especially fond of Kristoff, who was twenty-two at the time and an orphan since birth.

Even though the fair-haired young man never had a real home or family, Kristoff possessed inner strength and compassion, which undoubtedly had attracted Alexei. He was selfless and did whatever he could for others. One night, without consulting anyone, Alexei brought him home to the brood after turning him.

Although furious that Alexei did this without consulting him, the young German charmed him immediately. Kristoff never asked anything from other members of the brood, even though he did not know how to feed on his own. Not surprisingly, Alexei lost interest in Kristoff after a few weeks. He always wanted new blood and new adventures.

Magnus took him under his wing and taught him how to survive. Kristoff followed him around, trying to learn as much as he could about their kind. Magnus in turn told him story after story about his own history.

After spending an hour scouting potential victims at a bar on Chestnut Street, they moved on, finding nobody suitable. As they walked toward South Street, Magnus took in the current fashion crazes. He blended in on South Street where freaks with big hair, tattoos and piercings were the norm. People did not even give him a second look.

They started off at *Downey's*. Magnus inhaled the scent of fresh lobster. A breeze from the Delaware River cooled him. They weaved through the normal foot traffic past the shops and restaurants. He smiled at the sight of a young couple in their early teens. The girl had blue and purple hair that was long in the back and shaved on the sides. She wore a black lace dress and combat boots, and had a chain that extended from her nose ring to her exposed navel. The boy wore military fatigues and had his green hair in pointy spikes. Oh how things had changed since the Middle Ages.

He could tell Ursula was enjoying herself. Once upon a time, she had been a singer and dancer in Prague. Magnus first saw her when he and Gabriella went to the ballet. Magnus was moved by her pure beauty and graceful movements. He returned to the ballet repeatedly to see her dance. He knew the manager of the theater and arranged to meet Ursula. He discovered she had a radiant personality that matched her talent.

Magnus watched Ursula from afar. Occasionally he would approach her, and they would speak for hours. He took her out several times and bought her expensive Western clothes. They continued this relationship for a year. When Ursula expressed a romantic interest, he backed away. He couldn't trust himself around her, and she might wind up dead.

He had not seen her for a couple of months. One night when they were strolling along the river, Gabriella asked, "Why don't you see that dancer anymore? I know you're fond of her."

Magnus didn't respond.

Gabriella tilted her head. "Don't deny it. I know you far too well."

He tried to evade her questions, but she had none of it.

Finally he said, "I don't think it's a good idea to spend time with her anymore."

Gabriella would not relent. "You clearly care for the girl. Why don't you make her one of us?"

Magnus refused to say anything further on the subject.

He wasn't opposed to turning mortals into the undead, but rarely did it. Besides Gabriella, he had turned four others. Mostly, he didn't think his kind should be abundant. If there were too many, their chances of discovery would increase. And his sense of morality made it difficult for him. Unlike Alexei, he never fully reconciled killing people. Even for him on occasion, it happened when feeding. It had always been a moral dilemma for him to balance the possibility that he would kill someone while satisfying his own needs and desire for blood.

Unbeknownst to him, Gabriella took it upon herself to visit Ursula one evening after a performance. She gave Ursula the same choice Magnus gave her hundreds of years ago. She returned a week later, and Ursula told her she wanted to become a creature of the night. Later that evening, Gabriella brought to their home outside of Prague a weakened Ursula, who she just turned. Magnus was delighted. She did for him what he would not do for himself.

Ursula was reluctant at first to go out and feed despite it being vital for her survival. She was still too human. As a result she became weakened and near death. For her sake, Magnus lured people into their cavernous mansion and killed them so Ursula could drink their blood. If they were already dead, then what difference would drinking their blood make?

Ursula became so weak and haggard in those early days, Magnus was concerned she would not live long. Convinced that she was reluctant to feed on her countrymen, he moved his brood. He didn't like spending too much time in one area anyway. Eventually suspicions would arise after an increasing number of people went missing. Once they left Prague and moved to a beach area in southern Portugal, Ursula developed a taste for human blood.

Now Ursula lacked those old inhibitions and delighted in feasting on humans.

After strolling a few blocks, Magnus spotted two women who were older than the usual crowd. One looked to be in her mid-forties. She had bleached blonde hair and fake breasts. Magnus had yet to understand the cosmetic enhancements of this era. It was a disfigurement of people's natural state. The other woman was a redhead who'd had too much to drink. Her face was flushed and her eyes blood-shot. Both wore skimpy outfits. From their looks, he suspected they would be willing victims.

He stopped walking as Ursula and Kristoff stayed close behind. He waited until the two women approached him.

"What lovely ladies I see here tonight," Magnus said.

The two women giggled like schoolgirls.

"None more than you two."

"Wow, aren't you exotic looking," the blonde said.

"Pretty cute, too," said the brunette. "Do you have a name?"

"Magnus, my sweet."

"That sounds so powerful. I'm Suzie. This is my friend Pam. We were walking by and I said to Pam, now that's an interesting looking guy. I bet he has a great story to tell. So Pam said to me, let's introduce ourselves."

Pam smiled. "Now we normally aren't so forward, but I said to Suzie, this guy looks big and strong and safe to be around."

"So we just had to introduce ourselves," Suzie said.

"You made a wise choice, ladies."

"Magnus, what an interesting name," Suzie said. "You're not from around here, are you?"

"I originally hail from Norway, but the world is my home."

"Ooh, I like that," Pam said. "So who are your friends?"

"This is Kristoff and Ursula."

Suzie said, "You guys are like a regular United Nations convention. So are you interested in showing two old gals a good time?"

They drove in Pam's car to an Irish pub in Rittenhouse Square. As the night wore on, Magnus did his best to seduce the two older ladies. He told stories of his travels around the world. When he said the world was his home, he was not kidding. He had lived in every habitable continent.

He could sense the blood lust inside Kristoff and Ursula. If he were alone, he would have let these two women go, but his young protégés would not be satisfied.

During the course of the evening, the older women drank five margaritas each. Pam hung onto Kristoff, while Suzie seemed more interested in Magnus and Ursula.

An Irish band came on stage. The music was atrocious. Magnus was a classically trained musician. He found it difficult to listen to the band butcher their music. Suzie and Pam seemed to enjoy it, or were too drunk to care.

At midnight, Pam suggested they go to her apartment.

Magnus paid the tab and they left the pub. He was an old-fashioned gentleman and would not allow the women to pay. Magnus then met the rest of his party outside.

They walked to Pam's car, located five blocks away. Normally reserved, Magnus felt the blood inside his veins shimmer.

They walked on the sidewalk past the shops and restaurants. Pam held Kristoff's strong arm. Ursula and Suzie flanked them on one side, and Magnus on the other. They turned onto a side street. Magnus surveyed the area. It was filled with houses and apartments. The street was otherwise empty.

Coming from behind, Magnus suddenly appeared in front of the two ladies by moving with preternatural speed.

"Wow, how did you do that?" Pam asked.

"This guy is like magic," Suzie said.

Even Kristoff blinked.

Magnus smiled. "I'm like the wind."

Suzie gasped when Magnus disappeared.

"I'm here one moment and gone the next."

Suzie stepped back as if she were dizzy from Magnus disappearing and reappearing. He drew up closely until he could feel her hot breath. He listened to her heart beat and felt the rhythm of her blood flowing through her body. She closed her eyes and leaned in toward him, before running her hands through his wavy blond hair.

"What you feel now is nothing compared to the pleasures I hide," Magnus said.

Pam momentarily left Kristoff and rubbed her body against Magnus.

"Will you take what we have to give?" Magnus asked. "A pleasure so intense that you will feel like leaping out of your skins and soaring through the heavens. Whatever you have experienced in your life will feel dull in comparison."

Suzie nodded.

Pam said, "That would be wonderful."

Suzie lifted her head and looked into the cloudless sky as if inviting him to do with her as he pleased. Magnus opened his mouth and sunk his fangs shallowly into her neck, getting a taste of blood. Not a long swallow or a draught, just a taste. It gave him a rush. Even after all these years, it was a feeling like nothing else. He withdrew and let Suzie fall into Ursula's arms. Ursula dug her fangs deeper into the skin and drank fully.

Pam did not turn in shock or revulsion. Instead she had a look of wanting.

As Suzie faded from consciousness and fell into the deep abyss, Magnus drew Pam toward him. "And what of you, my sweet? Would you like what we have given to your friend? Do you want pleasure beyond all else?"

Pam swayed between Magnus and Kristoff. She nodded, a dreamy smile on her face. Magnus grabbed her shoulders and buried his fangs in her throat, closing his eyes and relishing the sweet sensation of blood trickling into his mouth. He would thank Gabriella for persuading him to go out tonight.

As with Suzie, he consumed only a small amount of blood and left the rest for Kristoff. He smiled at their unbridled joy, remembering his early years.

He waited and watched. Before Suzie faded too far, he pulled back Ursula.

"That was intense. I feel like I'm on top of the world."

Magnus nodded. "So you are. There's nothing better than human blood."

Kristoff took several droughts than pulled himself off Pam. He had more restraint than Ursula. Her body wilted. A few moments later, he lowered her to the ground.

"Kristoff, remember that Pam's blood is more than just for your nourishment, because one day you will no longer need it for sustenance. Instead you'll need it to give you vitality and a thirst to live. When you get older, that desire can fade. Don't allow that to happen."

"I won't," Kristoff said.

Magnus looked deep into Suzie's eyes. "You will not remember meeting the three of us. You and your friend went out and had a fun, chaste, safe evening. You will now be going home."

Suzie had a distant look. "We had a safe evening. We're going home now."

Magnus smiled and did the same to Pam. She seemed as if in a trance. The women walked to their car and left.

Kristoff grinned. "How do you that? Whenever I try, it never works out so easily."

Magnus put his hand on Kristoff's shoulder. "It comes with time and experience. These ladies will hardly remember what just happened. They will only have vague, blissful memories. And why did I just glamour these ladies to forget what just happened?"

"To preserve our secrecy," Ursula replied. "Because humans would not accept our existence and would try to eliminate our kind."

Magnus nodded. "We must protect ourselves against those who would seek us harm. We are different from them, and they will never accept that."

Unlike Alexei, these two would never give him problems.

Chapter VIII

Mark Andrews gritted his teeth when he arrived at the murder scene and found Detective Glen Brown conducting the investigation. The last thing he needed was to deal with that cock-sucker. Brown was negligent at best and corrupt at worst. In his various dealings with the Philadelphia Police Department, he learned Internal Affairs had conducted several investigations on Brown for the use of excess force when questioning witnesses, but he always escaped punishment. Twice, they had investigated him on bribery charges, but in both cases the prosecutor's office had nothing more than circumstantial evidence. Mark saw enough corruption to discern the good from the bad. Brown wore a badge and represented the law, but he was not one of the good guys.

Nikki Staretz's fiancée, Enrico Pineda, made the discovery. After calling her numerous times, Pineda contacted one of Staretz's co-workers, who told him she had not shown up for work or called out sick. According to Detective Brown's report, Pineda, a construction foreman, finished working and went to a pub to eat dinner. He then drove to the apartment late that evening to find her dead. He called 911, and seventeen minutes later Detective Brown and his partner arrived and took control of the crime scene.

They questioned Pineda in addition to Staretz's neighbors, but no one could shed light on the murder. Pineda spoke incoherently during questioning. Brown claimed he was a suspect in the homicide, but Mark was certain he had no involvement. The tears he shed were genuine.

Pineda had to be innocent based on the condition of the body. It had been drained of blood. Also, the perp sliced open her abdomen and consumed part of her heart and kidneys. Staretz had been the fourth victim killed this way in over a week. Although there were slight variances in the three crimes, Mark had no doubt the same perp did all three. There were too many glaring similarities. The earlier questioning by the detectives showed that he had no connections to the other victims, as well as solid alibis for the times of the other murders.

Mark did not want to get involved in a serial murder investigation since it was out of his normal scope of operations, but he couldn't back out now. Initially, he only cared about Johnny Gunns. With this fourth victim, Mark had stumbled on something more important and deadly than the world of organized crime.

Three days ago, he and Rick had investigated the murder of a young Vietnamese woman, Thuy Pham, whose body had been found in a row home in Kensington. Much like Nikki Staretz's apartment, there were no signs of forcible entrance. Her body exhibited similar drainage of blood and puncture wounds on her neck. Also like Staretz, someone or something had partially consumed her organs.

They searched the entire house. The furniture was undisturbed, and there were no signs of a struggle. The neighbors had not heard anything unusual. The resemblance of the Thuy Pham case to Nikki Staretz was uncanny. The most peculiar thing was that both victims had smiles on their dead faces. They seemed blissful. In neither case was there signs of sexual assault.

Mark was still trying to arrange a meeting with mob boss Enzo Salerno. He had little doubt that Salerno was conducting his own parallel investigation. With Salerno's resources and connections, he could uncover things law enforcement officials couldn't.

Over the past few days, Mark sent feelers through his underground network to see if Salerno would accept a sit-down at a neutral territory. Salerno would probably reject a direct contact.

He stared at the corpse. Here she was, dead and drained of blood, yet she seemed perfectly content. No sign of forced entry or a struggle indicated she knew the killer, but why would she allow the perp to puncture her neck?

While other forensic experts and police officers milled about looking for more evidence, Mark sat in the kitchen kicking around ideas in his head. Maybe Staretz had been drugged. He wanted to see the toxicology report. They ran one on Thuy Pham, and she came up negative for drugs or alcohol.

Perhaps these were ritualistic killings. The two victims could have been part of a cult that practiced human sacrifices. That would explain why there was no forced entry or violent resistance, but that did not hold true with Johnny Gunns and Tina Monterullo. Every path he took led him nowhere. He had to get out of his normal mode of thought. Mark was used to dealing with mobsters where everything was calculated and the ultimate purpose was financial gain, power or revenge.

Special Agent Rick Carroll was speaking to Detective Brown. As much as he detested the man, he had to speak with him also.

"That boyfriend, what's his name, Pinera, he's got to be behind this," Brown said. "That sick fucking bastard. I'm going to book him on murder charges."

"Based on what?" Carroll asked. "Pineda has an alibi and he had no blood on him."

"You're going to find his prints all over here," Brown said.

Mark could no longer take this. "Of course his prints are going to be in the apartment. He was her fiancée, for Christ's sakes."

"The guy's a hothead," Brown said. "He had probable

cause. The neighbors said they fought all the time."

"Lots of couples fight," Mark said. "That doesn't mean he killed her. The similarities to the Pham girl and the Debenedetto and Monterulo murders are too similar. Does he have any connection between them? If so, I'd like to hear it. Any other murders you want to pin on Pineda while you're at it?"

Brown grinded his teeth. Mark almost wanted the detective to take a swing at him.

"What's your problem? I'm just trying to take another piece of shit off the street."

Mark went face to face with him. Nicotine stains covered the man's teeth. "The kid didn't do anything. You're looking for a nice, easy answer to this problem. Arresting Enrico Pineda won't make it go away. Why don't you do your job and investigate?"

"You got some kind of nerve coming in here and telling me how to do my job. I don't care what your badge says."

Rick Carroll stepped in between them. "This isn't going to solve anything. Look, Brown, we're going to talk to the suspect. You have no grounds to arrest him, so I'd strongly suggest you back off. If you find any evidence to substantiate your claims, we would be happy to listen to them. Until then, I strongly advise you not to press charges against the kid."

Carroll grabbed Mark's arm and dragged him away.

When they were outside Mark said, "That guy's a complete asshole. Except he's an asshole with a badge, which makes him dangerous."

"Cool it, Mark. The last thing I need is for one of my agents to get into a fist fight with a dick at a murder scene."

They stepped into Mark's government issue Chevy Impala. For a while neither said anything. Mark's mind was troubled with thoughts, theories, and ideas. None seemed plausible.

Before they arrived at the station off Spring Garden Str' where Pineda was held for questioning, Carroll asked¹ what are we dealing with here?"

Mark sighed. "The hell if I know."

"Come on, we're smart. We have nearly fifty years of Bureau experience between us. You're telling me we can't come up with something?"

"You ever hear of victims having their blood drained? I mean completely drained."

"No," Carroll replied. "I've witnessed some pretty exotic killings, but these are unique. Three in one week. It's only a matter of time before this leaks."

"I'm surprised it hasn't already with that idiot Brown investigating."

"Any connection between Johnny and Pham?" Carroll asked.

Mark shook his head. "I don't think we'll find any."

"You think these are random."

"Not in the sense that there's no purpose behind the killings. What throws everything off is Johnny. The other victims are young, attractive females. How did he get into the mix?"

"Maybe he was at the wrong place at the wrong time," Carroll answered. "His girl Tina was an exotic dancer. The perp attempted to kill her, and Johnny got in the way."

"But he was killed the same way as her. The loss of blood, the consumed organs. If he was just in the wrong place at the wrong time, a bullet in the head would make more sense." Mark hit his palm with his fist. "There's something here we're not seeing."

"When you figure that out, let me know."

They walked into the police station. Mark had a good relationship with the cops in the city. He tried to foster an environment of cooperation, since he often worked cases with them. Brown was an exception. The man was crooked. Mark didn't mind playing fast and loose with certain procedural rules in order to get an arrest or secure a conviction, but bribery, extortion and confiscating drugs in order to sell them made a cop just like thugs on the street.

They walked into the interrogation room. Enrico Pineda looked visibly shaken. This kid had nothing to do with Staretz's murder. He'd stake his reputation on it. He and Carroll sat at the opposite end of the table. The room was sterile, poorly lit and smelled of perspiration. Mark turned on additional lights to make the questioning seem less adversarial.

"Sorry to hear about your girlfriend, Rico," Carroll said.

Rico nodded. His eyes were red and his face was pale.

"We have a few questions to ask you," Mark said.

"Cigarette?" Carroll asked.

"Yeah, please."

Carroll handed Pineda a cigarette and a lighter.

"I don't have any idea who killed her. I mean, who'd want to kill my Nikki." Pineda paused and let out a muffled sob. "She never hurt no one. She was a good, kind person. Everyone liked her, and now she's gone forever."

Mark gave him a few minutes to regain his composure. "Did you have any indication that Nikki may have been in danger?"

"No way. Like I said, everyone liked her."

"Do you know if she met anyone unusual in the last few days?" Mark asked.

"No. She don't get out too often. Usually, she just goes to work, and then I come over, and she cooks me dinner and we stay in."

"Detective Brown indicated you went out tonight," Mark said. "You went to a bar, had dinner and a few beers."

"Yeah, you know, just trying to unload a little. There's been a lot going on at the job site."

"Yet, prior to that you called Nikki and had no reply. You also called one of her co-workers who indicated she hadn't been to work that day. So why did you wait until a quarter to eleven to see if Nikki was okay?"

"Look, sometimes she gets a little high strung. After we get into a fight she might go a couple of days without talking to me. Sometimes I'll call, and she don't pick up, so I figured she was mad at me. Nothing to worry about."

"In that case, why did you drive over to her apartment?" Carroll asked.

"Ah, you know, I figure if she's mad at me, then maybe we could make up. That's when it's the best, after we fight and make up." Rico buried his face into his open palms.

"You weren't at all concerned about her?" Mark asked.

"Nah, she just went with some friends from work to the Rock Lobster a couple days ago, so I figure maybe they put some ideas in her head like I'm a bad dude or somethin'."

"She went out to a club two nights ago?" Mark asked.

"Yeah. I guess she needed to get out."

Mark glanced at Carroll. "Can you give me the names of the people she went out with?"

"Sure." Pineda wrote the names on a legal pad. "I can't believe my baby's gone."

They thanked Pineda for his time and left. Mark felt sorry for him. He obviously cared for her. Brown put the guy through the ringer. To lose a loved one and then to be questioned as if he were the murderer just wasn't right.

On the drive back to the Federal building, Rick sighed. "I should turn this case over to some other field agents."

Mark frowned. "Why?"

"It's out of your jurisdiction. I think we can rule out Johnny Gunns as a mob hit, so there's no connection to organized crime."

Mark looked out the window. "I don't think we can rule out anything."

"Come on, Mark. Who are you kidding? Whoever did Johnny did these two girls as well. It's more than obvious they're not connected. You said as much back there."

"Fine. Call it what you want, but I can't let go. Not yet. Something crazy is happening out there, and I don't want to rely on that dickhead Brown. Let's keep investigating. It's now four victims in over a week. Whoever's doing this, we have to stop it. Can you just walk away after what you've seen?"

Carroll opened up his window and lit a cigarette. "I suppose not. All right, let's roll with it for now and see what happens. You do this job long enough and you think nothing can surprise you. Then something like this comes along."

Chapter IX

Enzo finished the escarole soup his wife Gina made for him. He brought his bowl to the sink and kissed her cheek.

She smiled and kissed him back.

He had not gone to his Center City office today, opting to handle business from home. It was past noon, and he only received one phone call from Vito Anastasia, also known as the Wiz. Vito got the nickname because he had an uncanny ability to add, subtract, multiply and divide numbers in his head. He was great at mathematical formulas and equations. In his mid-twenties, he looked barely out of high school. The kid was smart as hell. Enzo encouraged him to enroll in Villanova or Drexel to pursue a mathematics degree and then come back to work for him, but the Wiz wanted to be a part of the action. The problem was the kid didn't have the stones for this lifestyle. If the Wiz was forced to pull the trigger in a tight spot as Enzo had in the past, would he be able to do it? He doubted it.

The Wiz called to let Enzo know he wouldn't be able to drive him tomorrow. Sophie needed him. Of late, she had been using him as a hacker to get into databases and decode information from corporate and government offices.

He was about to go to his study, but before he entered, his four-year-old daughter Angela charged at him full speed. Just as she was about to collide with him, Enzo reached down, grabbed her by the waist and hoisted her in the air. He twirled her, and she squealed with laughter. This was their daily ritual.

No matter what was going on, he always made time for Angela, seven-year-old Eddie and eleven-year-old Donna. He especially liked playing with Angela. She was headstrong and full of energy.

Gina walked by and shook her head. "She's going to hurt herself one of these days."

Enzo waved his hand. "You worry too much. Kids are resilient. They take a tumble and keep going. Right, sweetie?"

Angela giggled. "Right, Dad."

"It's my job to worry. Someone around here has to."

Gina wore a severe frown.

"What's wrong, baby?" Enzo asked.

"Nothing."

Enzo threw Angela in the air like a projectile and caught her before she splattered on the floor. Winded, he sat on the leather sofa. Angela ran outside to play on her swing set.

Enzo accompanied Gina to the basement where she had some ironing to do. He put his arms around her waist, careful not to touch the iron. He kissed the back of her neck. "So what's the matter?"

Gina sighed. "Donna's been asking a lot of questions lately."

"Kids are naturally inquisitive. When I was her age, I wanted to know about everything."

"I'm talking questions about what her father does. She knows that I don't work, so how does Daddy make money? I think some of her friends have planted ideas in her head."

Enzo drew away from her. "I'm a businessman, plain and simple."

"Not everybody sees it that way."

"Let them think what they want."

Gina frowned. "What happens when her friends start saying otherwise?"

"I doubt they will. People don't know who I am. I'm invisible, like Average Joe Citizen. The media wants violence and bloodshed. I don't give that to them, so they ignore me."

"Some people know who you are."

Enzo shrugged. "Unless their parents are in law enforcement, I doubt it. If the time comes when more explanation is necessary, then we'll say that I operate in a slightly different manner than most businessmen."

"People talk."

"Let 'em talk. Since when does that bother you?"

"It doesn't bother me any," Gina said. "You know I'm one hundred and ten percent behind you. I just worry about the kids. How will they handle it?"

"They're strong."

"I hope so." Gina finished ironing and carried the basket of folded clothes up from the basement as Enzo followed.

He knew there were risks associated with his lifestyle, and some involved his family. He tried to shield them from scrutiny. So far, he had been successful.

Enzo tried to go the corporate route after having graduated from the Wharton School of Business but couldn't play by corporate America's rules. It was not for someone of his talents and abilities. He and Gina had not been married for long when Donna was an infant. Between his income and what Gina made working as a receptionist for a computer design firm, it did not provide the lifestyle they wanted. So he came home to South Philadelphia and found what once had been one of the premier organized crime syndicates in the country was in a sad state. Ruthless killings and guys flipping had plagued the local mafia. Most bosses and major players were dead or in jail.

Growing up in South Philly, he looked up to the mafiosos in the neighborhood. They had respect and a glamorous lifestyle. Angelo Bruno, the Docile Don, was revered by everyone. Bruno's successors were feared. They owned the neighborhood. Tales of the mob fascinated him in his youth, but he never thought the lifestyle was for him. He was the valedictorian at his high school and received several full scholarship offers.

That made it even more difficult when he did not find success in the business world. Maybe if he was more patient, he would have gotten his break, but he was not about waiting for a break. He was about creating his own.

Enzo's entire family was connected in some way. In fact, his uncle Johnny was a high ranking member of the Rabito family in New York. That was how he got his start. His ascension through the ranks was rapid. After a couple of years, he made his play to take over the Philadelphia crime scene.

Whoever controlled the Philadelphia area could only do so with the blessing and the approval of the New York bosses. His uncle Johnny set up a meeting with the bosses of the Rabito and Torello families in New York on his behalf.

He knew he was facing an uphill battle. He was still new at this game and was unknown to many of the major players, so they were naturally suspicious. He had to wow them.

Enzo used his business smarts. He created a slide show presentation. He spoke eloquently and commanded their attention, using his street smarts to figure out what would appeal to the mob bosses. Seven people including his uncle Johnny sat in the room with their eyes locked on him. Halfway through, he knew he had them hooked. When he finished, they said their good-byes and hugged and kissed him.

The next day, Vince Torello called him. "We want you to come to New York tonight."

If Vince Torello called, you didn't refuse him. When Enzo arrived, numerous members of the New York and New Jersey families greeted him warmly and gave him their blessing.

He never looked back. He was under control, organized and had fresh ideas. Under his leadership and vision, his organization rose in national prominence.

Before Enzo stepped into his office, the phone rang. Gina walked down the stairs to get it. "Hello... Oh hi, Sophie. How are you doing? Good. Good ... Eddie's earache is much better. Thanks for asking ... Hey, I wanted to let you know that I tried out the meatloaf recipe you gave me ... Oh, it was delicious. Where did you get it from? Well thank your grandmom for me ... Okay, just a second."

She handed Enzo the phone.

"At the office?" he asked. "I'll call you right back."

Over the years, Enzo developed a growing paranoia about people listening into his conversations. He conducted weekly electronic sweeps on his home, office and vehicles to detect hidden devices. Worried that the feds would develop new, increasingly sophisticated bugs, he always used the latest, most advanced bug detectors. Once he found a listening device planted underneath the steering wheel of his Jaguar XJ8.

Despite his confidence that his home office was not tapped, he still went outside when discussing business matters. It was more out of habit than an actual need for secrecy.

He took out a disposable cell phone and dialed Sophie's number. He would use the disposable cell phone for a couple of weeks, toss it and get a new one. Khalil, his Saudi Arabian supplier of stolen high tech gadgetry, assured him they were completely untraceable.

Sophie answered on the first ring. "Good news."

"That's the only kind I like."

"It seems that the distinguished Councilman Stephen O'Leary has a thing for underage girls. Most of them are eighteen and nineteen, but some as young as sixteen and seventeen. And we have the pictures to prove it."

"Really? Give me the details."

It was crucial that this real estate development deal go through. He owned several construction companies, one of which would get the bid for this project. When he figured in the cost of overruns and other "unexpected costs", he could make a nice profit. He also owned the lots where the land development would take place. He bought them a few years ago at a low price with the idea of forcing a development project in the area. After several years of negotiations, he'd finally made progress.

The only thing he needed was approval by the city council, and his point man was Stephen O'Leary. Enzo didn't trust the man. Yes, he was on his payroll, but the councilman was getting cold feet on the deal.

"Well you remember when I was telling you about that spa I go to out in Wayne. One of their male customers, who by the way isn't gay, just so happens to have a business relationship with O'Leary. For a fee, he provides teenaged girls for him. O'Leary meets them in the same room at the City Hotel on Tuesday and Thursday afternoon. I got The Wiz to install cameras into the room and activate them at the rendezvous times. Bada-bing, now we have the goods on him. I sent Fat Paulie to show O'Leary the pictures."

"I wish I could have seen his reaction. That would have been priceless."

"So, we won't have any problem with the legislation. It will pass through City Council nice and easy, and O'Leary is going to do whatever it takes to get the mayor on board."

"I would say so. O'Leary's got big aspirations. Leaking this would crush him. So the Wiz set this up. How about that?"

"I had him update our computer networks. He does some hacking on the side, so I figured this would be up his ally. He disguised himself as an HVAC mechanic who was called in to fix a ventilation problem. He snuck into the room. Fifteen minutes later, he set the whole thing up, and nobody knew any better."

"It's a good thing he's on our side. I wouldn't want him working for the bad guys."

After Enzo hung up the phone, he went inside and looked over the project plan for the land development proposal he wrote three years ago. Before legislation of this magnitude passed, he had to grease certain hands and line some pockets with gold. That was fine with him, because he would make more money from this project than working for ten years in the legitimate business world. Who said crime didn't pay?

Enzo kept busy for the next couple hours looking at outlines and blueprints. He wanted to start construction the day after the legislation passed, and he had to hire sub-contractors — his people of course — and get his crew on the payroll of the union handling the job. He would give the Wiz a special gift, maybe a new sports car, as a sign of his appreciation.

When the front door bell rang, Enzo walked out of the study, but Gina beat him to the door. Tony Scrambolgni was at the front door with Angela clinging onto his back. He swung her around, and she squealed with laughter. Tony raised her high above his head. She shrieked as he brought her close and planted a kiss on her forehead. He lowered her to the floor and greeted Gina with a kiss on the cheek.

"Anthony, so nice of you to stop by."

"I happened to be in the neighborhood and I saw the prettiest little girl I know."

Angela raised her arms. "Lift me up again."

Tony hoisted her onto his shoulders.

"I just made biscotti." Gina opened a Tupperware container. "Would you like some?"

"Ooh, you know my weak spot." Tony devoured a piece. "Excellent." He licked the crumbs off his fingers and put down Angela.

Angela looked at him with wide, expectant eyes. "Uncle Tony, wanna see my new bike?"

"Of course I would. I just have to talk to your daddy first."

"Okay, Uncle Tony." Angela ran out the front door.

Gina put away the remainder of the biscotti. "So how's Tricia?"

"She's doin' fine, 'cept she keeps bugging me about getting these collagen treatments. I tell her she looks fine. You know if I live to be a hundred, I'll never understand women."

"Be happy," Gina said. "She's trying to look good for you. A lot of women just give up and their looks go to hell."

"I guess."

"Well, I have work to do so I'll leave you two alone." Gina went upstairs.

Enzo gave Tony a half hug. Without speaking they went outside.

Tony handed Enzo an envelope filled with hundred dollar bills. "I was able to get Slim Jimmy to pay up plus a little extra that I squeezed out of him."

Enzo put the envelope in his shirt pocket. "Good, but that isn't what brings you here. You could have given me this tomorrow."

Tony nodded.

"It's about Johnny. You know something, but you're reluctant to say it. Come on, Tony. Whatever it is, you can tell me."

Tony lit a cigarette. He offered one to Enzo, who declined. "You remember I told you about the old lady who saw the man walking outside of the house shortly after Johnny got killed? Well, I told her to call if there was anything else she wanted to let me know."

"And?"

"She called and, um, said there was one thing she didn't tell me. You see, she was afraid to say it, thinking I wouldn't believe her, but she had to tell me. Wouldn't feel right if she didn't." Tony puffed his cigarette. "The man she saw, he was there walking on the street with his pale skin and blood on his shirt and then, he just disappeared."

"Disappeared?" Enzo asked.

"That's what the woman said. Poof. Just like that."

"That's consistent with The Goat's story. The guy was choking him and then disappeared."

Tony nodded.

"The plot thickens. We might need to get Perry Mason on the case."

"Yeah, well there's more." Tony threw his cigarette to the ground and crushed it with his shoe. He produced an envelope from his jacket pocket and handed it to Enzo.

"What are these?"

"Photos. Two more done just like Johnny and Tina. Some Vietnamese broad, Pham, and some chick Nikki Staretz."

Without changing expression, Enzo examined the photos.

"Brown gave me them." Despite the cool breeze, a trickle of sweat ran down Tony's cheek.

After Enzo finished looking at the pictures, he put them back in the envelope and handed it to Tony. "What makes Brown certain it was done by the same person?"

Tony put the envelope back into his jacket and wiped sweat off his forehead with his sleeve. "He said the way the killings were done made him think it was the same guy who offed Johnny. Almost all their blood was gone."

"I noticed the neat little puncture marks on the neck. Now I may not be a detective, but they look like bite marks."

Tony sighed. "Yeah, that's what Brown said. They were made by teeth, actually fangs."

"What about the torn abdomen?"

"He said that markings on the body suggest they was done by sharp talons or claws or something."

"Johnny's liver and Tina's kidneys were consumed. Did that happen with these two?"

"Yeah, same deal."

Enzo smiled. "I'm a reasonable man. Wouldn't you agree, Tony?"

"Sure. You're the most fair and reasonable guy I know. That's what everyone says even when they don't like your decisions."

"Then why is it that when I look at these pictures, combined with The Goat's story and what you're telling me about the old woman, that I come to an insane conclusion? If I put everything together, what was done here was the work of a vampire, or at least someone who fashions himself as one."

"I don't know what to tell you, boss. I ain't one to believe in ghosts or creatures of the night or shit like that, but I gotta admit, this is fucking creepy. It makes my skin crawl just looking at those pictures. What a fucking way to go, huh?"

"I want to talk to The Goat again. Before I make any rash conclusions, I want to think this through. Find out more about those two girls. Talk to their families. See if they met anyone unusual lately. Give them the guy's description. He sounds Eastern European from The Goat's description. Check out the Czech and Russian clubs in town. Also, go back to Joe Senneca and find out if any recent customers at the *Cat House* match that description. Don't rule anything out just because it sounds crazy, because this shit is crazy."

"I gotta tell you, boss, I don't like this one bit. I've been in some tight spots before. I can deal with the heavy hitters, but what the fuck's going on here?"

"I don't like it either, but I assure you we'll find Johnny's killer. I told his mother at his funeral that his death would not go without retribution. I told her I would deal with her baby boy's killer in a manner the legal system couldn't. We'll get whoever's responsible. Right?"

Tony looked down, then back up at Enzo and nodded. "Sure, we'll get him." His voice showed a complete lack of confidence.

After Tony left, Enzo went back inside his office and put aside the work blueprints for the Delaware Avenue land development deal. He logged onto the Internet. He prided himself in being well prepared for every situation. He wanted to be able to handle all eventualities. Although he did not believe Johnny's murderer was a vampire or some supernatural being, he would learn everything he could about the subject. If the impossible was true, he would know how to face this enemy.

Chapter X

For the second time this week, Alexei sat in the audience watching the musical *42ⁿᵈ Street*. He came back because of the spellbinding play of the flute player in the orchestra. He had long been a fan of the arts and had seen plays in dozens of cities. His ears were so keen that he could pick out the sounds of individual instruments within an orchestra.

Alexei worked his way back stage using his charm. These mortals couldn't resist him. He chatted with several performers, then asked where he could find members of the orchestra.

He found her near the rear exit to the theater, a bottle of water in hand, talking to a trumpet player. The trumpet player's musical abilities were not so impressive, but he had a soft spot for all practitioners of the arts. He worked his way into the conversation.

The woman was a fiery, red head named Denise McKenna. Her skin was fair and lightly freckled. She spoke softly and possessed a quick wit. Alexei could tell she was passionate, but careful with whom she let into her world.

The trumpet player had a baby face. He was probably close to thirty, but appeared more like twenty. His name was Troy and he was a native of Philadelphia.

Their conversation lingered, as members of the cast and crew exited. In the middle of Alexei's story about some time he spent in Mongolia, a security guard told them the building was closing down and everyone had to leave.

Troy smiled. "Let's go back to my place."

They took a cab to Troy's apartment. They conversed and drank coffee until the early hours of the morning. "I have enjoyed your company immensely, but I fear I must depart. Perhaps we could meet again tomorrow night."

Denise had a look of desire, as if the last thing she wanted was for Alexei to leave. "We have a matinee performance. Maybe you can come by after the show."

Alexei smiled. "I'm afraid I'll be occupied. How about after the Thursday evening show."

"That'll be great," Denise said. "I look forward to seeing you again."

He left them each with a kiss on the forehead.

He met Denise after the Thursday show. Troy was ill and did not make the performance.

"Would you like to take a boat ride on the Delaware?" Alexei asked.

"I'd love to."

"Great, bring your flute." Alexei thought at that moment she would have loved to peel potatoes with him. He commandeered a luxury boat on Pier fifty-three off of Delaware Avenue. He told her it was his, but he had no idea who actually owned it.

Even though he hadn't sailed a boat in some time, it did not take him long to figure out its inner workings. He still preferred sailing to flying. It was difficult to find flights that entirely traveled in darkness.

As Alexei sailed down the river, Denise played her flute. He felt at peace as the melody bounced off the walls of the ship and onto the water. He leaned back against the cushion of the captain's seat and watched the soft moonlight glisten off her face.

When Denise finished, he held her in his strong arms as if she were a child. Her eyes beckoned for him to give his sweet embrace.

"Take me now," she said.

He kissed her. "Patience, my precious. When the time is right, I'll give you such intense pleasure you won't be able to handle it."

She leaned her head onto his chest. Within minutes she was asleep. Alexei carried her to a cot in the lower deck of the ship. He then sailed the boat back to the dock.

He took Denise back to her condo and returned to the mansion in Gladwynne, expecting to find everybody asleep as day was ready to break. The house was still, but he sensed a presence. A slight rustling in the air told him he was not alone.

Alexei looked around the living room. It had thirty feet ceilings and an overhanging balcony. The floors were hardwood and carefully treated. The room was adorned with expensive furniture, some modern, some ancient. Members of Magnus' brood often shipped their favorite items when they moved. To fill the rest of the house, members of his brood purchased furniture, decorations and artwork. As for Alexei, all he needed was his gold-plated coffin.

The main living room featured a large plasma television and stereo system. Nearby were a baby grand piano and an antique grandfather clock. A plush, leather sofa sat next to an old armoire that was in immaculate condition. The centerpiece was a jade chalice Magnus attained hundreds of years ago. In the corner was a juke box from the fifties.

In the next room, two criss-crossing swords that Magnus had taken from a baron in Romania who had tried to kill him over a land dispute were positioned above the walk-in fire place. Alexei rolled his eyes. It was a feeble attempt by Magnus to show his ability to vanquish his enemies. Alexei needed no such symbols.

As Alexei sat on the solid oak rocking chair, he again felt the presence of another. He closed his tired eyes, knowing he should retire to his coffin. The hungry rays of the sun would soon be shining. For most of his kind, sunlight exposure was fatal. For him, it was merely painful.

Despite Magnus' claim, Alexei was at least as old as the brood leader. He barely remembered the time when he could freely walk in the sunlight. Those days were so long gone, it seemed as if they never happened.

Born and raised in the Ukraine, Alexei's life was a simple one. He worked on a farm with his many siblings, raising cattle and sheep, growing potatoes and cabbage. He remembered being content. He thought he had been married, but was not sure.

One night while tilling soil, he heard strange noises. He wanted to go inside, but could not ignore it. He walked in the direction of the noise and spotted blood on the ground. He followed the trail and found a calf lying on the dirt with a massive gash near its throat. It was still alive. Before Alexei could react, a creature sitting on a branch of a tree pounced on him. He could scarcely defend himself, grabbing at its jaws as it tried to bite him. The creature's eyes held a look of insanity. What manner of beast was attacking him?

He threw the creature off. This thing looked human, but it appeared wild and unintelligent. It grunted and moved in a frenzy. Blood dripped from its stubbled chin. It had torn apart the calf with its own teeth.

It leaped into the air, an inhuman leap, and pounced on him again. He tried to use his fists to fend off the attacker, but it overwhelmed him with incredible strength. He fought with desperation, but could not stop it from burying its fangs deep into his neck. Alexei closed his eyes and felt his life escape. Yet it felt good. Peace and contentment replaced his initial terror.

His eyes went wide as blood surged through his body. He felt weak, but death had not won this round. Slowly, sensation returned to his limbs and extremities. He could move his fingers, but did not have the strength to stand. He opened his eyes. The creature was on top of him. Alexei's mouth was cupped on its wrist, and he sucked its blood. It was this very blood that dragged him from the shadows of death.

When the creature left, tears welled in his eyes. He never felt so alone in his life.

It took a great effort to rise to his feet. He was certain he was still alive, but unsure how he escaped death.

The calf next to him did not share his fate. Alexei tried to move, but it was too strenuous. He stared at his big farm house, which now seemed foreboding. He then looked at his tattered clothes and torn flesh. He did not know where to go, but did not want to go back. He was tainted.

When Alexei regained some strength, he walked away from his farmhouse. His memory of that time was murky, but he remembered walking through fields, meadows and farms with no real destination in mind. He grabbed a chicken and crushed its neck with his hands. Instead of cooking it over a fire, he tore its head off and drank its blood.

He continued in this haze for some time. He could not bear for his family to see him like this. His condition deteriorated. He killed farm and wild animals, drinking their blood for nourishment. As he moved away from the farms and closer to the city, finding sustenance became more difficult. Physically, he was weak, but he was also on the verge of madness. He was alone and afraid, no longer part of the human race. It was unnatural to live with an unquenchable thirst for blood.

Before sunrise each day he managed to find shelter, usually an old farmhouse or shed. The light was no longer his friend. Just thinking about the sun hurt.

When his physical and mental fatigue reached its peak, he stopped walking and wept. He wanted to return to his old life. He was a despicable creature, wandering the lands in search for blood.

He landed in the streets of Kiev looking like a vagrant. Lying huddled in the street, a constable arrested him. He would die in jail. How could he satisfy his insatiable blood lust inside of a prison?

"Why are you arresting me?" Alexei demanded.

The constable slapped him hard across the face. "You're being arrested for abducting two missing children, you loathsome fiend."

Could he have been responsible for these missing children? He could barely remember how he got to Kiev. Perhaps he killed them without realizing it.

If he had the strength he would break free from his shackles. Prison would kill him for sure. How was he going to avoid coming out during the daytime?

As the constable ushered him to the prison, a figure shot down from the top of a building like an arrow. Alexei made a feeble attempt at getting out of the way, but he was not the target.

The assailant knocked the constable to the ground. With an awesome display of strength, he lifted the constable with one hand and flung him to the opposite side of the road. The constable met the outside wall of a house with a thud, instantly rendered unconscious.

Alexei cowered in fear. The newcomer looked human, but how could a person possess that kind of strength?

Instead of killing him, the man lifted Alexei and stood him on his feet. With ease, he broke Alexei's shackles.

He tried to thank the stranger, but could not form the words. Not having the strength to stand, Alexei slumped to the floor. The man picked him up as he faded from consciousness.

He woke up at night in a warm and cozy cottage lying next to a fire. He coughed fitfully and shivered despite the warmth of the flame. Alexei looked around, but did not see anyone. Maybe the stranger who saved him was the owner of this place. He called out, but no one answered.

He tried to keep himself warm, but had a difficult time no matter how close he got to the fire. He wanted to search the cottage, but could hardly stand.

A door opened. Alexei's rescuer entered, but he was not alone. Cradled in his arms was an older woman with grey hair and wrinkled skin. She appeared to be unconscious.

He brought the woman closer to Alexei and sat her on a chair. He slashed her wrist with his teeth, then took her wrist and brought it to Alexei's mouth.

Alexei shrank back from it. "I can't ... ."

"Do you wish to live?"

Alexei nodded. He did not come this far to die.

"Then drink. Your transformation is incomplete. If you do not, you'll die."

Alexei looked into the man's hard blue eyes and saw his concern. He had not seen himself in a mirror lately but could only imagine what kind of ghastly sight he looked like.

Once more the man brought the bleeding wrist to Alexei's mouth. He swallowed a mouthful of blood and felt energized. It was like he had been in the desert dying of thirst, and someone had given him water. No longer cognizant of the presence of the other in the room, he tore deeper into the woman's flesh with teeth that had recently grown in size and sharpness. The only thing that mattered at that moment was the sweet elixir coming from her body.

The woman fidgeted and shook as Alexei drained her blood. The rhythm of her heart pounded inside his head.

Before her life expired, the man took her away.

Alexei frowned.

"Enough for now. There will be more later." He took the woman and exited the back of the cottage.

Alexei licked the blood off his mouth and chin. He inched closer to the fire, which now warmed him. He felt more alive than he had since being attacked by the creature at his old farm.

Nearly an hour later the man returned. "How are you?"

"Good." Alexei rose. "Thank you for saving me from the constable and for what you did just now."

The man smiled. "There are not many of us. We have to look out for our own."

"Us? What exactly are we?"

The man roared with laughter. "You still do not know what you have become?"

Alexei shook his head.

"My name is Ivan. Tell me your story."

Alexei started with the fateful evening he was attacked. He told him everything he could remember, although many details were sketchy. Ivan told him today's date. He had been gone from his farm for nearly a month. Had his family gone looking for him? Did they think he was dead?

Alexei said, "You told me you would reveal my true identity."

"You and I are creatures of the night, my friend."

Alexei shook his head, feeling a mixture of confusion and fear.

"You're unfamiliar with the term?"

Alexei nodded.

"But you understand the concept. You have sought shelter during the day?"

"Yes."

"When your transformation is complete, you won't be able to go out during the day at all. Our kind is destined to walk the night for all of eternity and never see the sun. It is our curse, yet we are blessed with immortality."

"You mean I can't die?" Alexei shifted nervously.

"Oh, you can be killed. We're not invincible. If you don't meet an unfortunate demise, you can live forever, for you are undead. We have incredible speed, strength and agility. We can do things mortals can only dream of. As you advance in age, your powers will grow. The physical boundaries of the world mean nothing to us. With time you will be able to scale buildings and move so fast people won't be able to detect you. You will know pleasures that humans can never experience. How did you feel when you drank of that lady's blood?"

"Vibrant. Rapturous."

"That feeling only intensifies over time," Ivan said.

"What happened to the old woman?"

"I gave her a proper burial."

Alexei shook his head as a tear formed in his eye.

"Don't weep." He put his arm on Alexei's shoulder. "You'd perish without her blood."

"But I killed her. How can you tell me not to weep?"

"Because we need them to survive. We can drink the blood of animals, but it's not the same. People sustain us."

"But I murdered her," said Alexei.

"Don't think of it as murder, since you're no longer human. To us they are animals to use as we see fit."

Alexei's eyes narrowed. How could Ivan be so callous?

Ivan told him about his own history, as well as things he needed to know to survive.

"Are there many like us?" Alexei asked.

"Not many. About a dozen in Kiev. Our numbers must be small, or we would overrun the human population. I have met others in my travels. We are small and silent, yet strong and powerful."

For a while Alexei said nothing, numb to his new reality. Ivan sat beside him wordlessly providing comfort.

"That thing that attacked me, it didn't look like you or I. It was a twisted, demented creature."

Ivan stood up with his arms folded and paced the room. "Although I've never seen any, I have heard of them before. I believe the wretched beast had been made a creature of the night, then abandoned and left to fend for itself. The early period of one's conversion is crucial. From the first time I laid eyes on you last week, I knew you were recently turned."

"I have been in Kiev for a week?"

Ivan nodded. "At least. If I did not find you to help you through this difficult time, the same fate could have befallen you. That beast is probably crazed and unintelligent. A violent and destructive being whose only concern is to feed. You would not want to live like that."

"But why did it make me a creature of the night? Why didn't it kill me?"

"Good question. Perhaps it was an inner need to propagate the species."

Over the next few weeks Ivan mentored Alexei. Each night, he would bring Alexei a fresh kill. Eventually he grew in strength and could hunt on his own.

Alexei stayed with Ivan for a few years. He met others of his kind in Kiev, but he never returned to his old family. That part of his life was over.

Alexei wanted to explore the European continent and meet others of his kind, but Ivan did not want to accompany him. He had already traveled throughout Europe and Asia and wanted to stay put. It was with mixed sadness and excitement that Alexei embarked on his own. Before he left, he needed to do one last thing.

Alexei ventured to the Ukrainian countryside pretending to be a law enforcement official. He asked the citizens if they had seen a wild and dangerous beast, giving them a detailed description. They would not speak about it until one day a blacksmith in a small village told him this beast fatally wounded his daughter. The blacksmith wanted revenge.

Three days after meeting the blacksmith, Alexei found his target lurking in a cave. It had slaughtered a lamb and was drinking its blood. Alexei called out to it. It looked at Alexei with a lack of comprehension in its eyes, then howled in a frenzy. Alexei felt pity, but that did not stop him from fulfilling his mission.

Alexei lunged at it. He grabbed the creature and hurled it against the wall of the cave. Before it could recover, he picked up a stone and smashed its skull. It fell to the ground dazed and badly wounded. Alexei smashed its skull repeatedly with the heavy stone.

Ivan explained about their amazing ability to recover from

injury. Alexei did not want to give it a chance to recuperate. He wanted to end its misery, so he pulled out a sword. With one swift motion, he decapitated it and watched its head roll down the cave. This creature was a liability to him and others of his kind.

Alexei smiled when he spotted his elusive visitor standing in the shadows. "Gabriella, I thought you would have retired by now. It's late."

"I was waiting up for you." Gabriella slithered toward him like a feline. "Did you enjoy your evening out?"

"As always. You should come out with me."

"Perhaps I should." Gabriella's voice would be barely audible to human ears, but Alexei heard her with perfect clarity. "You've been making the news."

"Is that right? Andy Warhol said everybody would achieve fifteen minutes of fame. After nearly a millennium, it looks like I have mine."

Gabriella's voice was soothing like a cat's purr. "You know we can't afford any unwanted attention. That's what happened in Lisbon, and we had to make a hasty departure."

Alexei's pale face darkened. "Let me guess. Magnus told you to talk to me. He wanted you to get me to tow the line. The coward can't even speak to me himself."

"I'm acting of my own accord. I care for you and want a harmonious existence for all of us. What you've done makes that difficult."

Alexei turned away from her. "Magnus has forgotten what it's like to live. I never will. He may still live, but he's dead in his heart and mind. He's jealous of me."

Gabriella leaned her head onto his shoulder. "You misconstrue his intentions. We need secrecy. You would not have been able to live for so long if you were visible to the outside world. Nobody is asking you to stop living. Just be discreet."

"I'll take your suggestion under advisement. Now if you don't mind, I must retire."

Gabriella sighed as he walked away.

Chapter XI

The Goat woke up with a groan. His thudding headache prevented him from getting out of bed. How could he have been so stupid?

His girlfriend Karen was already awake. Of course, she had not been out with the boys last night, drinking and smoking heavily.

She wore a wide smile. "Wake up already, Patrick. I can't believe Enzo Salerno is actually coming to our apartment. I'm so excited."

The Goat struggled to sit. His stomach churned, and for a moment he thought he was going to vomit. Eventually the queasy feeling subsided, but his head still spun. "When Enzo comes to your home, that ain't always a good thing." He buried his face in his hands as nausea returned.

"Whaddaya mean it ain't a good thing?" Karen asked. "You didn't do nothing wrong."

The Goat groaned.

"I told you not to go drinking, but would you listen to me? No. You had to make an ass out of yourself to impress your friends."

"Don't remind me." He couldn't get mad at Karen for nagging him. For once, she was right. Enzo called him at seven last night after The Goat returned from closing the books and taking the last bets. There had been little action with only a handful of baseball games on the schedule. Things would pick up next week when the NFL preseason started.

The Goat couldn't believe Enzo called. He spoke to few people, and The Goat was not part of his inner circle. The boss told him he would stop by his apartment at noon to discuss business matters.

This news stunned Karen. She took off from work to prepare a lavish feast, even if it would be for three people. The Goat had already made plans to go out with his boys. They always got together on Tuesday, so he told Karen he would still go out, but he would take it easy.

They started out at the *Cat House*. If he had any sense, he would have suggested alternate plans. After several lap dances, he knew he would regret this night. Four beers in, he was already half lit up.

After leaving the strip joint, they drove across the Betsy Ross Bridge and into Jersey. A friend owned a bar across the river. Inside the bar, they had their own private room. The tequila flowed and to make things worse, one of The Goat's friends brought a dimebag of pot. He should have said no, but he was already ripped, so what difference would it make? That turned out to be another bad decision.

By the time they left the bar, he could hardly walk. He stumbled into the apartment at two in the morning, not remembering anything after that.

The Goat rubbed his eyes and tried to stand. "What time is it?"

"It's nine o'clock." Karen started a pot of coffee. "Come on. Let's get going. Mr. Salerno is going to be here before long. You have to get yourself ready."

"I don't think so." He lunged for the bathroom and vomited into the toilet.

"You all right, Patrick?" Karen's voice had a hint of annoyance. "You know you shouldn't have gone out partying last night. This is what happens when you do stuff like that." She hovered outside the door, while he leaned his head against the wall. "You don't look so good. Why don't you take a shower. I'll have some black coffee ready for you."

The Goat shook his head and flushed the toilet. "I ain't feeling so good."

"Of course you ain't feeling good. You were drunk as a skunk. What do you expect?"

"How about some sympathy?"

"Sympathy?" Karen helped him to his feet. "You did this to yourself. You have to grow up."

"You sound like my mother."

"When we get married, you're not going to go out with your friends all the time."

Still bleary eyed, he jumped into the shower. When he finished showering, he put on clothes and took a sip of the coffee. "I don't think that's so good for my stomach. Do we have any Tums?"

Karen opened a cabinet door and took out a container of Tums. "Mr. Salerno is going to love this lunch. I'm making Escarole soup, Portobello raviolis and veal chops. Then we're going to have some Tiramisu I made last night while you were out gallivanting."

"Thanks, Karen. I appreciate it."

"Well, you can show your appreciation by picking up some Romaine lettuce. And don't mess the place up. I've been cleaning the apartment since yesterday while ... "

"I know, while I was out gallivanting. You made your point." He tried to sip more coffee. It tasted like mud. "All right. I got to pick up some cigarettes anyway."

"So what do you think he wants to talk to you about? I don't think Mr. Salerno goes around making social calls."

"I don't know. It's not like I ever deal with him. Everything goes through Sophie which then goes to Tony and gets filtered down to me. Probably something to do with Johnny."

Karen lowered her eyes. "God rest his soul."

"Yeah, Johnny was a great guy. All heart, I tell you."

"So, does he believe what you told him?" Karen asked.

"I don't know. I guess we'll find out."

The Goat went on his errands. The fresh air made him feel better. He walked to the corner grocery store, a dying breed still alive in this tight-knit South Philly neighborhood.

"Holy mother of God." He picked up the *Philadelphia Daily News*. On the cover was a young Vietnamese woman. The headline shouted at him in big, bold print. "Vampire Killer Slays in Kensington."

The Goat dropped the Camels he just bought. "Motherfucker. I can't believe this shit."

"Hey, whatsa matter?" Angelo, the elderly Italian gentleman who owned the store, asked. "You no use that language around here."

"This is crazy."

"Oh, you talk about the killer who take the blood. These kids, they no respect any more."

The Goat felt sick. "I gotta go." He made a hasty exit with the newspaper and lettuce, but left the cigarettes behind.

"Hey, you no pay for the paper."

"I'll pay you next time," The Goat yelled.

As soon as he reached the apartment, he rushed to the bathroom and heaved.

Karen ran to him. "You okay, Patrick? I just finished cleaning the bathroom. Now I'm going to have to clean it again."

He staggered to her. "Fuck the bathroom. Look at this shit." He handed her the newspaper.

"Oh my God," Karen said in a slow and exaggerated fashion. She sat down and flipped to the page with the article. Although the article didn't spare any gory detail, it neglected to mention Johnny Gunns or Tina.

Karen hugged him. "This is the same guy who killed Johnny, ain't it?"

"I think so. When I saw that picture on the cover, man, I got the chills. It took me back to that night when I saw that guy. What a scary son of a bitch."

"I hope they catch this bastard."

The Goat reached for a smoke, before realizing he left them at the store. "I don't think they can do anything with him even if they found him. When he grabbed me by the throat, that was stronger than anything I've ever felt, and I've gone head to head with some pretty strong dudes."

The Wiz dropped off Enzo and Tony at The Goat's apartment. Tony knocked on the door and Karen Ferrano greeted them with a wide smile. Her body language changed when she saw Tony. *Must be bad blood between them.* It wasn't his business, and he didn't want to know.

"Mr. Salerno, it's so wonderful for you to come over today."

Enzo greeted her with a kiss on the cheek. Tony followed suit.

"Patrick told me so many great things about you. I'm honored to meet you. Come inside."

"Thank you." Enzo wiped his shoes on the door mat. The scents of a home-cooked Italian meal bombarded him, whetting his appetite. "You didn't have to go to the trouble of cooking such an elaborate feast."

Karen blushed. "Oh, it's no trouble at all. I hope you enjoy it."

Patrick emerged from the bedroom, his face drained of color. "Tony, Enzo, it's good to see you." He greeted each of them with a half hug. The Goat led them to the living room where they sat on the sofa. Karen brought over a tray of olives and smoked capicola.

They talked business until the food was ready. Karen ushered them to the small dining room table, which was barely large enough to hold the food.

"So, Pat, I owe you an apology." Enzo broke a piece of fresh bread and dipped it into the marinara. "It appears there may be some credence to your story. When you first told me the other day, I lashed out at you."

The Goat held up his hand. "Hey, you don't have to apologize. Believe me, I know what I told you sounded absolutely fucking nuts. I wouldn't have believed it if I didn't see it myself."

Enzo smiled. "I didn't say I believe your story. All I'm saying is that under the circumstances, I can see how you drew those conclusions. At the very least, you were dealing with someone who is deluded into thinking he's a vampire."

"Not for nothin', but he is a vampire." The Goat handed Enzo the newspaper.

Enzo's face tightened. "Who the fuck leaked this?" He sighed and handed the paper back to The Goat. "She's not the only one. There's at least one other victim. And yes, I think it was done by the same person who killed Johnny Gunns. There are too many similarities. But is this guy a vampire? I don't think so. I want an entire recount of what happened that night. I want it from the beginning, and don't leave out a single detail."

The Goat nodded. "Okay." He told the same story as he told Enzo the first time. Karen clutched his arm while he spoke.

Enzo said, "So you're telling me when you shot him, it had no effect. But then he heard the siren and disappeared. He didn't just run real fast, he disappeared?"

"Yeah, vanished. Like here one second and gone the next."

"So, he takes a bullet without any problem, but vanishes when he hears police sirens. Sounds like our boy doesn't like the heat. Why?"

"The hell if I know," The Goat replied.

"'Cause if he's a vampire then he don't want nobody knowin' about him," Karen said. "You know, they probably want secrecy."

Enzo shrugged. "If this guy believes he's a vampire, then I

suppose it would be disadvantageous for him to have his identity known. This freak was seen at the *Cat House* the day before the murder, right, Tony?"

"Yeah. Sam, one of the dancers, said she saw him."

The Goat frowned. "Get the fuck out of here. He gets a hard on for Tina and wants to kill her. Johnny must have been at the wrong place at the wrong time. So what are we gonna do?"

Enzo wiped his mouth. "We're going to find the son of a bitch and kill him."

The Goat's eyes opened wide. "Woh, Enzo, you know I respect the hell out of you, but I don't think you realize what you're dealing with here. I shot the motherfucker, and it didn't phase him. If you think you're going to kill him just like that, well you better have a plan B, because it ain't gonna happen."

Enzo smirked. "We'll see about that."

Chapter XII

As he waited for his wife to meet him for lunch, Mark stared at the photos. His investigation was going nowhere. It was like chasing sand in the wind. Why couldn't he let go of the case?

The corpses of Johnny Gunns and Tina Monterullo looked like extras in a slasher movie. He could relate to their violent ending, but the last two were another case. Their faces haunted him. They seemed perfectly content dying. How could two young attractive women be so happy before they died? Why was there no struggle?

How many more would die? If it could happen to Thuy Pham and Nikki Staretz, it could happen to others. No matter what the cost, he had to stop the killer.

He already spoke to family members, friends, neighbors and co-workers of the victims. No one had useful information. The deceased didn't have enemies or stalkers or anything typically seen in murder cases. Yet they were dead just the same.

He tracked down Staretz's co-workers who had gone with her to the *Rock Lobster* the night before she was murdered. They had not noticed anything unusual, although they said she was separated from them while speaking to an old friend from school. Mark pressed for a name for this old friend, but they drew blanks. To add to his frustration, security cameras at the club came up with nothing revealing.

He snapped out of his daze when Victoria came into view.

She had been alarmed when he told her he was working on the case. Not wanting to discuss it in front of their young daughter, Sarah, he told her they could discuss it over lunch at the faculty dining room at Villanova.

Mark put away the photos.

After their food arrived, Victoria sat and stared at him. "So how are you even involved in these vampire killings? What does this have to do with organized crime?"

"I think the person who killed this woman also killed a member of Salerno's crime regime, but the killings are coincidental."

"I can't imagine Salerno is too happy about that." Victoria took a bite of her grilled chicken.

"Probably not." Mark's stomach had been acting up since he took the case. He probably had an ulcer. He did not want to eat anything abrasive, so he had ordered a house salad.

"Is this really a vampire?" Victoria asked. "That's all my colleagues have been talking about. It started a roaring debate on vampire literature."

"No," Mark replied. "We just have a very exotic killer on our hands. Probably looking for attention. He has it now, but we're going to nail the son of a bitch."

"I hope so. I know you'll be able to do it."

Before long, reporters would find out about the other victims and magnify this story. The media loved shock value, and this case had it in abundance.

Against his better wishes, he went to the Roundhouse after lunch. Detective Brown was a dick, but he might know something useful. He chewed on a couple of Tums, but they were becoming less effective in fighting his stomach problems. Before he had his chance to see Brown, a frantic young man at the front desk caught his attention.

"Come on, you have to get into her apartment."

The police officer at the front desk rolled his eyes. "Listen, Mr. Zutaut, your friend has not been gone long enough for her to be considered a missing person. I'm sorry, but we have to follow protocol. If you ask me, you're overreacting. She probably went off with this guy you were telling me about. We see this all the time. Girl meets guy. She falls for him, and they run off."

The kid shook, his anger visible. "Denise isn't like that. She's responsible. She would never miss a performance without letting the conductor know ahead of time. Something must have happened to her."

The police officer ignored him, jotting notes on a pad of paper.

Zutaut shouted, "I'm telling you, there was something seriously wrong with this guy. I can't put my finger on it, but he's dangerous."

"Did he issue any threats?"

"No," Zutaut replied.

"Did he say anything that would lead you to believe he was going to harm your friend?"

"No."

The officer's vein protruded from his forehead. "Then why are you wasting my time?"

"Because this guy seemed almost, I don't know, unreal. When I spoke to him, it was hypnotizing, but there was something dark and destructive inside him."

"If you're so concerned, then why don't you get the landlord to open up her door?"

"I already told you, the landlord's out of town and won't be coming back until next week."

"Then wait."

"I can't wait." The kid threw his hands in the air. He appeared as if he was going to grab the officer by the throat.

Mark's eyes narrowed. From what he could gather, this kid's friend was probably a young, attractive female. If she wasn't, then he wouldn't be so interested. She was missing, just like the other victims. It was probably a long shot, but it was worth looking into.

Mark approached the desk. He flashed his badge. "Special

Agent Mark Andrews. Perhaps I can be of some assistance here."

"Yeah, get this punk away from me."

"Gladly." Mark turned to Zutaut. "Please follow me."

"Where are we going?"

"Away from here." Mark led him out of the lobby away from Brown, down the stairs towards the dingy cafeteria. The smells suggested the cafeteria contained something edible, but having eaten there twice, he doubted it. Mark sat at an empty table, but the kid stood. "Take a seat, please."

He did not move.

"Listen, I'm here to help you, Mr. Zutaut."

"Troy."

"Troy, you'll find I'll be more helpful than that cop. Now take a seat."

Troy sat opposite him.

"I overheard part of your conversation. What's your friend's name?"

"Denise McKenna."

"What makes you so sure that something bad happened to her?"

Troy leaned back on the stiff plastic chair and closed his eyes. "You have to know Denise. She's rock solid. There's no way in hell she'd run off with some guy she just met. Something about him scares me."

He described their first outing when they went back to Troy's apartment following their performance of *42ⁿᵈ Street*. "This guy had a mystical quality. I was like in a trance when he spoke. The same with Denise. Time just flew by that night. I thought we had just arrived, and when I looked at the clock, a few hours had passed. We were supposed to get together again the next night, but I had the flu. A couple days later Denise is gone. Nobody's heard from her. I have this cold feeling that the man harmed her. Whenever I think about him, I break into a sweat."

On its face, the story had no merit, but Zutaut radiated

intensity as he spoke.

"All right. Tell me more about this fellow. What's his name? Where's he from?"

"His name is Alexei. He told some wild stories. It's like he's been everywhere and has done everything. He's charismatic. Talking to him makes you feel at peace. It's like he could get you to do whatever he wanted by suggesting it."

That last statement caught Mark's attention. That could explain how the last two victims failed to put up a struggle. He had not considered the possibility of hypnosis. Even if they were in a trance, it should break once they were in physical pain and their lives endangered.

Mark heard enough. "Let's take a ride. We'll poke around and see what we can find."

"But I said that …."

"Let's just go and take a look. You never know what's going to happen."

"Okay," Zutaut said.

They drove to the apartment. Zutaut fidgeted in the passenger's side. He was a nervous bundle of energy. It was obvious his feelings for Denise McKenna went beyond friendship.

They walked to the third floor. The only noise in the building was Zutaut's heavy breathing. Sweat dripped down his face. If they found Denise's corpse, he doubted the kid could handle it.

"So now what do we do?" Zutaut bounced from foot to foot, staring at Mark.

"I'm going to see if the door is open. I know you tried before, but maybe I'll have better luck. Why don't you go down the hall? I think there's a window. Get some air."

He nodded and walked to the end of the hall. Mark knocked on the door. When there was no answer, he went to work. He was skilled at picking locks, but this was ridiculously easy. It took less than a minute. He cracked the door open and called out to Zutaut. "Hey, what do you know? I was able to open it. Knob's a little tricky. You might not have turned it right."

"Thank God." Zutaut took a deep breath. "I don't know if I can do this."

"Would you like me to go in alone?"

Zutaut closed his eyes. "No. I'll go with you."

"Okay, stay close behind. Don't touch anything." Mark entered the apartment. The living room was in perfect order, but based on the last two murder scenes, that didn't mean anything. A half-filled tea cup was on the kitchen table. It looked cold. Unwashed dishes covered the sink and uncut strawberries were in a strainer. Not good signs.

Mark approached the bedroom. Zutaut followed, not saying a word. The door was slightly ajar. Mark pushed it open. Inside, Denise was underneath the covers of her bed. She had no visible clothes and a dreamy look on her face.

"Hey Denise, it's Troy. Wake up."

He walked toward the bed, but Mark grabbed his arm. "Stand back."

Zutaut's brow furrowed. "Why? What's going on?"

Mark felt Denise's wrist for a pulse. She had none. He then lifted her head and found puncture marks in her neck. He took a brief look under the covers. Like the other victims, her abdomen had been mangled. This had all the markings of his perp, and now he had a name for the killer. Alexei. Soon, he would have a face to go along with the name.

Tears streamed down Zutaut's face.

"She's dead," Mark said. "I'm sorry."

He dropped to his knees and wailed. "No. Please no." He inched toward Denise on his knees. Before he could reach her, Mark intercepted him.

"This is a murder scene. I'm going to have to ask you to step back."

Mark gave the young man a few minutes to grieve before he asked him once more to back away. He helped Zutaut to his feet and led him out of the room. He then called Rick

Carroll. Another victim, but at last he had a break in the case.

Chapter XIII

Magnus had a hard time concentrating on the keys as he played the baby grand piano. He would never be a great piano player. He played competently because of his experience, but he did not have the natural talent he needed to excel.

He could hardly take his eyes off Ursula, who did a ballet routine to the music. He remembered those days in Prague when he first discovered her. Ursula won him over before they ever spoke. She had been so timid at first. Now her personality was vibrant and infectious. She was one of his favorites.

When they finished their routine, Magdalena, the dark haired vixen, kissed Ursula lightly on the neck. "That was beautiful. Don't you think, Magnus?"

He smiled. "I couldn't agree more."

Magdalena pranced toward the piano and sat on Magnus' lap. She wrapped her arms around his neck. "You know what would be funny? If she joined a ballet. She could do the Nutcracker. That would be something to see. A vamp in a ballet. Think of what the newspaper critics would say."

Magnus frowned. With the *Daily News* article implying that the vampire killer murdering Thuy Pham, he had to do something. Alexei's path could only lead to destruction. He had been reckless in the past, most notably in Lisbon, but he had never gone this far. Some elder vampires would have killed Alexei in the past, but this was a different era, and vampires did not kill one another. Gabriella had thus far persuaded him not to confront Alexei, but he could no longer stand by and do nothing.

Last night, Kristoff, who still resented Alexei for converting and then abandoning him, told Magnus that the vampire killer was a popular topic of conversation around town. Kristoff frequented clubs and other social gatherings. He also attended meeting groups, such as Alcoholics Anonymous, claiming to suffer from the same ailments as these individuals. Because of his frequent contact with people, he had his finger on the pulse of society. Whereas Magnus relied on the wonders of the Internet and other modern media, Kristoff stayed plugged in the old fashioned way, by talking to people.

Because of their heritage, Alexei and Magnus shared a kinship, something he could not easily dismiss despite personal feelings, but he had to do what was in the best interest of his brood. They looked to him for leadership and guidance.

Maybe the difference between the two was that Magnus was more cognizant of his own origins and the time he was able to walk in the daylight.

The Kingdom of Norway –
est. Tenth Century A.D.

Magnus glimpsed his homeland for the first time in many months. He had sailed to edge of the world, crossing the great ocean. Just like his father before him, the red men across the sea greeted him upon arrival. His friends told him he was crazy for undertaking this voyage. His mother begged him not to go. Undaunted, he had the journey of a lifetime.

He turned around when a strong hand gripped his shoulder.

His cousin Oddi wore a wide smile. "We must make a

return trip."

Magnus' brows furrowed. "We haven't set foot back home yet."

"I know and I already want to go back."

Magnus grinned. "I see that the red woman Chipoya has put you under her spell."

Oddi crossed his arms. "You're mistaken. I merely enjoyed the adventure."

"You could have brought Chipoya home."

Oddi looked forlorn. He turned and walked away.

Magnus would return, but for now, all he wanted was to see his family.

He told his crew to unload their bounty. It would take all day, so he and Oddi rode on horseback to the family manor. As a child he spent countless hours in the summer wandering around the sprawling estate. His father, a Viking chieftain, amassed a sizable fortune raiding and plundering lands across the Black and Caspian Seas. As a young boy, he accompanied his father on these expeditions.

He called out, but the manor was unusually silent.

Oddi frowned. "Is there some festival that we did not know about?"

Magnus shrugged and continued to call out. He expected his mother and his sister, Rakel, to throw a grand celebration for his return. The last thing he expected was an empty house. He was about to ascend the stairs when he spotted his mother. Her eyes were bloodshot, her hair tangled, and her face appeared to have aged ten years.

Magnus' heart began to pound in his chest. "Mother, what's wrong?"

She put her hand to her face and sobbed.

Magnus ran up the stairs and hugged her. "What is it?"

"Oh, Magnus, you've returned. It's Rakel. She's missing."

Blood rushed from Magnus' face. "What do you mean missing?"

"She's been gone for a week. Your father and brothers are

searching for her, but they haven't found her."

Magnus held onto the rail of the staircase for support, his hands trembling. "When was she last seen?"

His mother wiped tears from her face. "Rakel and a servant left one morning last week to visit a friend. She never reached the friend's house, and the servant was found dead. She had been decapitated."

Magnus stepped back, his body shaking. "I have to find Rakel."

He forgot about Oddi until his cousin put a hand on his shoulder. "Let's find her."

One afternoon, months later, rain poured on Magnus' covered wagon.

Oddi scanned the horizon. "We should stop at the nearest inn. It will be impossible to find Rakel in this weather." Oddi's face was raw and unshaven. Normally, he was vain with his appearance. Magnus could only imagine how he looked. For the past three months, he and Oddi scoured the countryside in search of Rakel. They had been to hundreds of towns, villages and outposts talking to constables, townspeople and farmers, but no one had seen her.

Magnus closed his eyes. "We must keep searching."

"I realize you're close to Rakel, and I'll go with you to the ends of the earth if necessary, but I don't think we will find her."

Magnus clenched his fists. "I can't accept that." He took a deep breath. "My head tells me you're right, but I can't bear the thought. When we were young, Rakel used to go hunting and fishing with me. Mother scolded her since these weren't womanly tasks, but Rakel never cared. I love her."

The wagon shook and careened off the road.

"What happened?" Magnus called out to the driver. When he didn't receive an answer, he peered up front and gasped.

The driver had a gaping wound in his chest.

There was no way he could grab the reigns in time, so he clutched Oddi's arm. "We've been attacked. We have to get out now."

They jumped out of the wagon and rolled onto the dirt road. Magnus limped to his feet and reached for his axe, which he had strapped on to his back. Meanwhile, the horses collapsed and the wagon slammed into trees.

On his injured ankle, he hobbled to the horses. Blood spurted from their necks.

Oddi ran after him, his sword drawn, his face pale. "A demon has attacked us."

Magnus scanned the area. Something moved in front of him like a blur. He held his axe with two hands, ready to strike. A long-haired phantasm with a white face appeared in front of him. Before he could react, it struck him. He had been in many fights, but had never been hit so hard. He fell backward, wincing in pain. It felt as if his whole face had shattered. Before he could get up, the thing kicked him in the ribs.

Another appeared. This one looked more like a man, but there was something unnatural about his appearance. He stared in revulsion as the thing bared fangs and bit Oddi's throat, killing his cousin. Magnus issued a muffled scream that was cut short when his attacker kicked his ribs again.

The demon or phantasm or whatever it was, grabbed his throat and squeezed. Magnus choked under its grip, blood spurting from his mouth.

The world went dark until a familiar voice penetrated his head. "Stop it, now."

The grip slackened.

"Leave him be."

His attacker dropped him to the ground.

The voice. It was Rakel. He whispered her name before losing consciousness. When he woke up, she was gone.

Magnus found it increasingly difficult to overcome his guilt about Rakel. If he had been home, he could have saved her.

Four years after her disappearance, Magnus married his first love. She was a Dane, the daughter of a merchant he traded with. The merchant considered Magnus unworthy of his daughter's hand, so Magnus kidnapped her and brought her to his homeland where they had a lavish wedding ceremony.

Nine months after his wedding, he sailed to Greenland. He returned to find his young wife on her deathbed. She was extremely ill, and the healers couldn't determine what ailed her. When she died, he was left broken hearted again.

He could barely function after her death. For three years he rarely left the manor, his mind and soul rotting. The only way to save himself was to get back to the open waters. Physically he would live, but mentally and emotionally he would not survive unless he resumed his old life.

Magnus had a wide smile as he stood on the deck of the longship, feeling alive again. His fleet had just raided the Welsh coastline, plundering several towns. It was his first voyage in years. He had been sullen and withdrawn for too long. It was time to restart his life, and the best way to do it was to go out to sea.

He captained his fleet's longship. In his teens, Magnus supervised the construction of these warships. They were large wooden boats ninety feet in length with portholes along the sides for oars and a single mast, which carried one, large square sail. Their speed was unmatched. They were designed to land on shore even when there was no harbor. The rest of his fleet consisted of knórrs, which were cargo ships.

Magnus spent much of his early years at sea. As part of his father's crew, he traveled to distant places in trading voyages and plundering missions. By age twenty-one, he had become a seasoned Viking warrior.

A member of his crew tapped his shoulder. "Magnus, you must look at this."

He followed the man to the back of his ship. A single Viking longboat trailed him. He did not recognize the emblem on its flag.

Magnus' fleet pulled into a harbor, and the ship followed. As they unloaded their merchandise, a messenger from the ship told him the captain requested to meet him. His curiosity overcame him even though there was much work to be done.

He expected the captain to be a fellow Viking who wanted to trade or join his fleet. Magnus nearly stopped breathing when he entered the captain's quarters. Standing across the room was Rakel, looking exactly as she had when he last saw her. Her age, height and weight had not changed, but there was something different about her. Her skin tone resembled porcelain and she looked ... inhuman.

Magnus lost his balance and nearly tumbled to the floor, but Rakel caught him with her powerful arms. He gasped. How could she move from one side of the room to the other so fast?

"Brother."

He was not imagining this. It was truly Rakel. Her appearance had not changed in over a decade.

"But how can you ... " Magnus could not finish his question.

"How can I be here?"

Magnus nodded. His head felt ready to rupture.

She lifted him to his feet as if he were a child. "I have returned to find you. You can't imagine how I've missed you."

"I can imagine, for I've missed you the same." Magnus touched her face to convince himself she was not a figment of his imagination.

Her smile reminded him of their childhood. "It's good to see you. It's been so long."

"What happened? I searched for you for months to no avail."

Rakel walked to the other side of the room, her blonde hair glistening in the moonlight. "I chose not to be found. I didn't want you or mother and father to see me in my current condition. I would not have been accepted."

Magnus frowned. "What do you mean? I would always accept you."

She hugged him fiercely. "I know you would have, Magnus. I could always count on you, but the others wouldn't. I would be a danger to myself and those around me."

"Why? And what are you doing here?"

"I have no regrets about my new life, but I'm lonely. I want you to join me."

"Join you?" Magnus frowned. "Where are you going?"

"I want you to become what I am?"

Magnus scratched his beard. "What have you become?"

"I am one who walks in the darkness. If it were daytime, I would not be here, for I can't be out in the sunlight. I don't age and can't die by natural means. I am undead."

"That's not possible."

"You're wrong, brother." Rakel disappeared from his sight. "It is possible."

Magnus jumped at the sound of his sister's voice coming from behind him. He turned and found her standing behind him.

"Don't be afraid. There are things I can do which you would scarcely believe possible. I have changed, but I'm still your sister whom you loved."

"How did this happen?"

"Marauders ambushed me. They killed and drank the blood of the servant I traveled with. I thought they were going to kill me. The leader of the pack drank my blood, but before my life was extinguished, he revived me by having me drink his blood.

"This was the same group that attacked you and Oddi. Fortunately, I stopped them from finishing you. They made me a member of their brood. They convinced me that humans would not accept our kind. That's why I stayed away for so long.

"After a few years, I realized that I did not like my new family. They were self-centered and arrogant. They did not care about humans and stepped on them as if they were ants. I could never be like that, so I left.

"I could not return home, but I desperately wanted to see you. Knowing how fond you are of sailing and plundering, I purchased my own boat and organized a crew, hoping we would cross paths. When I arrived at a port city, I would ask if you or your fleet had passed through. I've finally found you."

Magnus lowered his head. "I stopped sailing for a few years after my wife died."

Rakel cradled his head against her shoulder. "I heard. It's time for you to move on. I want you to roam the night with me forever."

"You want me to become a blood drinker like you?"

"Yes. You'll become powerful, no longer bound to this worthless flesh."

When he lost Rakel, part of him died. With the death of his wife, he felt purposeless and hollow. Now Rakel could make him whole again. He did not like the idea of living off blood or never seeing the sunlight again, but he was enamored with the adventure this new lifestyle would bring.

"Yes, let's do this, Rakel. Let's be together again."

Centuries later, he and Gabriella toured Luxor.

Gabriella kissed him. "I'll see you later tonight."

"I anxiously await your return," Magnus said.

Gabriella had arranged a private tour of the pyramids.

Since Magnus already toured them numerous times, he opted to haggle with merchants.

He walked through the crowded marketplace and came to a sudden stop when he sensed another of his kind. He kept a close watch with his keen eyes.

Magnus encountered a merchant peddling Egyptian artifacts. Surprisingly, there were authentic pieces mixed in with the fakes. While negotiating with the merchant, a shadowy figure blurred past.

Magnus scanned the area, but whoever he had seen was gone. He smiled. "I'll return later." He left the table, moving with stealth through the crowd. When he exited the market he found his stalker standing next to a red building. He was no stranger.

"Heinrich, what a pleasant surprise."

Heinrich stepped out into the cool moonlight. "Magnus, my friend, we meet again."

They clasped hands.

"Just happen to be in Egypt?" Magnus asked.

Heinrich's smile disappeared. "Unfortunately this isn't a chance meeting. I've been searching for you for months. I come with bad tidings."

Magnus studied Heinrich's placid face. "Speak, my friend."

"I was in South America and passed through Sao Paulo, when I learned your sister Rakel lived there." Heinrich took a deep breath. "I sought her out and was stunned to find out she had died."

Magnus felt as if he had been stabbed. He could hardly breathe. "But how … what happened? How did she die?"

"She was killed."

He fell backward, and Heinrich prevented him from hitting the ground. Tears streamed down his face. "Who did it?"

Heinrich sighed. "A night dweller named Silva was angered that she *invaded* his territory. It's stupid, but the broods in Brazil operate differently. He told Rakel to leave and she refused. In a direct confrontation she would have destroyed him, so he hired local gangsters he uses in the rubber trade. They attacked her during the daytime. The sun weakened her, and she was left vulnerable. The gangsters butchered her, stabbing her repeatedly and decapitating her."

"My Rakel," Magnus whimpered. He raised his head and gazed at Heinrich. "I will get vengeance. Will you accompany me to Brazil?"

"You need not even ask," Heinrich replied.

As the cool night air from the ship blew on Magnus, Gabriella put her hand on his shoulder. "We'll pay them back for what they did to Rakel."

Magnus frowned. "It won't bring her back."

Gabriella shook her head.

"I feel guilty that we fell out of touch."

After Rakel made him a blood drinker all those centuries ago, Magnus continued his Viking ways. His men had questioned why he and Rakel were never around during the day, but they feared him and he paid them well, so they heeded his order to never enter his quarters until he emerged in the evening. They sailed at night, becoming the scourge of Europe.

After years of pillaging, he and Rakel returned home. Their parents were elderly, but he and his sister still looked young. This caused an uproar. The villagers and the servants in the manor claimed that demons possessed them. Sensing their outrage, they made a hasty exit in the middle of the night and settled in Scotland, purchasing a vast estate. They amassed incredible wealth during their Viking days and could live off of it for generations.

They never stayed in one area for long. People became suspicious when long periods of time passed yet they did not age. They moved from Scotland to Finland to Iceland to

Russia. Later, they lived in France, Belgium, Holland and Germany. Occasionally, they turned a human into one of their kind. Their brood fluctuated, but never numbered more than a dozen.

Rakel was free spirited and traveled on a whim. Sometimes Magnus accompanied her. They toured the entire European continent as well as Asia and Africa. He and Rakel mingled with the social elite in Europe. They whined and dined with royal families, seducing them and giving them a sweet gift with which to remember them.

During the sixteenth century, Magnus and Rakel had parted ways. After five hundred years together, they needed to move on.

Magnus lived alone. When he visited Rakel, there was always friction.

When travel became easier, Magnus lived in North America, many centuries after his previous visit as a Viking. He preferred European society and sophistication to the wild frontiers of America so he did not stay long.

He went back to Europe and continued to be a loner until he met Gabriella. When Gabriella agreed to walk the night with him, he needed no one else.

He saw Rakel infrequently. She was a drifter, and he preferred a less chaotic life.

Magnus, Heinrich and Gabriella completed their voyage, crossing the sea and arriving in Brazil. They rented a house in Sao Paulo and located the thugs responsible for killing Rakel. Magnus posed as a wealthy European investor who wanted a piece of the rubber exporting business, not wanting to go through the traditional channels because they wanted too much bribe money for him to set up his operations.

He traveled in an expensive, chauffeured vehicle and wore impeccable suits. When he went to restaurants and clubs accompanied by the striking Gabriella, he threw money around. He arranged a meeting with the ringleader, Roberto Angiolini.

They met in an empty warehouse. Gabriella and Heinrich accompanied him. Thankfully, Angiolini surrounded himself with his henchmen. He wanted to kill as many as he could.

Angiolini wore a flashy blue suit and a loud hat that matched his overbearing personality. Magnus would enjoy watching him suffer.

Angiolini spoke in Italian. "My associates tell me you're interested in doing business."

Magnus chuckled. "I'm sorry, but you're mistaken. I've come here to kill you."

Angiolini dropped his smile. The gangsters drew their guns. "Is this a joke?"

Magnus laughed loudly.

"You'll pay for this insult," Angiolini said.

The gunmen opened fire. In a whirlwind of action, Magnus, Gabriella and Heinrich dodged bullets and then pressed the attack. They slashed with their clawed fingers and pounced on their victims. Within minutes, the empty warehouse became a macabre bloodbath. Bullet holes ripped through the walls and windows, but none successfully reached their targets. Magnus relished tearing the flesh of the men who killed his beloved Rakel. He glanced at Gabriella, who had a gleam of satisfaction in her eyes when she bit the neck of a gunman.

When they were done, the only human left standing was Roberto Angiolini. He tried to run, but Magnus tackled him.

"Going somewhere?"

Angiolini begged for mercy.

"I'm here for Silva. Tell me what I want to know and you'll live."

"We have been business associates for many years." Angiolini wiped sweat from his brow. "Silva performs services for my syndicate, and we return the favor."

"Where can I find him?"

"If I tell you, he'll kill me."

Magnus smiled. "Look around. Could it be any worse than

this?"

Angiolini told him where he could find Silva.

"Thank you for your cooperation. By the way, I lied."

Magnus thrust his right fist into Angiolini's chest cavity. Blood flowed from his mouth as he collapsed to the floor. He grabbed the gangster's throat and squeezed. Angiolini's face was a mask of terror. "This is for Rakel, you pig." He picked up the gangster and threw him across the warehouse. Angiolini's head smashed against a wall and his skull cracked.

They did not immediately go after Silva. He wanted to terrorize the bastard, so they dumped the corpses of Angiolini and his associates in front of Silva's house.

Silva fled. They chased him across Brazil, through the Amazon basin into Ecuador and Columbia. They finally pinned him down in Venezuela. Silva sought refuge at an inn before dawn, but Magnus had already seized control of the inn. Heinrich posed as the innkeeper and directed Silva to a room. When he opened the door, Magnus stood in front of him. He turned, but Gabriella and Heinrich blocked his exit.

Silva had a wild look on his face as he bared his fangs. "What's the meaning of this?"

Magnus' face tightened. "You killed my sister, Rakel. Claimed she invaded your territory. You made a mistake, one you'll pay for with your life."

Silva glared in defiance. "I won't go down without a fight."

"I wouldn't expect you to." Magnus motioned with his fingertips for Silva to come forward. Earlier on he told Gabriella and Heinrich not to interfere.

They battled throughout the lodge. When they were done, Magnus emerged holding Silva's decapitated head. They had destroyed the building.

Magnus never knew such satisfaction as that revenge. He was glad Gabriella was there to share it with him. It would not bring back Rakel, but he could live easier knowing her death did not go without payback.

Heinrich joined Magnus' growing brood. Although he was fond of Heinrich and others in his brood, he would be perfectly content if it were just he and Gabriella again.

Chapter XIV

Sophie Koch ordered a Cappuccino and a sesame seed bagel with jam at an eatery in the Reading Terminal Market. She was waiting for Jimmy Two Tone, a street hustler turned FBI informant. Jimmy was now directing porno movies. Several local strip joints supplied the actresses. He usually took the role of the lead male actor. His new business endeavor was lucrative. It didn't matter. She was beyond judging people's occupations.

Normally Sophie did not run in the same social circles as Jimmy Two Tone, however, she had hired Jimmy in the past to perform a few jobs.

One was bugging the office of a union leader who was cutting side deals detrimental to Enzo's regime. She suspected the union head was operating on his own, but had no proof. Jimmy Two Tone, under the guise of a heavy equipment dealer, planted four bugs in the union leader's office. Over the next few weeks, she found out that he was embezzling funds, cutting corners on materials and had fictitious employees on his payroll.

She gave Enzo the tapes, expecting to see anger seep through his normally calm demeanor. Instead he told her he had his own suspicions but could not act unless he had proof. In an offhanded way, like he was asking his wife to pick up milk from the grocery store, he told her to give Fat Paulie the order to take care of the situation. A week later, the union boss vanished. Nobody heard from him again.

Enzo operated in a cold and calculating manner, not allowing emotions to control his decisions. He employed whatever means were necessary to accomplish his goals. His rivals and business partners did not dare cross him. Once when Sophie spoke to the New Jersey mob boss, he described Enzo as being silent but violent.

She first met Enzo when they were students at the University of Pennsylvania. She studied law, and he attended the Wharton School of Business. They met at a debate forum where the topic was capital punishment. She argued against capital punishment. Enzo, with his Sicilian heritage, took the other side. He impressed her with his well thought out approach and passion. They became friends after the debate, and went out a few times for coffee.

They kept in contact after graduation. She never thought Enzo would ask her to be his closest advisor and confidant in his organized crime family. It was a bold move that raised eyebrows in families across the country. But times had changed, and Enzo was a different kind of mob boss, determined to take organized crime to new heights.

Sophie cared deeply for her boss. Her range of emotions toward him drifted from like to lust to love to everything in between. Not that she would admit any of this to him. She would never damage their relationship or hurt his family.

Since she could not have the one man she cared for, she had many others. She did not care how others viewed her conquests. Men had been doing this forever. If they could do it, she could too. She exercised wealth and power like any man would.

She scrawled through the morning edition of the *Wall Street Journal*, waiting for Jimmy Two Tone. Just as she finished her bagel, Jimmy Two Tone walked through the entrance. His dark eyes glanced around nervously. He found a waitress and ordered scrambled eggs and hash browns, before sitting at Sophie's table. "It's been too long since I last saw you. How have you been keeping yourself?"

Sophie did not look at him. "I've been waiting eight minutes. That's eight minutes less that you have with me, so cut the chit-chat and tell me what you need to say."

"Sure, sure. No problem there. Don't want to keep the lady waiting any longer."

Sophie glared at him.

Jimmy diverted his gaze. "Right, right. As you may know, I work for a certain benefactor. I'm not mentioning any names, but you know who I'm talking about."

Sophie nodded. He was talking about his connections with the FBI, specifically Special Agent Mark Andrews. Jimmy had sold out a few years back, and it was no longer safe for him to operate as a street hustler.

"You see my benefactor has information your boss might find interesting. If the conditions are right, he would like to meet your boss. Friendly terms, nothing official. Just an exchange of information between two interested parties."

Sophie raised her brows. Why would Andrews want to meet with Enzo? If he had something on Enzo, then he would issue a subpoena or an arrest warrant. Andrews was a straight shooter. "What for?"

"A friend of yours met an untimely demise. My benefactor has information that could help your boss. Surely he's interested in knowing who clipped your friend."

Strangely enough, Enzo had not mentioned Johnny Gunns since the funeral. It had to eat away at him to see one of his associates go down like that, just like it ate away at her. She could not be emotionally detached when one of her people got killed. She had learned to be cold, but not that cold.

Enzo's tension had visibly increased since Johnny's death. She hadn't pressed him on the issue. If he wanted to say something, he would do so in his own time frame.

"There is a possibility that something could be arranged," Sophie said. If Andrews had information related to Johnny, Enzo would want to hear it.

"Good, good. I hope so." Jimmy Two Tone handed her a slip of paper. "He can dial this phone number at the specified time. My benefactor will answer the phone during that fifteen minute interval. If he doesn't call, then no further contact will be made. Got it?"

"He'll get the message."

"Great." Jimmy softened his tone. "You know, you're looking mighty fine. That sweater that you're wearing … whew, it's working for you. I've turned to the more artistic side of life these days, making film, and I think you would be a great actress. We could do a dress rehearsal at my place."

Sophie rose from the table after finishing her coffee. "Look down at my shoes."

"Sure, baby."

"You see these heels. If you ever approach me with that kind of suggestion again, I'll bury them into your throat and crush your larynx. Got it?"

She could feel Jimmy stare at her as she walked away.

Fat Paulie eyed The Goat's Italian hoagie. "You gonna finish that?"

The Goat snatched up the hoagie. He put it down for half a minute and already the vulture was circling. "Yeah I'm gonna finish it. Man, you just ate one."

Fat Paulie shrugged. "Still hungry."

"Maybe you oughta think about going on that South Park diet." The Goat quickly ate the rest of his hoagie before Fat Paulie could get his hands on it.

"Hey watch it, you smart ass punk. You remember who you're talkin' to."

The Goat felt like saying, *Yeah, I'm talking to a fat, fucking slob who has four chins and his head stuck squarely up his ass.* Instead he said, "Whatever."

Fat Paulie scowled. "I'm feeling a lack of respect. I suggest you think about where I stand in this organization and where you're at. From my spot, I look down at your worthless ass. So you best not be mouthing off."

"Fuck off," The Goat mumbled under his breath.

"What?"

"Nothing."

They finished eating lunch at *Tony Luke's* in South Philly, each opting for an Italian hoagie. Fat Paulie washed his down with a soda and an extra large order of cheese fries.

The Goat threw his wrapper in the trash. He brought the remainder of his soda with him as they got back into his BMW.

Fat Paulie pissed him off all the time. The Goat did not say anything to Tony Scrambolgni because he didn't want to seem like an ingrate, since this was an increase in his territory and responsibilities. He didn't know how much longer he could work with Fat Paulie, though. The man was an antagonistic, arrogant bastard. One of these days he was going to slug him in the mouth.

The Goat had been on edge since his meeting with Salerno. He thought he would be more relaxed after talking to the boss. After all, Salerno indicated he was inclined to believe his story might be true. He stuck his neck on the line because he knew the boss had the smarts and the means to handle the situation.

He couldn't stop thinking about the night Johnny died. That son of a bitch with the blond hair was inhumanly strong. He could have snapped The Goat's neck. Although the vampire had scared him shitless, he wanted to redeem himself and avenge Johnny.

With Salerno asking questions about the killer, that meant he was going after him, and that meant people would die. People who were like brothers to him. If Salerno thought he was dealing with a man pretending to be a vampire, then he was making a big time mistake.

"Let's make this quick," Fat Paulie said. "I want to get

another bite to eat."

"Ain't your old lady making dinner tonight?"

"So what?"

The Goat frowned. "Don't you want to save your appetite?"

"I got plenty of appetite. Don't you fucking worry."

The Goat turned onto Market Street. "Well I don't want to rush this and fuck it up. You know how the boss gets when you don't do things the right way."

"Don't you worry about that either. You answer to me, and I answer to the boss. Just do what I tell you."

"Why the fuck does everything have to be an argument with you?" The Goat asked. "Can't we ever do something without a hassle? Man, you're worse than a woman."

"Quit your yappin' and drive."

"What does it look like I'm doing? Picking my ass?"

As The Goat passed City Hall, neither spoke. Eventually Fat Paulie broke the silence. "So what happened when you met with Vladie?"

"He's almost set up now. He's going to be hacking four sites at the same time. This way, if whoever regulates that shit catches onto him, he can dump one site and move on to another. He's a strange cat, but he's got his shit together."

"I wouldn't mind hitting that broad of his."

The Goat grunted.

"What, she ain't good enough for you?"

"I don't know. She's freaky." Almost like a vampire.

"I'd do her," Fat Paulie said.

"I ain't sayin' I wouldn't. All I'm sayin' is that she's a little freaky. Not my type."

"Hey, as long as she makes our pal Vlade happy, then she's all right."

"I thought you didn't like Vlade. Didn't you call the Ukraine a big cesspool?"

"I'm sure it is. As long as Vlade makes big bucks for us, who gives a shit."

The Goat smiled. "Amen to that."

"So when can we expect some return on our investment?"

"He said maybe a few weeks before he can go operational. And then just keep collecting for as long as he can run this scam."

Fat Paulie grinned. "Scam is such a harsh word. I prefer business endeavor."

The Goat pulled up to an electronics store on Cambria Street. He eyeballed the *iPads* on display. He would take one and consider it as interest on the money owed.

The owner of the store was a Korean named Yeo See Choy. Coming up short on his mortgage payments, Choy was desperate for cash. A supplier turned him to Fat Paulie, who lent him cash.

For the first month, Choy made his payments. He had not made a payment since. Fat Paulie sent his people to give Choy a "friendly" reminder that the money was due. Choy still neglected his payments, so it was time to pay a not so friendly visit.

Years ago, they might have chopped off a finger to send a message, but Enzo Salerno was fostering a kinder and gentler regime.

They entered the store. Choy was in the back trying to sell a laptop computer to a customer.

"Hey, Choy, we need to talk," Fat Paulie yelled from across the store.

Choy's smile dissipated and his face became pale. "I be there. Just a minute."

"Sorry, Choy," The Goat said. "We need to talk to you now."

Sweat formed on Choy's brow. He scanned the store, but didn't move.

They moved quickly through the store, went on either side of him, grabbed an arm, lifted him off his feet, and carried him to the back office.

"Why you do that?" Choy asked. "Can't you see I with

customer?"

"Shut the fuck up, Choy," Fat Paulie said.

"You can't do that."

"I said shut your filthy, fucking gook mouth before I put my fist down it."

They threw him onto a swivel chair. The Goat cracked his knuckles.

"My boss has been patient with you, but your time's running out," Fat Paulie said.

"I need more time." Tears formed in Choy's eyes as sweat streamed down his face.

The Goat gave him a back hand slap. He could not stand seeing a grown man cry. This gook was pathetic.

"I come up with money." Blood seeped down from Choy's lip.

"You don't want to disappoint my boss," Fat Paulie said. "It would be bad for you and your family. I would hate for something to happen to your two young sons. So if you care about your family, you'll come up with the cash."

"You leave my family alone."

"They'll be fine if you pay back what you owe. You see my associate here." Fat Paulie pointed his thumb at The Goat. "He ain't as nice as me. Sometimes I can't control him. You don't want to see him again."

The Goat punched Choy in the jaw, causing him to give out a sharp cry. He took out a knife from his back pocket and brought it perilously close to Choy's face.

"Now I can tell him to put that knife away, but I'm not sure he'll listen." Fat Paulie shook his head. "These kids today."

The Goat pressed his knife against the back of Choy's ear. Choy screamed as he sliced the surface of the skin. Slowly he circled the knife around the perimeter of his ear, not enough to do any real damage.

Choy shrieked.

"Put the knife away," Fat Paulie said.

"Come on, Paulie, let me hurt him." He waited briefly before putting it away.

Choy cowered in his swivel chair.

"Next time, I don't know if he'll listen to me. Don't make him come here again."

Fat Paulie and The Goat exited the front of the store leaving a sobbing Choy in the back. They had no intention of hurting the man or his family just yet, but try convincing Choy of that. If he did not pay, they would give him an alternative to violence. They would swallow up his store and take control of his assets.

Chapter XV

Enzo glanced at his watch. He had fifteen minutes to decide whether or not he would take Special Agent Andrews' offer. He had been pondering this since he spoke with Sophie, hating his indecisiveness. He would rather act quickly, even if it meant making the wrong decision, then hesitate.

Yesterday morning Sophie relayed the information from her meeting with Jimmy Two Tone. When she finished, she looked at him expectantly. He still had not said anything about The Goat's story or Tony Scrambolgni's investigation.

"This is about Johnny's murder," Enzo said.

"I figured as much." Sophie smiled. "What's Andrews' angle?"

Enzo folded his hands. "The nature of Johnny and Tina's murder was unusual. Most of their blood was drained from their bodies and their organs were partially consumed."

Sophie's smiled dropped. "The vampire killer."

Enzo nodded.

"My God."

"There's more. The Goat arrived at the house shortly after the murders and before the police arrived. He went face to face with the killer."

Sophie's eyes went wide. "What happened?"

"The Goat said the murderer nearly choked him out. He heard sirens and disappeared."

"Disappeared?"

"Yeah, vanished. The Goat said that the man is a

vampire."

"What the hell's going on here?" Sophie asked.

"That's what I want to find out. Tony's investigating."

"This is crazy."

Enzo nodded. "One of Jim Debenedeto's neighbors provided a description of the killer. The woman said he looked like a vampire. Tony also spoke to the Vietnamese woman's sister. She described her sister meeting a man earlier that week who was a demon."

"A demon?"

"That's how Tony said the woman characterized him. He couldn't get out of her why she thought that, only that he looked inhuman. Anyway, this 'demon' also matched the description of the killer. She warned her sister to stay away from the man, but she wouldn't listen and wound up dead. Also, Tony talked to a bouncer at the club the Staretz girl was at the night before she was murdered. He said she had been talking to a man. After Staretz left, the bouncer said the man disappeared."

"So what are you telling me? You think this killer really is a vampire like the newspapers are saying?"

"Of course not." Enzo hesitated. "There's no such thing as the undead."

"Then how do you explain it?"

Enzo put his hands in the air. "The fuck if I know."

"You think Andrews knows something?" Sophie searched her purse for a cigarette but came up empty. She was always trying to quit. At first, she smoked casually when she was out with friends. By the time she graduated law school, she became a pack a day smoker.

Enzo stroked his chin. "This is out of his league. I can't imagine he's knows anything."

"He must have something, or he wouldn't contact you."

"He must have an agenda. I don't know his game, but I don't like it."

"Maybe he's trying to figure this out just like you."

"Then why would he want to talk to me?" Enzo pulled out a pack of cigarettes and offered one to Sophie.

Sophie took the cigarette and allowed Enzo to light it for her. "He knows you want to find out who killed Johnny so you can exact revenge. Maybe he thinks you have information he could use."

"Or maybe he's using this opportunity to get something on me."

"I don't think so," Sophie said. "So what are you going to do?"

"I'm not sure."

Since their conversation, he had ample time to think about the offer. He looked at his watch. Nine minutes until the window expired.

Growing up in South Philadelphia, he had an inherent distrust of cops. Tales of law enforcement corruption were common. For the past five years, Andrews had been investigating him, but Enzo always stayed one step ahead of him.

Three minutes left. Enzo scolded himself for procrastinating. He was the leader of an empire. It was about time he acted like one.

He picked up his secure cell phone.

Andrews answered on the third ring. "I was starting to think you wouldn't call."

Mark's stomach had been acting up all day and was getting worse. He chewed on a couple of Tums and wrote a note to remind himself to make an appointment with his doctor.

His actions of late were unconventional, and his peers would frown upon them. Not that he cared. He was after results, not career advancement.

He consulted Rick Carroll, not wanting to have this decision backfire, and Rick find out afterward. Not only was it professional courtesy, but he wanted Rick's advice.

Rick was reviewing Thuy Pham's file in his office. Mark was not the only one who couldn't get this case off his mind. Officially, two agents in homicide in the Philadelphia Police Department were in charge, but Mark was not ready to give up on the case and neither was Rick.

Rick laughed when he told him he was planning on talking to Salerno. "So you're considering sleeping with the enemy?"

Mark folded his arms. "I have to do *something* about this vampire killer. People are dying, and we're not getting far on our own. Neither are Robinson and Price. So, I can sit back and wait for more people to die, or I can do something. If I know Salerno, he won't rest until he gets vengeance for Johnny Gunns. If I can get him to share info, then we'll be one step closer."

"What makes you think Salerno will talk to you?"

"If he doesn't want to talk, I can't make him. If he does, I might have something."

"I'm not going to stop you. I trust your judgment, but you need to watch your step. You're going to be walking a tight rope if you're dealing with Salerno. Certain people in the Bureau would frown upon your collaboration with a reputed mob boss."

Mark smirked. "Fuck them. I've already pissed those people off anyway."

Rick sighed. "Be careful, Mark. He's dangerous."

Mark took his boss's advice to heart. Salerno was devious, but he had nothing to lose. The worst that could happen was that Salerno would not respond or tell him to go to hell.

He met Jimmy Two Tone yesterday afternoon. Jimmy was in his debt since Mark had gotten him off the hook for using a sixteen-year old girl in one of his movies. The girl's older sister found out she was "acting" in porno movies. She wanted to press charges against Jimmy, who had been working for Mark as an informant. He pleaded with Mark to help him, claiming a local strip club supplied the girl, and he had no idea she was underage.

Mark spoke to the girl. She admitted to lying about her age. When Mark asked if she thought the police should press charges against Jimmy, she said no.

Mark was satisfied Jimmy was not lying. Since the stripper felt she had not been wronged, Mark intervened and squashed the charges.

He met Jimmy at the food court in the Galeria on Market Street.

"I met Enzo's broad," Jimmy said. "She assured me Enzo would get the message."

Mark nodded as he chewed on hard pretzels. It was the only thing that wouldn't upset his stomach. "You wouldn't be trying to scam me by saying you met Ms. Koch when you actually didn't. Because if Salerno doesn't call, I'll be checking to make sure this meeting took place."

"Come on. I ain't that stupid. Plus, it's in my best interest to deliver Salerno to you. I don't know what business you have with him, but I want to see this work out."

"I'm sure you do," Mark said.

"So if Enzo tries to reach you, then I'm off the hook."

"That's right."

"We'll be even."

Mark nodded.

"Good. I can't believe that bitch tried to have me arrested. How did I know her sister was only sixteen? You see the jugs on her? She sure looked older."

It pained him to deal with pond-scum like Jimmy Two Tone. "Haven't you had enough brushes with the law? I might not be able to help you next time. Why don't you get into a legitimate enterprise for once in your rotten life?"

"Hey, I'm an artist. I make cinema. I'm just expressing my artistic abilities."

"Porn isn't art. Especially the hard-core stuff you make. I'm sure that if you put your mind to it, you could succeed at an honest endeavor."

Jimmy waved his hand. "Come on, that's for chumps. You expect me to wear a three piece suit and work a nine to five? I ain't doing that. No sir."

"Have it your way, Jimmy. If you ever wind up in the can, I feel sorry for you. You've made a lot of enemies. They don't like snitches in prison."

"I can take care of myself."

"Of course you can."

He slept poorly last night, constantly fidgeting. He kept waking Victoria, so he went downstairs and slept on the couch. It was no more conducive for sleep than his bed. Since he was up anyway, he went over what he would say to Salerno, remembering Carroll's advice to go into this with his eyes wide open.

This whole morning, his attention span was short. When Victoria asked what was wrong, he did not tell her about his potential meeting with the mob boss. Mark was not sure why he was so anxious. He had spoken with Salerno before.

At work he watched the seconds tick by. At ten, he left his office and went for a ride in his car, not wanting to be in his office to take the call.

As time dragged on, he wondered if Salerno was going to call. With three minutes left, Mark no longer thought Salerno would call. He pulled over to a playground at Seventh and Shunk. He felt like a fool for thinking he could bargain with the devil.

Mark jumped when the phone rang. "I was starting to think you wouldn't call."

Salerno snickered. "I wanted to make you wait. Where are you?"

"At a pay phone on Seventh and Shunk."

"To what do I owe the pleasure of this stimulating conversation?"

"Let's cut the shit, Enzo. You know why I want to talk to you. You have links into the police department, so you already know I've been unofficially investigating Johnny's death along with the other ones that have happened lately."

"I'm glad you're keeping yourself busy. It beats keeping tabs on me."

"Real funny," Mark said.

"How does this concern me?"

"We have the same goal. I know you want payback for Johnny. So that means you've been doing your own investigating."

"You don't know the first thing about me. You may think you know me, but you don't."

Salerno was trying to bait him into an argument. "I don't want to fight with you. I want to work with you. My investigation hasn't progressed the way I'd like, and I don't want to see more people die. It's in our best interests to collaborate."

"Thank you for your concern, Mr. Andrews."

"Stop patronizing me."

"Mark, it's touching and all, but I don't need your help. What I choose to do regarding the death of my associate is not your concern. I'm more than capable of handling the situation. I don't need to go through the system to get justice."

"Cut the Godfather shit. I have information you can use. I would be willing to share it if you meet me."

"Somehow I find it hard to believe that you have info that I don't already know. You should know after chasing me all these years that I'm always a step ahead of you."

"Is that so? A young lady was killed this past weekend. The details of her murder have been kept private. I'm the only one who knows about it. I know the killer's name and have a good description of him."

"I'm glad you're doing your job. I wish you well, but I don't need your help."

"Listen, Enzo. Forget about who I am and who you are. People are dying. I want to put an end to it. Because of that, I'm willing to swallow my pride and ask for help. I don't feel so morally superior that it's beneath me to deal with you. I'm willing to do whatever it takes to stop this killer. If you have any decency and compassion, you'll meet with me. That's all I'm asking for. I give you my word that if we work together, I'll temporarily suspend any investigation into your activities. Anything that I learn during this time I won't use against you."

Mark's heart was beating quickly. That was not part of his script.

"Okay."

Mark blinked rapidly. "Okay what?"

"I'll meet with you. Despite what you may have fictionalized about me, I'm not a bad person. I want to see whoever is responsible for this stopped before others die."

Mark's hands shook. He tried to calm himself. "I'm glad."

"Tomorrow at seven in the morning at Fairmount Park. Go alone to the bench near the sculpture of Joan of Arc. If you're with anyone, I walk."

"It's a deal. I have photos and drawings you might be interested in. See you then." Mark hung up the phone and breathed a sigh of relief.

Chapter XVI

Alexei leisurely strolled out of the townhouse on Rittenhouse Square with the taste of blood in his mouth, humming a tune from *42nd Street*. The woman whose house he had visited was a model, who recently returned from the Cayman Islands from a photo shoot for a new swimwear line. She was married to a sugar daddy — a wealthy, middle aged attorney who specialized in medical malpractice litigation. There were things he could not provide, and for that she turned to Alexei.

Alexei met Nora Brooks at a dinner party celebrating the birthday of a magazine publisher. As usual, Alexei managed to nestle his way into the city's social elite. He was a mysterious stranger that everyone wanted to know. His wealth, enchanting looks and magnetism drew people to him like flies to a light.

After Alexei arrived at the party, people gathered near him. He had a Long Island Iced Tea in hand, although alcohol had no effect on him. He found it amusing when others were wowed that he could drink so much while maintaining his coherency.

He spotted Nora across the room. She had a look of extreme melancholy. He sauntered toward her and offered her a drink. She was perfect. Young, beautiful and looking for more in life. That entire evening she clung to his side laughing at his jokes, enchanted by his stories. They danced, took a stroll in the moonlight walking hand in hand.

Alexei did not leave with her that evening since her husband was home. Nora gave him her phone number and an open invitation for the following evening, when her husband would be in Florida meeting a client.

He had made a habit of waking before the sun rose. Just like Magnus, the sunlight did not affect him as long as the shades were drawn and he stayed inside. It gave him time to himself while the others were sleeping. Although spacious, with sixteen others living in the house, it was difficult to be alone.

He walked to the computer room. He craved keeping up with news around the world and communicating with others of his kind through email. The house had high speed Internet connections and four state of the art computers. Magnus always insisted on getting the most advanced technology available.

Alexei's eyes narrowed as he entered the room. Much to his chagrin, Magnus also tended to wake before sunset.

Alexei hovered by the door.

Not turning around, Magnus spoke in a cold voice. "Hello, Alexei."

"Good afternoon, Magnus."

Icy silence ensued. Magnus continued typing. With his keen vision, Alexei could see he was typing a letter, although he could not identify to whom it was addressed.

Although Alexei wanted to check his email, he did not want to be in the same room as Magnus. He walked away without saying another word and went to the library.

The library had thousands of books in stacks and shelves. It had reference books, works of fiction, biographies and volumes of ancient literature. Some pieces were hundreds, even thousands of years old.

Alexei devoured all kinds of books. He was especially fond of vampire novels. He enjoyed seeing how humans viewed his kind. He had read every book in Anne Rice's *The Vampire Chronicles* and now was reading through Laurell K. Hamilton's collection.

After reading a few chapters, he took out his cell phone, but couldn't get a signal inside the library. He walked down the hall until he picked up a signal and dialed Nora Brooks to take her up on her offer from the previous evening.

He drove to Nora's house in his vintage '69 Mercedes convertible. He treasured material objects. Living in excess and maximizing pleasure were his only concerns in life.

That night, he said to Nora, "You do realize I'm a creature of the night, what you might call a vampire."

She looked deeply into his eyes. "None of that matters to me."

After an exhilarating sexual escapade, Alexei promised her something more intensely pleasurable. She begged for it, but he wanted her to wait in eager anticipation. Just before leaving, he gave her a small kiss to remember him by. It was just below her neck and above her chest. He left behind two puncture wounds, and took a gulp of her blood in an exercise in self-discipline. He had trouble exerting control over himself lately, acting like a crazed animal while feeding. He wanted to prove to himself that he could stop once he started. He left Nora somewhere between agony and ecstasy.

He drove home feeling on top of the world. Nothing could bring him down. That was until he stepped into the house. The usual cast of characters had assembled in the living room to watch some inane movie on the large screen television.

He was about to go upstairs to his room when Magnus stood in front of him with his arms crossed, drilling laser beams at him with his eyes. Alexei moved forward but Magnus blocked his path.

"In my room, now."

"I have things to do," Alexei said.

"You can do them later." Magnus' gaze never wavered.

Alexei reluctantly followed. The last thing he needed was Magnus lecturing him.

Magnus closed the door after they both entered. He paced around.

With a bored tone, Alexei asked, "What do you want?"

"You have been spending time recently with a high profile model named Nora Brooks."

Alexei's lips curled. "How do you …."

"How do I know?"

"Yes. You never leave this place. You remain holed up in the house for days at a time."

"Very little escapes me. I have eyes and ears everywhere."

Alexei's eyes narrowed. "So what's it to you?"

"This woman is somewhat famous and keeps a high profile. You have been seen with her. If I know about it, others will also. Therefore, if she winds up missing, they will look for you, and you will once again expose our identity."

Alexei turned his back. "If that's all, then I'll be leaving."

A strong grip on his shoulder prevented him from moving. Magnus turned him around. "I'm not making a suggestion. If I find out this woman has been harmed, there will be trouble that you do not want to deal with."

Alexei stood face to face with Magnus. They were inches apart and neither flinched. "Is that a threat?"

"Take it any way you'd like. It doesn't matter to me. The only thing that matters is that the woman goes unharmed. Understand?"

"I would suggest you choose your enemies wisely. You don't want to cross me."

"Then don't give me a reason."

Alexei and Magnus continued to stare at each other.

Gabriella opened the door. "There you two are. I've been looking for you. Heinrich brought guests over that he would like everyone to meet. They're quite interesting." Gabriella grabbed Alexei's hand. "Come on."

He allowed her to lead him out of the room. Magnus stayed behind, his gaze unwavering.

Downstairs, Alexei glanced at the dark haired twins that

Heinrich brought to the house. Although the others in the brood seemed to find the twins amusing, Alexei could not get over his confrontation with Magnus.

He slipped out the front door and left the house. As he walked along the quiet streets of their sleepy neighborhood, he thought about leaving the brood. He didn't want to leave. He liked the others, especially Gabriella. If he and Magnus had a problem they could not resolve, why should he leave? Perhaps he would force a confrontation, and the stronger of the two would stay.

He had joined the brood fifty years ago. If not for Gabriella, he wouldn't have bothered. He lived in Berlin through both World Wars. It was a great time to be there. With the country on the brink of devastation, he could make fresh kills without being noticed. However, when the wars ended and the communists entered the country, he could not stay, not in a country under the rule of Josef Stalin.

He first encountered Gabriella on a cold winter evening on his way to attend the opera at a theater that had yet to fall prey to the communists. He knew the owner of the venue, and guaranteed his theater's protection in exchange for premium seats whenever he wanted them. The owner called upon Alexei when members of the Party tried to squeeze him.

Alexei enjoyed the mile walk from his apartment to the theater as communists wearing combat fatigues drove by in military vehicles. He relished the bitterly cold weather. It reminded him of his early days in the Ukraine.

A few blocks away from the theater, he detected the presence of another of his kind.

Most night dwellers residing in Germany left prior to the Second World War. He had not seen or heard from another in some time. Although he enjoyed humans, he missed the company of his species.

He quickened his pace and did a double take when he spotted one of the most gorgeous creatures he had ever seen.

She appeared to be haggling with someone at the ticket office. She stood next to another blood drinker of German ancestry. As he got close, she abruptly stopped arguing and turned in his direction. He smiled as their eyes met.

The theater employee greeted Alexei warmly.

"What's the problem?" Alexei asked.

In a professional voice, the employee said, "I am trying to explain to the gentleman and the lady that tonight's performance is sold out. There is not a single ticket available. It is most unfortunate, but they can purchase tickets for future performances. However, they insist on seeing the show tonight."

"Such small problems. These are my friends, and will be guests in my box."

"Well, if they are friends of yours, then an exception can be made. Please follow me." The man led them to Alexei's private box.

"That was most kind of you … "

"Alexei. And you are?"

"Gabriella. This is my friend Markus."

Alexei greeted Markus, but he only cared about Gabriella.

"I thought the undead community in Germany had disbursed long ago," Alexei said.

"We were passing through on our way to Zagreb. Markus is originally from Germany and he wanted to show me the home of his youth."

Markus smiled. "Thank you for your kind gesture."

"It's the least I could do."

Alexei watched the opera with his new friends, but could not keep his eyes off Gabriella. Afterward, he led his two guests backstage where they met the performers. Markus hit it off with a singer and went back to her apartment that evening. That was fine with Alexei, since it gave him an opportunity to spend time with Gabriella alone.

Alexei gave her a late night tour of Berlin. Before dawn she returned to her hotel. By that time, Markus also returned from his escapade with the opera singer.

The following evening they got together, and Alexei told them he would like to accompany them to Zagreb. These were difficult times in Eastern Europe, and there was safety in numbers. Markus and Gabriella agreed, and they departed a few days later. They traveled by train to Zagreb, and extended their tour into Turkey and Asia.

When they returned to Germany, Gabriella invited him to live in Spain with Magnus' brood. Alexei did not have any compelling reason to stay, and this gave him a perfect excuse to depart from Germany before it fell further into the hands of the Soviets. He packed his belongings and had them delivered by rail.

In the early years, he got along well with the others, even Magnus. After a while, his eccentricities wore on some of them, yet nobody ever told him to leave. For better or worse, they accepted him. This long running, silent feud between him and the brood leader was coming to a head. If Magnus wanted to force the issue, he would oblige him.

Chapter XVII

Mark Andrews sat alone on a bench near the Joan of Arc statue in Fairmount Park. Although he was sure the mob leader would not attempt foul play, he was still armed. He stretched his legs and cracked his neck. Enzo was late, probably watching nearby.

At peace with his decision, Mark slept well the previous evening. He was confident that since Enzo was willing to go this far, he would agree to work together.

He looked at his watch. Salerno was seven minutes late. When he glanced up again, Salerno approached wearing khaki pants, a polo shirt and sunglasses.

He sat next to Mark and took out a pack of cigarettes. "Care for a smoke?"

"No thanks," Mark replied. "I quit."

"Smart move. Here I am. I have a busy schedule, so I hope this will be worth my while."

Mark nodded. "What I'm about to show you has to be kept strictly confidential."

Salerno glared at him. "What do you think I'm going to do, find a reporter after we're done? Come on, Andrews."

"I know you won't, but I had to say it."

"And you wonder why I'm reluctant to work with you."

"I'm not going to waste your time with the early victims. It's a safe assumption that you've seen them already." Mark opened a briefcase and took out a picture. "This is the latest victim. Her name is Denise McKenna. She's a member of the orchestra at a local theater. Like the others, she was murdered in gruesome fashion."

Salerno picked up the pictures. "Our killer likes to carve up beautiful young women." He stared at the next picture. "This definitely fits the pattern. Did he go for the organs?"

"Yes. He partially consumed the liver and kidneys."

"Sick bastard." Salerno continued to flip through the photos. "Was the blood drained from the body?"

"Yes."

"What does he do, suck it out or use an instrument?"

"The evidence suggests he sucked the blood from small puncture wounds below the neck."

"You've been around a while. You ever seen anything like this?" Salerno asked.

"I've seen other brutal serial killers in the past," Mark replied. "But never any as sick as our boy. He takes it to another level of depravity."

After he finished looking at the photos, he handed them back to Mark. He took a deep drag from his cigarette. "Fascinating, but this is nothing new."

"This is where it gets interesting. Troy Zutaut, a friend of the deceased, took me to her apartment. Prior to Denise's death, they spent an evening with the suspect. Zutaut was pretty shook up when we reached the apartment."

"I would guess so."

"He said that the man had a mesmerizing quality about him. They were in his apartment for hours and he said it felt like minutes, like he had been in a trance the whole time."

"Maybe he uses hypnosis," Salerno said. "That would explain why there has been no forcible entry."

"Except for Johnny Gunns. In that case, there was a struggle."

The mob boss nodded. "Johnny was a fighter. Have you found any hallucinogenic drugs in the toxicology reports?"

"No."

"What about the hypnosis angle? You think there's

anything to it?"

"I wouldn't rule it out. The kid said the suspect had been around the world and told wild tales. Judging by some of these stories you would think the killer was really old, except that he didn't look old."

Salerno crushed his cigarette butt and tossed it into the trash can.

"The killer used the name Alexei," Mark said.

"Sounds Russian."

"We're running a search on anyone in the area with a criminal record that has a first name of Alexei, Alexander or some variation."

"Okay, since you shared some useful information, I'll tell you what I know, as long as you agree that anything I say here can't be used to implicate anybody."

"You have my word."

"On the night Johnny Gunns got wacked, one of my associates, Patrick Adesso, had a run-in with the killer."

"The Goat?"

"You do your homework. You know everybody I deal with?"

Mark shrugged.

"Anyway, the man nearly killed Patrick. In his words, he choked him with an inhuman grip. The kicker is that once he heard sirens, the man vanished."

"So I take it The Goat got a good look at him?"

Salerno nodded.

"We have an artist's sketch. I want you to show this to him and verify whether or not it's the same person." Mark took the sketch out of his briefcase and handed it to Salerno.

He brought it close to his face. "It fits the description he gave."

"Can you show it to The Goat?"

Salerno nodded.

"What else can you tell me?"

"Several neighbors saw our guy prior to the time Johnny

and Tina were killed. He had blood on his shirt, and they described him as a vampire."

Mark frowned. "We're not dealing with a vampire. This guy's flesh and blood like you and me."

"I didn't say otherwise."

Mark's brows creased. "We talked to everybody in the neighborhood. Nobody told us anything."

Salerno chuckled. "They don't talk to your kind. I guess you do need my help."

"You have anything else?"

"Nothing that you don't already know."

"So, Enzo, I'm glad you decided to meet me today. That shows character and integrity."

"Let's not make this a love fest."

Mark ignored the sarcasm. "We can make progress if we work together. I want your help nailing this killer."

Salerno put his index finger to his chin. "I'm not sure this is a good idea, seeing as how you're always trying to arrest me. That's not conducive to a working relationship."

"Enzo, I'm not going to lie to you. I'm desperate to get this guy. If it takes your help, then so be it. I'm willing to suspend my investigations into your illegal activities."

"Alleged illegal activities. My record is clean. I've never been convicted of anything."

"Yeah, and I'm the Tooth Fairy. Regardless, I'll suspend my investigations in anything you may or may not be connected with until we catch the killer or dissolve our partnership."

"Let's say I agree. How would we go about doing this? What are we going to do, ride in a squad car together?"

Mark hesitated, not sure if Salerno was being serious.

"It'll mostly be what we're doing now, sharing information. If I come up with something useful, I'll let you know. If we put our heads together, we'll nail this guy. There are things I can't do that you can and vice-versa. We can share resources. Basically, whatever it takes to get this bastard."

The mob boss nodded. "You know, I've thought about this since the other day when you told me to cut the Godfather bullshit. I don't have faith in the law. Your hands are tied because of legalities designed to protect the bad guys. There's too much corruption for law enforcement to be effective. I know many cops and judges on the take. But I respect you. I want justice for Johnny, so, I'm going to take you up on your offer as long as you give me your word that you're not going to turn on me."

Mark smiled. The road ahead would be bumpy. "You have my word. You're going down at some point. That's as inevitable as the sun rising and setting, but for now you're safe."

Salerno chuckled. "I like your false bravado." He extended his hand, and Mark shook it.

"I'll be in touch. We've got work to do. Alexei doesn't seem to take much time off between kills. That means we have to keep our eyes and ears open."

"We'll have people looking for our friend. He won't be able to move without being seen."

"Good."

Mark turned to leave, but before he could go anywhere, Salerno grabbed his arm, pulled out a large silver cross from his breast pocket and handed it to him.

"What's this all about? I thought that you didn't believe in this vampire nonsense."

Salerno smirked. "It never hurts to be careful."

Chapter XVIII

Fat Paulie took the envelope from a trembling Yeo See Choy and handed it to The Goat. "All the money better be here, you fucking gook bastard."

The Goat counted the money. He didn't think Choy would come through, but it was all there. They must have scared him shitless last time. "That's all of it. Too bad. I was hopin' to slice you up today." He pulled out his switchblade and rubbed the blade against his palm.

"You leave me alone," Choy said.

"Don't tell us what to do," Fat Paulie said. "The next time we come here, you better have the money again." Choy had three payments left to settle his debt. "'Cause like I said, I can't always control this guy. You know how young people are. They do what they want and don't have respect for their elders."

"I will have money! Now go. I have customers in store."

"Relax. You think we don't have better things to do than bother with a useless gook?"

The Goat waved the knife close to Choy's neck. "See you next month. By the way, I'm taking a Blackberry. Consider it a penalty for your late payment."

"How am I supposed to pay if you take merchandise?"

"That's not my fucking problem. You're the fucking business man. You figure it out."

As promised, The Goat took a Blackberry on the way out. Meanwhile, Fat Paulie took a camera. They put the goods in the trunk of The Goat's BMW.

Fat Paulie looked at his watch. "Shit, we gotta go. We're running late."

The Goat pulled onto the Schuylkill Expressway and stepped on the gas. "Don't worry. We'll get there in time. So what do you think the Boss wants?"

Fat Paulie shrugged, his double chin sagging. "We'll find out when we get there. All I know is that all the capos will be there."

"So then why does he want me there?"

Fat Paulie's head snapped back. "What do I look like, a fucking mind reader? He didn't tell me. All the fucking questions. It feels like I'm on the goddamn witness stand."

They made it to the parking lot of Santucci's restaurant ten minutes later and walked to a private room. Santucci's was owned by Tony Scrambolgni's cousin.

The Goat's spine tingled at the sight of all of Enzo's top guys. Mario "Ice Pick" Lazaro sat at a table next to Vinnie Mascaro with his glass eye. He had supposedly lost his real one in a knife fight in high school. Sophie Koch stood on one side of Enzo, and Barry Horn on the other.

The Goat couldn't hide his smile as he sat next to "Mad" Sal Demonte. He had never been this close to the Salerno family elite.

After everybody sat, and the waiter took their orders, Enzo addressed the capos, opening with a few jokes. When he finished he said, "I'm sure by now many of you have heard rumors about the death of Johnny Gunns, may God rest his soul. Although some of what you heard may be accurate, I doubt you know the full story. That's why I've invited our associate Patrick Addeso to give a detailed account of what transpired."

The Goat's brow furrowed. "Say what?"

"Did you not understand what I just said? Then I'll say it slower. I want you to tell everybody what happened from the time you arrived at the house."

"Um, sure." The Goat took a deep breath. He put his shaking hands in his pockets and rushed through his narrative. From time to time he glanced at the cold eyes of the men sitting at the table and lost his train of thought.

When he first mentioned the vampire, Vinnie Mascaro said, "Yo, pal, back up. What the fuck you talkin' about?"

"I know it's crazy, but you shoulda seen this fucker. If someone woulda told me that a month ago, I'd think the same thing. After I shot him, he grabbed my throat and then vanished. There ain't no way it could be nothing else."

"You gotta be shitting me," Vinnie said.

"I swear it's the truth."

Enzo stared at Vinnie. "We'll reserve judgment on the nature of this person for now. I can tell you that this is the "vampire killer" you've been hearing about on the news."

"Get the fuck outta here," "Ice Pick" Lazaro said.

"My personal belief is that the killer is a man just like the rest of us, despite what the reporters want us to believe. He just happens to have a demented way of taking his victims." Enzo removed a folder from his briefcase and handed it to The Goat. "Open it."

The Goat opened the envelope. His eyes bulged out. "Holy shit."

"Does that look like the man you saw that night?" Enzo asked.

"Hell yeah. Where did you get this from?"

Enzo removed a stack of papers from his briefcase and passed them around the table. "I know everyone here wants revenge for Johnny, nobody more than me. These are copies of an artist's sketch. His name is Alexei. This son of a bitch is our killer. I suspect he's Russian or Eastern European. Pass these around to your associates. Be on the lookout for this bastard. If any of your associates finds this guy, have them call you immediately, and then you call me. I don't care what time it is or what's going on. This is our top priority. Understand?" Everyone at the table nodded. "One more thing. We're going to work with Mark Andrews and his people from the Feds on this."

Shouts of dissension spilled from the table.

"Settle down," Enzo shouted.

"What?" Spit flew from Mad Sal Demonte's mouth. "Work with the Feds?"

Ice Pick Lazaro slammed his fist on the table. "Back in the day, you talk to the Feds and that's a one way ticket to your grave."

"This is fucking nuts," Mad Sal said.

Enzo stood. "Enough already. This is a one shot deal." He glared at his capos. "The best way to get this Alexei is to work with Andrews. After we kill this fucker, we part company."

Barry Horn removed his glasses. "What makes you think we can trust the Feds? By working with us, they can dig up dirt. We all stand to lose."

"Believe me, I don't trust the Feds either, but Andrews is a stand up guy. I believe his sincerity. I can read people. Let's not forget, I sniffed out that rat Dom Capesso when he was trying to sell us out, and I cut his fucking throat. There have been other cases where I cut off people we couldn't trust, and you guys know it. So right now, I'm telling you to believe me when I say you have nothing to worry about from the Feds."

Sophie Koch said, "Enzo's right. Andrews won't screw us on this."

"What have you two been smoking?" Mad Sal asked. "This is treason."

"Sit down, Sal." Enzo stared at him, his face tight. "I'm the boss around here, and that's what we're doing. If you stand against this, you stand against me."

Sal stood defiantly.

"You either sit down now or leave. Once you're gone, there's no coming back."

Mad Sal gritted his teeth. He looked around at the other capos, but they looked away from him. He took his seat.

"Think about poor Johnny's mother. Her son was unjustly put in his grave, and it's up to the people in this room to make things right. If Andrews or any of his agents are playing us, then we pull the plug, but that won't happen. Put your trust in me. I haven't steered you wrong in the past, and I've put you in position to earn a good living for your families."

The Goat stared at Enzo, entranced by the boss's power of persuasion. Just minutes ago, he had a full scale mutiny on hand, and he skillfully diffused the situation. He was glad he talked to the boss. So transfixed by what went down at the meeting, he did not even mind when he got stuck with the bill at the end of the meal.

Later Tony Scrambolgni sat at a table at the Reading Terminal Market with Enzo and Sophie, drinking a cappuccino and eating a cannoli from Termini Brothers. "You know I trust you, Boss. If you give me an order, I'm going to follow through. You've earned my respect and the respect of the other captains, but I have to say, I'm leery about your plan." Tony gestured with his hands. "I get a little nervous around those Feds. They're out to bust our balls, and the last thing I need are RICO charges."

Enzo put his hand on Tony's shoulder. "No one here has more to lose than me. Don't forget, I'm the one they're after. The rest of you guys would be used to get to me. If I'm okay with this arrangement, you should be too."

"You're worried about the wrong thing," Sophie said.

"What do you mean?" Tony asked.

"I've been doing a lot of reading about this vampire killer. Look at his victims. Their bodies have been drained of blood, organs consumed or removed. There have been no forcible entry into the homes, and that kid Troy said Alexei was mesmerizing. The Goat claims he vanished, and witnesses said he has the appearance of a vampire. If it looks like one, acts like one, and smells like one, then call me crazy, but I think we're dealing with a real vampire."

"You can't be serious." Enzo smirked as he drank his espresso.

"I'm dead serious," Sophie said.

"You're pulling my chain," Tony said.

"You believe in God, right?" Sophie asked.

"Of course I do."

"And you believe in Satan?" Sophie continued.

"Sure."

"You believe in saints. I see you're wearing a cross."

"Yeah, so what?"

"If you're willing to believe in God, the devil, and saints, then why is it so hard to believe in vampires? There are lots of things we have no explanation for."

"Because God and Satan, you know, those are things that exist in the afterlife. I'm talkin' about the here and now in South Philly, and there ain't no vampires."

"Vampires aren't a concept some movie director invented. There are versions of these creatures reported in regions separated by distance, religion and culture. Most major cultures have tales of vampires. It can't be a coincidence."

"She makes a good point," Enzo said. "Why would all these different cultures have stories about the undead?"

"Come on, Enzo. Don't tell me you're falling for this crap."

"No. Vampires are just old fables designed to scare primitive people. The serial killer we're dealing with is truly demented."

"Thank God," Tony said. "I was starting to get worried."

"Back to your point. I'm fully confident about our deal with Andrews. I could see it in the man's eyes when we were talking. He's like an addict, and his addiction is catching this murderer."

"I'll follow you wherever you lead me. I know those guys acted like you were nuts, but the other captains will back you.

I just hope it's all worth it."

Chapter XIX

Gabriella glanced at the photo in her wallet, then stared at the man at the bar. He was short, balding and overweight. His cheap blue suit accentuated his appearance. She had been searching for him for the past week.

As she stepped into the bar, heads turned and men ignored the women they were with. She was used to that reaction. She sat at an open spot at the bar, ten feet from Jack Williams.

Jack stared at her in his not so subtle way as she ordered her drink. She made eye contact with him. The man practically drooled. How classy.

She got up and sat on the open stool next to Jack and introduced herself. "I finished my drink. Would you like to buy me another?"

"Uh, sure. Of course. How about we sit at that table?"

Gabriella went to the table as Jack got their drinks. She engaged him in small talk, pretending she was interested in what he had to say.

"So, Jack, do you have a wife you're hiding back home?"

"No. I've been searching, but I haven't found a woman who has captured my heart."

Gabriella smiled at his lie.

"What I need is a great gal like you." Jack ordered another gin and tonic. "So, Gabriella, that's a pretty exotic name. You must not be from around here."

"I was born in Spain."

"I have important clients in Spain. I travel around the world quite a bit with my job."

"Is that right?" Another lie. Jack Williams told her he was a marketing manager for a pharmaceutical company. She knew he peddled insurance.

"Yeah, I fly to different countries to meet clients. I'm hoping to do more teleconferencing in the future. Still, you can't beat those frequent flyer miles, let me tell you, and it's a good idea to get close to the customer. So do you have a significant other?"

"I did, but he died."

Jack recoiled, sweat beading down his forehead. The man's hygiene left much to be desired. "Well, um, sorry to hear that. You know what they say, you gotta get back on the old horse."

She took another sip of her drink and held his hand.

"You probably get this a lot, but you're a real looker."

"Not really," Gabriella said. "I don't meet many people."

"Well, I'm all ya need. I have a certain way with women. I treat them like angels."

"I can tell."

Jack looked at his fake Rolex. "I was thinking we could go somewhere more private. There's a hotel downtown I like to go to. Maybe you and I could get to know each other better."

"I thought you weren't married."

Jack smiled. "No ring on this finger. My condo's being renovated, so this'll be more cozy."

She leaned back and crossed her legs. "I'd love to."

He paid the bar tab, leaving no tip. They got into his beat-up Pontiac Bonneville. Gabriella held her comments that this was hardly the car a marketing manager of a multinational pharmaceutical company would drive.

During the drive, Jack bored her with false stories of major deals he brokered in the business world.

They parked in a garage and walked toward the seedy hotel lobby. She stayed behind while he checked in, but remained close enough to listen to the conversation.

"Charlie, I picked up the most amazing babe ever," Jack said. "I'm talking off the charts. Hook me up with my special room."

Charlie, the beak-faced clerk, had a stupid grin. "No kidding. I gotta check her out. You're in luck. I have a bottle of wine you can take up to the room."

"You're the best."

Jack met her outside and led her up the elevator toward room 313. He took out the bottle of red wine, poured two glasses and handed her one. "You know, I don't do this often. Most of the time, I'm flying around the world. It's hard to find a meaningful relationship, but I think that might change."

"Jack, I have a confession to make. I've been following you. It wasn't by chance we met tonight. I thought you might be there, and I had to see you."

Jack nearly tipped over his glass. "Really?"

"Now that we're here, I can hardly wait." Gabriella ripped his shirt open.

"Woh, aren't you aggressive." Jack put his glass down.

She kissed his chest and bit his shoulder.

"Ow, that hurt."

"You don't mind, do you? I like it rough."

"I can take it."

Before he could react, Gabriella gave him a backhand slap to the face. His head jerked back in a whip-like motion.

He touched his face and glared at her. "What the hell was that?"

Gabriella winked. "I was just getting in the mood. We can stop if you like."

"No, I can play that way. You're nothing like I thought you would be."

"You can't judge a book by its cover. For instance, by looking at you, I would never guess that you like to beat up women."

Jack stepped back. "What are you talking about?"

"You left Katie a real mess. And you nearly killed your first wife, you sick bastard. Then there was Susie, Dianna and Alicia, other women you abused. I've done a little investigating." She punched him in the ribs with such hand-speed that he could not defend himself. He dropped to a knee, clutching his ribs and gasping for breath.

"You're a real piece of work, Jack. Physically, I find you unattractive, but inside, you're truly repulsive. I've been following you from afar ever since I saw the court proceedings when you pleaded no contest to beating your wife. God only knows why she still lives with you. Since the court system did not provide justice, I will."

Jack groaned.

She grabbed a fistful of his hair and tilted up his head. "I have contacts in the police force, and through them I saw the court photos of your wife. It looked like she had been run over by a Mack truck. You tore her left retina, separated her shoulder, broke her jaw, and knocked out her teeth. As if that wasn't bad enough, you ripped most of her hair out of her scalp, you filthy animal."

Gabriella glared at him. "I looked deeper into your background. At the time of your separation from your ex-wife, she had cigarette burns all over her body. At the divorce proceedings, she said that if she did not leave, you'd kill her."

Jack staggered to his feet. "You crazy bitch!" He balled his hands into fists, but before he could strike, she kicked him in the groin, causing him to crumple to the floor. She waited until he rose and then punched his face repeatedly until blood covered her hands. She licked the blood off and smiled.

He yelled incoherently, spitting blood, and stepped toward her. He lunged at her, but she deftly sidestepped him. When he turned, she clawed his neck, tearing flesh. Before he could scream, she covered his mouth with her free hand. She sank her teeth into his throat and closed her eyes, relishing the taste of blood. She pulled back and snapped his neck. She wanted to give him no pleasure, only pain. He was not worthy of her seductive gift.

She crossed her arms, tilted her head back and licked her lips. Regardless of how despicable the victim was, it was still sweet, delicious, life-sustaining blood. Gabriella only fed on the worst of society: rapists, child molesters, murderers and other predators. It started when she was living in Lisbon. For weeks she hunted down and finally killed a serial rapist that had eluded the Portuguese police. Since then she had become an amateur sleuth.

After cleaning up in the bathroom, she gathered his body and wrapped it in the bed sheets. She bundled him and scanned the floor for blood. There had been some splatter from when she had smashed his nose, but otherwise she had been careful to consume most of it.

She looked for soap and a towel to clean up the blood when footsteps sounded.

"What the hell's going on here?" the front desk clerk yelled.

Gabriella stopped moving, hoping he would go away. She listened to his fast beating heart and heavy breathing. *Damn.* The man wasn't about to leave.

Gabriella's eyes opened wide at the click of a shotgun. She had seen what happened to another of her kind who had been shot with a shotgun. It took him months of deep sleep to recover from the wound.

She dashed into the bathroom when the clerk opened the door. He walked into the room, shotgun in hand.

"What the ... ."

Before he could finish his sentence, she jumped out of the bathroom and landed a clean blow to the back of the head. He crashed onto the carpeted floor. She bent down and felt for a pulse. He was still alive. She bared her fangs and lowered her mouth to his neck, but pulled back, sweat dripping from her brow.

No. She had just fed. She had to control her urges. Years

ago she had decided to feed only on those who deserved it. Although this guy was a scumbag, he had done no wrong.

Keeping a close eye on the clerk, she went to the window and waited until the streets were empty. After a few minutes, she raised the window, put Jack's body over her shoulder, jumped down three flights and landed on her feet. The street was clear of people and traffic. She moved quickly to the parking garage. Using keys from Jack's pants pocket, she opened the trunk of his car and dumped his body.

She drove to an unused quarry near the Delaware border, where she weighted the body down and threw it deep in the quarry, hoping no one would find him soon.

Tonight, Jack Williams provided her not only with nourishment and an opportunity for justice, but a diversion. Tensions were mounting between Alexei and Magnus. The strain of playing the role of the peacemaker was wearing on her. She wanted the others to live harmoniously, but their tenuous relationships were fracturing with little chance of mending.

After dumping the body, she drove back in Jack's Bonneville. She abandoned the car at an alley off of Sansom Street and took a cab home.

When she arrived, Magnus was hunched over the oblong kitchen table writing in his journal. "How did it go?"

Gabriella sat next to him. "Well. I disposed of the body discretely. It should be some time before anyone recovers it."

"How was he?"

"Tasty. What an overbearing jerk. How were women ever attracted to him?"

"There's no accounting for taste," Magnus said. "At least there's one less piece of human filth out there. So who's your next target?"

"I'm not sure. Kristoff was telling me about the victim of a good candidate at a woman's shelter."

"The streets will be safer for the mortals with you around. How ironic."

"And how are things with you?" Gabriella asked.

"I contacted an antiques dealer in New Hope. I'm looking to purchase a gargoyle statue for the front gate. The outside is rather drab."

Magnus swept her into his powerful arms and lifted her off her feet. He twirled her around gracefully and dipped her. "Do you remember that time in Monte Carlo when we entered the dance floor at the ball thrown for Prince Constantine? All eyes were on us. They couldn't stop staring."

Gabriella smiled. "Even the Prince was transfixed."

"Wherever we went, everyone was envious of us." Magnus brushed his lips against hers. "Sometimes I miss those days and wish we could once more tour the world and create our mark among the social elite, just the two of us."

"I know, but I care deeply for the others."

"As do I. Heinrich always puts me in a good mood. Kristoff has an impressive presence about him considering his young age. Magdalena is a siren. Still, I wouldn't complain if it were just the two of us."

"Perhaps some day," Gabriella said.

"No matter who else is in the Brood, you are always first with me. As long as I have you, I'll be happy."

Gabriella leaned against his chest. "And you'll always be first in my heart."

"I'm glad to hear it. Your tired eyes need to rest." Magnus lifted her into his arms and carried her to her room.

Chapter XX

"Stacy's hot for me," Vinnie said.

"She ain't hot for you," Tony Giordano yelled over the blaring music at Club Egypt. "You always say that whenever a girl talks to you. I'd watch out if I were you. Rita'll tear your balls off if you hit on her."

Vinnie shrugged as he drank his Seven and Seven.

"I'll tell you what, Stacy has one sweet rack," Mike Tarracone said. "I wouldn't mind taken a swing at her."

"Too bad you only got a Wiffle bat," Vinnie said, getting a laugh out of Tony.

Mike smirked. "That's not what your old lady says. She told me I'm packing two tons of dynamite."

"Yeah, with a one inch fuse. If anyone's getting a piece of Stacy's ass, it's me." Vinnie pointed at his chest. "She's outta your league."

They quieted when the ladies returned from the bathroom.

"Hey, where's my beer?" Vinnie asked his girlfriend Rita.

"You got two feet," Rita said. "You can go to the bar and get it yourself. Last time I checked, I don't have a leash around my neck or a ring around my finger."

"Always with the attitude," Vinnie said. "What's with you? I take you out and show you a good time, and all you do is break my balls."

"I was going to the bar anyway," Mike said. "I'll get drinks. No need to have a domestic situation here. What would you like, Stacy?"

Rita put her hands on her hips. "You can't boss me around."

"I ain't bossin' you around." Vinnie scowled. "I just asked you to get me a beer since you were up."

"You can get me a Margarita—frozen." Stacy batted her eyelashes.

"Anything you want, baby," Mike said.

"Take me home," Rita said to Vinnie.

"Take you home?" Vinnie's face reddened. "We just fucking got here. You was beggin' me to take you out, now you want me to go home. Make up your fucking mind!"

Mike smiled at Stacy as he sauntered toward the bar. She wanted to hook up with him. It was obvious. If only Vinnie and his woman would stop arguing. They were driving him nuts. They looked like they might come to blows, and he didn't want to get in the middle of it. Vinnie had a hot temper, and Rita's was worse.

As he neared the bar, he froze when he saw a guy with long blond hair. He knew that guy. Damn, he shouldn't have taken those pain pills. Now his head wasn't straight. Where the hell had he seen him before? He pulled out the sheet of paper from his jacket, then eyed the blond dude at the bar. It was Alexei, the Vampire Killer.

"Holy shit." Earlier that day, Tony Scrambolgni had told him and the members of his crew to keep a lookout for this guy. He reached for his piece before putting it back. He couldn't shoot him here. They were supposed to notify Tony if they saw Alexei.

He forgot about the drinks and walked back to his friends, keeping his eyes on Alexei. He called out to Vinnie and Tony.

Tony, who was hitting on Stacy, glared at him. "What the fuck do you want?"

Mike motioned with his head. "This is important. Now!"

Tony frowned, while Vinnie appeared to be relieved to escape from Rita.

"What's so damn important?" Tony asked.

Mike took out the drawing. "The Vampire Killer. He's by the bar."

Tony's eyes went wide. "Son of a bitch."

"Let's pop the bastard," Vinnie said.

Mike grabbed his arm. "No. The Wop told us to call him first."

Vinnie shrugged. "We call him and then we'll pop him."

The Wop's stomach growled as he smelled the fresh macaroni, Italian sausage, roasted peppers and broccoli rabe his *gumar* was cooking. He couldn't wait. First his *gumar* would feed him, and then she would satisfy his sexual appetite.

Tony Scrambolgni was proud of his nickname, The Wop. He had been doing time in Rahway State Prison for armed robbery. It was what an inmate had called him just before he knifed the guy. Since then he wore it like a badge of honor.

He needed to relax. He had too much on his plate. Besides the Vampire Killer, he was dealing with a dispute with the New Jersey syndicate over a shipyard contract.

When his phone rang, he didn't want to answer. Dinner was almost ready, and he was famished. He closed his eyes as the scent wafted into his nostrils. He cursed after the phone rang for the third time.

"Yeah."

"Hey, this is Mike Tarracone. I'm over here at Egypt with Vinnie and Tony."

"Yeah, what do you want me to do about it?"

"We saw the guy who you told us to look for."

Tony nearly dropped his phone. "Where?"

"Here at the bar."

The Wop ran his fingers through his thinning hair.

"You want us to do the job?" Mike asked.

"Cover him like a blanket. Don't let him out of sight even for a minute. Ya hear?"

"I hear ya."

"If he leaves, follow him. If you got a free shot, take it. Understand?"

"You got it."

Tony hung up the phone. He was no longer hungry. He was now hyped on adrenaline from the excitement of the chase. Caught up in the moment, he nearly forgot he had to immediately notify Enzo.

Enzo slid into the Jacuzzi. "This is nice."

His wife was inside, holding a glass of wine. "You didn't want to get a Jacuzzi."

"I thought it was a bit much."

"But now you're glad we bought it."

Enzo picked up his glass. "I am."

Having just put little Eddie and Angela to bed, they finally had time to themselves. Their oldest daughter, Donna, was allowed to stay up later. Enzo was experiencing angst because Donna had just asked for her own cell phone. At age nine, she acted like a teenager. She even wanted a manicure. She was growing up too fast.

"I was talking to Uncle Gino today. Aunt Carla's surprise party is next Sunday."

Enzo sighed. "I'm busy that afternoon."

Gina gave him a sad, puppy dog look. "She'll be upset if you're not there."

"All right, I'll be there. I'll be late, so you'll have to take the kids without me."

"Thanks, Enzo."

As she leaned in and put her arms around his neck, his cell rang. "Don't answer it."

Enzo kissed her forehead. "I have to."

He answered the phone. "Yeah ... Where?" He got out of the Jacuzzi. "Is he still there? We can't let him get away ...

I'm coming over."

Gina propped her arms on the ledge of the tub and rested her face on her hands. "Don't leave. We were just getting started."

"I'm sorry, baby, but I have to go. This is urgent."

Gina sunk back into the Jacuzzi.

"I'll make it up to you, I promise. I didn't want to tell you yet, but I booked that Champagne suite in the Poconos. It'll be just the two of us. No interruptions."

"You promise?"

"Cross my heart."

Enzo toweled off, put on his clothes and left the room. As he was leaving, he called Special Agent Mark Andrews.

Mark looked at the clock. It was time to go home. He put his file away. Victoria was understanding about his late hours, but this past week had to test her limits. His obsession with the Vampire Killer was unhealthy.

His agents were looking for Alexei. They were to canvass the neighborhoods and go to all the bars, restaurants, night clubs, and high end shops. Thus far they had no promising results.

As he was packing his briefcase, the phone rang. "Mark Andrews … When did this happen? Was he alone? Okay. I'll get right on it … I'll call you later."

His body surged with adrenaline after talking to Salerno. It would take fifteen minutes to reach the club. Agents Staples and Barton could get there quicker.

He called Agent Barton, who said they would be right there. Mark loaded his gun and took a deep breath. This was his chance to capture Alexei. He was determined to use whatever means necessary to stop the vampire killer.

"Sorry ladies, but we gotta go," Vinnie said.

"What do you mean, you gotta go?" Rita asked. "You always pull this crap. Something happens and you have to leave."

"The night's still young." Stacy winked.

"I wish we could stay," Mike said. "But something's going down."

"You don't know what you're missing," Stacy said.

Rita crossed her arms. "Just leave. Us girls will have more fun without you."

"Whatever." Vinnie led the others toward the bar, where Alexei was having a friendly conversation with a young man and woman.

"Each of you cover an exit," Vinnie said. "I'm gonna stick close by him."

They split up. Vinnie tried to act casual as he edged toward the bar. He glanced at his two associates, who were in position. He felt a chill when, for a brief moment, Alexei stared at him. Vinnie was locked in a trance. He broke free when Alexei turned.

Alexei and his two friends walked toward the rear exit, where Tony stood. As discreetly as he could, he gestured for Mike to follow.

Vinnie pursued Alexei as they weaved through the crowd. By the time he reached the exit, Alexei was outside. Fortunately so was Tony, who pretended to talk on his cell.

Mike hurried out the exit door, and they closed the distance on Alexei.

They walked in step, trailing Alexei. Vinnie pulled out his gun and pressed it against Alexei's lower back. Mike and Tony grabbed Alexei's two friends.

"We got business with your friend here," Tony said. "Take a walk."

They gaped as if they had seen a monster and weren't just talking to one.

"You best leave quickly," Mike said.

Alexei smiled. "Everything is all right. I'll meet up with you later." His friends left without arguing. "So to what do I owe this rude interruption? You claim we have business, but I've never met you. Perhaps you have mistaken me for someone else."

"No mistaking here, Alexei," Vinnie said.

"Ah, so you do know who I am. However, I don't know you. Perhaps you can enlighten me."

Vinnie kept the gun pressed on his back. "Keep walking and shut the fuck up."

"As you wish." They walked up Spring Garden past Second Street. "Thus far you have been rude, something I frown upon. Now tell me what this is about."

"This is about a friend of ours, Johnny Gunns," Tony said.

"Yes, Johnny," Alexei said. "A most unfortunate situation."

"It's time for a little payback, you son of a bitch," Vinnie said. "We're gonna go somewhere nice and secluded where no one will be able to hear you scream."

They made a left onto Third Street and then a right up a side street.

"You shouldn't underestimate me." Alexei was a blur. He turned, grabbed Vinnie by the neck, lifted him off his feet and hurled him. Vinnie flew head over heels in the air and landed on his back. After he hit the concrete, his gun flew onto the street.

Alexei punched Mike with lightning quick fists that sent him reeling backward.

When the vampire turned around, Tony shot him. The bullet pierced Alexei's chest. Its impact knocked him to the ground.

Tony helped Mike to his feet. "You alright, buddy?"

Mike had a dazed look, but he nodded. "What happened?"

"I killed the son of a bitch," Tony replied. "We gotta get rid of the body."

"Right. How's Vinnie?"

"I don't know."

As they moved toward their friend, they stopped in their tracks when Alexei stood before them. "You really shouldn't have done that. Do you realize how angry that makes me?"

"What the fuck?" Tony said. "I just shot you."

"Didn't work out for you, did it?" Alexei lunged at Tony and tore out his larynx, causing blood to erupt. He took a long drought of blood.

Tony fell to the ground and convulsed.

"Motherfucker!" Vinnie charged Alexei from behind, knocking the unsuspecting vampire off his feet.

Mike jumped on Alexei and smashed his head on the concrete. Alexei snarled, grabbed Mike by the throat and squeezed. Mike's face turned an unhealthy shade of red.

Vinnie grabbed his gun, prompting the vampire to release Mike. Alexei moved with preternatural speed and struck Vinnie with an open hand with such force that it shattered his sternum. With both hands he grabbed Vinnie's head and twisted his neck, snapping it instantly. Vinnie slumped to the ground, a blank expression on his face.

Alexei turned his attention to the remaining mobster and approached with a look of cold steel in his eyes. In the background a car came roaring in their direction.

Agent Ross Staples drove behind the rear entrance of Club Egypt. He couldn't find a spot, so he double parked alongside another car.

Gunfire sounded.

"Where?" Ross asked.

"Up Spring Garden," Agent Barton replied.

Ross put the car in reverse and backed away, nearly running over a civilian. He made a sharp left onto Spring Garden. "Where to?"

"I'm not sure. I don't know if it was to the left or right."

Agent Barton opened his window and leaned out his head.

Ross drove slowly until a shout sounded.

"To the right," Barton said.

The car screeched as he turned onto Second Street.

"Up ahead," Barton said. "Make a quick left."

Ross pulled into a narrow street. One man was on the ground, blood streaming from his neck. A tall blond held another man by his throat. Son of a bitch. It was the Vampire Killer. Alexei released the man. Ross blinked in disbelief when Alexei moved impossibly fast and punched a third man in the chest. He watched in revulsion as Alexei snapped the man's neck with ease.

Alexei strolled toward the remaining member of the trio he had been fighting when he made eye contact with Ross. His gaze captivated Ross, who momentarily forgot what he was doing. Alexei leaped into the air, disappearing from sight, causing Ross to slam on the brakes.

"Holy shit!" Barton yelled.

Alexei landed on the hood of their car. Ross undid his seat belt and reached for his gun when Alexei's fist shattered the windshield. He pulled Barton out of the car, raking him against the crushed glass. He held Barton over his head, then hurled him like a projectile. Barton sailed through the warm night air and landed head first against the brick wall of a building. A sickening crunch sounded upon impact.

Not bothering to get out of his car, he fired at Alexei, hitting him three times; the third shot sent Alexei staggering off the car.

Ross took a deep breath, relieved that Alexei was dead. He exited the car at the same time the last surviving member of the trio fighting Alexei approached him.

"He ain't dead yet," the man said.

"What are you talking about?" Of course Alexei was dead. He shot him three times at point blank range.

Ross searched for Alexei's body until his car lifted off the ground on one side.

Ross shot forward, avoiding the car as it tipped over.

Alexei walked forward as if nothing happened.

"What the hell are you?" Ross muttered.

Alexei approached them when three police cars roared onto the scene. He smiled. "I would love to stay and chat, but it appears I must go."

Right before his eyes, Alexei vanished.

Chapter XXI

Nora Brooks folded her arms and pouted as Alexei watched the news.

"The neighborhood is in shock in the aftermath of tonight's brutal violence." The camera showed a wide angle shot of the bodies being led away in gurneys. "Although it has not been confirmed, Channel 10 has information that leads us to believe that this is the work of the Vampire Killer."

The reporter interviewed a gray-haired woman who had been in the vicinity during the fight.

"Three in all are dead tonight at the hands of the Vampire Killer," the reporter said. "One is believed to be a Federal Bureau of Investigations agent. At this point it is unclear whether or not the agent was involved in the investigation of the Vampire Killer. The identities of the other two victims are still unknown."

Alexei turned off the television and paced around the room. He muttered a curse in Russian. If only he knew they were FBI agents, then he would have killed them both despite the sounds of police sirens drawing closer. Letting one live was the worst possible scenario. He would face unwanted repercussions, both from within his family and from outside. He smashed his fist into his palm. He couldn't have possibly screwed up the situation any worse, and now he was a marked man. "I have to go."

"You just got here." Nora provocatively showed her legs,

the same ones that earned her model of the year by a European fashion magazine.

"I realize that, my lovely, but I have to clear my head."

Nora grabbed his shoulders and rubbed her body against his. "You weren't lying. You really are a vampire."

"Why would I lie to you?"

"You're the one they're talking about in the news, right?"

Alexei smiled and bared his fangs. "Guilty as charged. Does that bother you?"

"No." She pressed her lips against his. "The media's wrong about you. You didn't kill those women in cold blood." Nora lifted her head, exposing her neck.

"No, I didn't." Alexei ran his tongue along her throat and closed his eyes. She was there for the taking, so sweet, so inviting.

"They wanted you to take them."

"They cherished every moment. Those men I killed tonight got in the way. I had no choice but to deal with them. I didn't ask for this trouble."

Nora drew him closer. "So what are you going to do?"

"I don't know. Needless to say, some people aren't pleased."

The phone rang, and Nora answered. He ignored her chatter and contemplated fleeing. He wasn't one to cut and run if the situation got dicey. That was what Magnus did, old, stale, pathetic, barely living Magnus. Let them pursue him. He was an ancient vampire, one of the most powerful in the world.

Nora clicked off the phone. "I don't want you to leave. I thought you might be coming so I invited a friend. She's nice. I think you'll like her."

His senses were already flaring from Nora's blood. This further piqued his interest.

"Won't you stay? She'll only be a few minutes. She's dying to meet you."

Alexei wrapped his arms around her slim waist. He

pricked her neck slightly with his fangs and took in a few drops of her blood, any thought of leaving gone. When Chelsea Sheppard, a seventeen-year-old aspiring model, arrived he was glad he stayed.

"So what do you think?" Nora asked, standing by Chelsea.

"I like what I see." Maybe this was what he needed, fresh young blood. He put a premium on beautiful people, and these two women were most exquisite. Alexei draped his jacket over a chair and made himself a drink. When the night was over, what occurred outside of Club Egypt was a distant memory.

A tired and frustrated Mark Andrews sat in Enzo Salerno's office on Market Street. He had not slept last evening.

"We have to rethink this whole thing," Salerno said.

"What do you mean?" Mark asked.

"Alexei the Vampire Killer. Our game plan's all wrong."

Mark finished his fourth cup of coffee and threw the cup in the trash. He chewed on two Tums. "What's wrong with the plan? We waited for Alexei to show up, and he did."

"Wake up, Mark. If we didn't capture or kill him tonight, then we're not going to using those tactics."

"So we send more men."

Enzo's voice rose. "Why? So more people can die? I don't know about you, but I don't want any more of my men getting killed by this bastard."

"I don't want mine to die either."

"You have to face facts."

"And what are they?" Mark asked.

"That Alexei is a real life, honest to God, fucking vampire."

Mark and Salerno each spoke to their men and compared notes. They had them go over every detail of what occurred in agonizing detail. Mark spent a few hours at the scene of the crime while Salerno had every available associate prowling the streets looking for Alexei.

"Come on," Mark said.

"What more do you have to fucking hear? Both Mike and Staples' stories mesh, for the love of God. If what they're saying is true, he can't be human. No human could do the things they said this bastard did. If you can't acknowledge that he's a fucking vampire, then we're done here."

Mark threw his hands in the air. "All right. He's a goddamn vampire. If he's not a vampire, then he's some super being. It's just hard to accept."

"The first step in solving this problem is knowing our enemy."

"Great, we know our enemy. Now what do we do?"

Enzo paced around the room and pulled out a cigarette. "It's obvious that conventional tactics are useless. Hell, we shot the son of a bitch so many times, and it just pissed him off."

"We have to find out everything we can about Alexei."

"Exactly." Enzo clenched his fists.

"The question is how. We don't know where he is, or how to find him."

"We start with the basics. If he really is a vampire, then we know a good deal about our friend. There are legends of vampires in almost every culture going back thousands of years."

"One little problem with all that. Out of these legends, myths and stories, how can we decipher what's real and what's bullshit. There has to be a better way," Mark said.

"If you got one, let me know, because I'd love to hear it."

Mark shrugged. "I don't think I'm about to tell my bosses I'm hunting a vampire. They'll think I'm nuts and they might be right. I'm going to have to come up with a good cover."

Enzo patted his shoulder. "Get some sleep. You look like shit."

Mark laughed. "You don't look so hot yourself."

"What a fucking night. We're going to get Alexei. By God, we'll get him."

Chapter XXII

The Goat was sprawled out on Vladimir Ustanov's sofa in a drug-induced haze. The crazy concoction he took last night when he was out with some friends had been a bad idea, but at the time he had an overwhelming need to numb himself. Now, he felt like he had been on the wrong side of an encounter with the Vampire Killer. He swore to himself he would never do that again.

As he feared, he told them Johnny's attacker was a vampire, and they laughed at him. They hadn't been there the night he encountered Alexei. They had made a foolish mistake pursuing Alexei like he was a normal person. If they listened to him, Vinnie Casso and Tony Giordano might still be alive. Now, even the most skeptical had to admit the truth — Alexei was undead.

The Goat's face cringed and he nearly vomited. Like his girlfriend Karen always said, he was self-destructive. Every time something good happened in his life, he screwed it up.

He sat up as Vladimir entered the room with his lady friend, Ksenya. Vladimir handed him two Tums and a cup of black coffee.

"Thanks, Vlad." The Goat swallowed the Tums. "I appreciate it." Even through the haze, he gawked at Ksenya. She wore tight shorts and a half tee shirt that revealed a bare midriff. She was hot, even if she did look like she belonged in Alexei's family.

"You had bad night?" Vladimir asked.

"Bad doesn't describe it. This was an all-timer. I feel like Humpty Dumpty."

Vladmir's brow furrowed.

"Never mind."

"Well, I make you happy." Vladimir handed him an envelope with cash.

The Goat didn't feel like counting. "How much?"

"Twenty five hundred."

The Goat raised his left eyebrow. "Not bad."

Vladimir nodded. "Business is good."

"That's good. If you do a good job here, we might have some more work for you. Maybe even with a better cut."

"I have other ideas to make money," Vladimir said.

"You keep it up, and we'll talk."

The Goat gingerly rose from the sofa. "Hey, you're from Russia."

"The Ukraine," Vladimir corrected him.

"Yeah, like I was saying, so you probably know all about this vampire shit, right?"

Vladimir smirked. "Vampires, witches, black magic, everything. I have vampire living next door."

The Goat detected sarcasm through the thick accent. "I'm not saying because you're Russian you know all about vampires. It's not like they're living out in the open there, or anything. But you must know about them."

Vladimir rolled his eyes. "If they have vampire in Ukraine, I would not know. I do not travel in those circles."

"I'm sure you don't. It's just that the Vampire Killer is Russian or something."

Vladimir shrugged. "I know nothing."

The Goat waved his hand. "Forget about it."

"I know of him," Ksenya said.

The Goat's jaw dropped. "Huh?"

Vladimir frowned as he stared at Ksenya.

"My grandfather had encounter many years ago in Georgia."

"I thought your family was from Russia." This conversation was getting confusing. It was the last thing The Goat needed after his bender.

"Georgia was part of former Soviet Union," Vladimir said.

"Georgia's in the South. What are you talking about? Have you been smoking something?"

"Never mind," Vladimir said.

The Goat grabbed Ksenya's arm. "Tell me about this deal with your grandfather."

"A vourdalak almost kill my grandfather when he was boy in Georgia."

"Voura-what?" The Goat asked.

"Vourdalak," Vladimir said. "It is vampire in Russian folklore. Vourdalak is beautiful but evil man or woman who preys on people."

"So how do you know its Alexei?" The Goat asked.

"Who is Alexei?" Ksenya asked.

"The Vampire Killer," The Goat replied.

Vladimir smiled. "Like I say, you know more about it than I do."

"I do not know if vourdalak who almost kill my grandfather is same as this one," Ksenya said. "My grandfather knows about them. He can help."

The Goat shrugged. "Alexei whacked two of our boys a couple nights ago. We need to figure out how to kill this son of a bitch or we're in deep shit."

Vladimir picked up the copy of the *Philadelphia Daily News* with the picture of Agent Barton's body being carried away in a gurney. "I think you are right."

Sophie Koch wore a black dress to Vinnie Casso's funeral, her second burial in two weeks. Tomorrow was Tony Giordano's.

She vividly remembered Enzo calling her to let her know

what happened. She could not tell if he was sad or angry. Perhaps it was frustration in his voice.

She wanted to console him, but that would be a terrible mistake. In that moment of weakness, he might succumb to her, and she would feel guilty as hell if he cheated on his wife with her. Sophie had been fighting this battle for some time, and her self-control always won. She chose not to pursue a relationship with Enzo years ago. Now that he had a family, that option no longer existed.

They spoke on the phone for a half-hour. They talked of ghouls and ghosts and things that go bump in the night, things she would have dismissed as nonsense a few weeks ago. Even before this attack, she was convinced Pat Adesso's story was authentic. Fortunately, Enzo now reached that same conclusion.

She glanced at Enzo, who was speaking with Casso's mother. She imagined he was saying something similar to what he told Johnny Debenedetto's mother. When Enzo finished speaking with the grieving mother, he walked in Sophie's direction.

She tried to smile, but couldn't. "I hope we don't have to attend any more funerals for a while."

He nodded. "You and me both."

Sophie clutched his arm. "Let's take a walk."

Enzo lit a cigarette. "It always hurts when I have to talk to the mothers. It cuts deep, to the bone. It doesn't matter how many bad things they've done. To the mothers they're perfect angels." Enzo crushed his cigarette. "I have to make sure this doesn't happen again."

"What did we get ourselves into? We run a business. We're not about hunting the undead." Sophie gritted her teeth.

"I didn't ask to have anything to do with this monster. He came to the wrong neighborhood and killed the wrong person. He started it, but I'll be damned if we don't finish it."

Sophie gave him an icy stare. "Enough bluster. Saying what we're going to do won't get us anywhere. We need a plan, or more people will get killed."

Enzo nodded. "You're right. We now know he's a fucking vampire."

"I would say so."

"Like you said, vampire legends exist in many cultures. Since vampires are real, many of these legends must be based upon fact. So we study them, find out what they do, how they do it, and uncover their weaknesses."

"Like garlic or sunlight or stakes."

"Precisely," Enzo said. "We'll find out how to identify and kill these vampires. I was reading some vampire lore that suggested they travel in packs called broods. It's possible our boy may not be flying solo."

"I certainly hope he's alone. I wouldn't want to deal with more than one vampire."

Enzo took out a cigarette. "Most of the men in our organization aren't the research type. They're more doers than thinkers. You need muscle or you need a guy plugged, they can do that, but figuring out how to kill vampires isn't their strong suit."

"We'll have to take that on ourselves."

"We have to do it quickly. Alexei won't be waiting. I want the Wiz to work on it."

Sophie raised her brows. "The Wiz?"

Enzo nodded. "This will be right up his alley."

"I'll let him know what we're looking for."

As they were walking back to the mourners, Sophie said, "I have to admit, I'm feeling a bit uneasy. We might be dealing with something we can't handle. All of us, including our families, could be in danger. It's not like we're fighting against another family or the Feds, where everybody follows certain rules and families are off limits. I'm guessing a vampire doesn't have any codes of honor."

"We can handle him," Enzo said with quiet confidence.

"What makes you so sure?"

"For one simple reason. If vampires have been around for

so long and they're so powerful, why haven't they overrun the planet by now? How come they aren't in control? They must have weaknesses that can be exploited."

Sophie gave him a hug before abruptly releasing. She needed comfort. Since that was as much as she would get from Enzo, she would have to look elsewhere. There was a young stud she met at the gym who was all bulging muscles and good looks with little brain activity. He invited her out for drinks. Tonight she would take him up on his offer for drinks and much more afterward.

Chapter XXIII

Kristoff arrived at the mansion out of breath.

Heinrich, who had been sitting on a plush leather sofa working on a puzzle, helped him off his feet. "What happened to you?"

Ursula, who had been drying off after swimming in the indoor pool, dropped her towel and approached him. "You look like you ran two marathons."

Kristoff nodded. "I feel like it."

The others gathered around him.

"Where is Magnus?" Kristoff asked. "I must speak with him."

Magnus emerged from the basement. "I'm here."

He took a couple of deep breaths. "Alexei has gotten into big trouble."

Magnus sighed. "What now?"

"I was at the comedy club on South Street with three mortal friends. Afterward, they wanted to go dancing. Always up for a good time, I obliged. We went to the Rock Lobster and then to Club Egypt. The area was crawling with cameras, reporters and police. Nobody would say it too loud, but I heard their whispers. This was the work of the Vampire Killer. I weaved my way inside and asked the bouncers, bartenders and waitresses if they had seen a man who fit Alexei's description. Not surprisingly, they had. He killed two members of the local crime syndicate as well as a law enforcement agent."

Magnus closed his eyes. "Wonderful."

"I imagine it's on the news."

When Heinrich turned on the large, flat screen plasma television, the local news channels were showing live coverage of the massacre.

Magnus trembled with fury. The local gangsters Alexei killed were bad enough, but killing an FBI agent was unacceptable. Alexei's arrogance would lead to their demise.

"He's gone too far," Kristoff said. "He has put us in jeopardy, and I don't want to suffer because he can't control himself."

"Alexei may have his faults, but he is a member of our family," Heinrich said.

"Yes, but unlike our original mortal families, we can pick ours," Kristoff said. "When you do harmful things to your family members, you don't belong."

Magdalena turned toward Kristoff, her lush brown hair whipping him in the face. "Why, because he killed a few mortals? You have killed before."

"In those regrettable incidents I have the good sense to not make the evening news. If we all acted like Alexei, we would have been hunted down and burned in a fiery pyre many moons ago. He lacks respect for our kind."

"You still harbor resentment because of what happened when he first converted you," Ursula said. "You have to get over it."

"What happened between us holds no relevance. I've learned to live with it, but I can't live with his disregard for us."

Magdalena stroked Kristoff's hair. "Our loyalties should be with our own. I'll take any blood drinker, even a stupid, mindless one, over a hundred mortals. They're nice as playthings, don't get me wrong, but they will never equal one of us."

"We have to live among the mortals," Heinrich said. "They outnumber us and their technology gets increasingly more sophisticated, which will enhance their ability to detect and hunt us."

"We have ascended the evolutionary chain," Magdalena said. "We're superior."

"Without them we would have no food supply," Heinrich said.

Kristoff shook his head. "We're getting off topic. Alexei must go."

Ursula folded her arms. "Will you stand against him? No offense, but he'd destroy you."

Kristoff's eyes narrowed. "I will."

Magnus raised his hand. "You'll do no such thing. The only one who can and will do something is me. I bear the responsibility of taking action against one of our members. You've made your points. Alexei is one of us, and therefore our kinship is strong, but that doesn't mean he can do whatever he wants."

"So what will you do?" Magdalena asked.

"I haven't decided, but it will be in our best interest." Magnus gazed at the other vampires and saw no dissent.

There was no point looking for Alexei. He was either on his way home or hiding. He was not reckless enough to be prowling the streets.

Magnus resumed his billiards match against Markus. His concentration was off, and Markus beat him easily. He did not allow the others to see how disturbed he felt. He had to remain their cool and unruffled leader. Gabriella was the only one who knew how much he despised Alexei.

When the sun rose the following morning, Alexei still had not returned. Magnus was not surprised. Different levels of vampires existed. The younger ones like Ursula had to be completely enshrouded in darkness during the day. They slept in a coffin or vault, something impenetrable to light. An older vampire such as Gabriella could sleep in a conventional bed in a darkened room. Exposure to sun light could be harmful, but not fatal. Ancient vampires like Magnus and Alexei didn't have to sleep during the day. Sunlight only weakened them. Magnus had ventured outside in daylight to experiment. Although he felt sluggish, he had not suffered any injuries. The same applied to Alexei. He could be in a hotel room or staying with friends. Either he was hiding from the authorities, or he did not want to face Magnus' wrath.

Tension and speculation about what happened to Alexei filled the house. Some speculated that he fled, although Magnus doubted it. Alexei welcomed attention. Others thought someone had killed him, but he was an ancient vampire and would not die easily.

Three nights after Alexei made headlines, he appeared at the Wyncotte mansion. A hush swept over the house.

"The prodigal son returns." Magdalena kissed him. "Welcome back."

"It's good to be home," Alexei said. "It's been a wild ride."

"I can only imagine," Magdalena said. "You've caused quite a commotion."

The others gathered near him.

Alexei engaged them in light conversation until Magnus approached from across the room and glared at Alexei. "You have some nerve pulling what you did."

Alexei looked away from Magnus and walked to the stairs. "I had no control over what happened. I had to protect myself. You would have done the same."

"You're no helpless victim. You fed in a careless manner and brought unnecessary attention upon yourself. You have killed one human after another without concealing what you've done. Of course the police are trailing you. We aren't living in the fifteenth century in some backward village. This is the twenty-first century, the information age. Discretion has never been more important."

"I did what I needed to do. That's the last I want to hear about it."

Magnus grabbed Alexei by his shirt collar and lifted him

off the floor.

"Get your hands off me," Alexei said.

"Did you even bother to watch if anyone was following? Half the city is after you."

"I said get off me."

Magnus tossed Alexei. Alexei sprung to his feet and without hesitation threw an overhand right to Magnus' temple. His legs buckled and he crumpled. His eyes rolled to the back of his head.

Kristoff stepped forward, but Heinrich grabbed his arm. "This isn't your fight."

Alexei grabbed Magnus by the neck and was about to punch him when Magnus landed an uppercut to Alexei's abdomen, knocking the wind out of him. Magnus lunged forward, causing Alexei's back to crash into a granite counter top. Pumping his fists like a boxer, he repeatedly punched Alexei's face until it was red and swollen. With his free hand, Alexei grabbed a glass jar and smashed it on Magnus' face, broken glass flying in every direction.

Alexei lifted Magnus over his head and flung him across the living room. His leg caught the leather couch, tipping it over, and he crashed into the fireplace.

Alexei moved forward, smiling. As he got close, Magnus picked up a poker hanging near the fire place, rose to his feet and swung it like a baseball bat. Alexei partially blocked the shot, but it still connected with his ribs. He gasped and fell to one knee. He drove the poker toward Alexei's chest, but Alexei held it back with both hands. It was a battle of wills as Magnus used his strength and leverage to stab Alexei.

Alexei swept his left leg underneath Magnus and knocked him off his feet. Gasping, Alexei stepped back, giving Magnus time to recover.

They circled each other. Alexei feinted, and Magnus went into a defensive posture while looking for an opening. Magnus flew at him, but the blond vampire leaped over the balcony onto the second floor.

Instead of jumping after Alexei, Magnus ran up the stairwell. Alexei ran toward him. Halfway up, they collided. They grappled, each trying to gain an advantage. Magnus lifted Alexei with one hand on his leg and the other around his waist. He attempted to throw him down the stairs, but Alexei held on, causing both of them to tumble, shattering the wooden railing.

They staggered to their feet like punch drunk fighters, then came at each other with fists flailing and exchanged punches.

The front door opened, and Gabriella walked inside. She dropped her shopping bag and stepped into the middle of the fight. "Stop it, both of you! I don't think you understand, but things have changed in the last few days. We are no longer invisible and can't go about doing whatever we want. People are on the lookout for our kind."

Magnus wiped blood off his lips. "I'm keenly aware of this. If not for Alexei ... "

Gabriella raised her hand. "Now is not the time to cast blame. We have to worry about our survival. We must stick together, or we're all in trouble."

"I don't need help from anybody," Alexei said.

"Don't let your pride overtake you," Gabriella said. "We need each other. Fighting will not settle anything. When this whole thing is over, if you two feel the need to part company or settle a score, then do so then. For now, you need to put aside your differences. You don't have to like each other, but you must cooperate for all of our sakes."

Magnus winced as he sat. "I would be willing, if he can exert self-control. That's how this mess started."

"I use self-control," Alexei said. "You're just jealous because your life is a flicker and mine is a burning flame."

Magnus was about to leap out of his chair, but Gabriella gave him a stern look. She turned to Alexei. "That won't get us anywhere. We're your friends, but you have to compromise. Being a creature of the night doesn't entitle you to do whatever you want. Are you willing, at least temporarily, to stop killing indiscriminately?"

Alexei sighed. "Yes."

She turned to Magnus. "Are you willing to stop casting blame and guide us through this situation as the leader of this brood?"

"Yes, I will, for the good of the family."

"Good. This is the last time I see you two battle it out. The next time it happens, I leave." She picked up her shopping bag and walked to her room.

Chapter XXIV

Enzo followed Sophie and Andrews into Vito Anastasia's apartment.

Andrews's brow furrowed. "You sure about this?"

Enzo nodded. "This kid knows his stuff."

They stepped through piles of unfolded clothes and electronics parts on the way to his office, which doubled as his living room. They then sat on folding chairs around the Wiz's desk as he typed on his keyboard. Clutter covered nearly every inch of the room.

"I spent two whole days at the Drexel library and did a thorough analysis on the history of vampires." The Wiz stopped and stared at Sophie. "Don't move." He flicked a spider that was crawling on her shoulder. It landed on the floor, and he stomped it with his foot. "I keep telling the landlord he's got to exterminate this place."

"Maybe you should clean up every once in a while," Sophie said.

The Wiz continued typing. "It's only temporary until I get a new place." His printer stirred to life. "Anyway, in order to get any kind of meaningful data, I discarded the information that was obviously crap. Some of the beliefs about vampires were ridiculous. Like in Ghana and India, they suck blood from people's thumbs and toes when they're asleep, which would make them a pain in the ass, but not really harmful. In Indonesia, all you got to do is pluck a strand of hair from their head to escape from one. My favorite was in Prussia back in the day, where they thought vampires are into problem solving, so they left them knots or puzzles in their graves, which kept them occupied for centuries."

"I get the picture," Andrews said. "But how do you know it's bullshit?"

The Wiz's brows creased. "I don't know for sure, but that's what this is about. We're trying to figure out what has the highest chance of succeeding. Am I right?" He stared at Enzo and Sophie.

"What did you come up with?" Enzo asked.

"I developed statistical models to analyze the data. I wasn't satisfied with the results, so I tried something different. I thought vampire mythology had some inherent errors because these people were primitive, so I incorporated vampire literature into the data analysis. I realize these are works of fiction, but I thought it would be pretty useful."

Andrews buried his face into his palm.

"I assigned a lower weight to vampire literature."

"Why would you use it at all?" Andrews asked.

"What these authors wrote had to be based on legend or word of mouth. I'm pretty sure they didn't pull it out their ass."

"How do you know?" Andrews asked.

"Are you always so negative? Dude, you gotta chill."

Andrews glared at the Wiz.

Enzo glanced at Special Agent Andrews, trying to reassure him. Andrews might be reluctant to believe the Wiz, but he had faith in the kid.

"Let's get to the good stuff. The first thing we need to know is how to kill them." The Wiz handed each of them a set of papers. "As you can see this is a long list. That's because we're dealing with vampire mythology from lots of cultures. For instance, the Chinese believe vampires could be contained by a circle of rice since rice is important in their culture."

"And he's a philosopher too," Andrews said.

The Wiz's jaw tightened. "Anyway, before I was rudely interrupted, there's no one thing that has an exceptionally high probability. Instead, there are four or five things that have a higher percentage, so you might want to concentrate on them."

"We'll worry about that," Andrews said.

"Some of these results were surprising. To start, there's a fifty-six percent chance vampires could get killed by beheading."

Andrews put his hand in the air. "Hold up. Is that your top thing, beheading?"

The Wiz scratched his head. "Yeah, that's right."

"Our best option gives us a fifty-fifty chance of killing him. Are you kidding?"

Enzo lit a cigarette. "At this point I'll take fifty percent. I know the shit we've done gives us zero percent, and fifty is better than nothing."

"I don't think anything we try is going to be a sure thing," Sophie said. "We just have to do our best with the information we have."

"Thank you. I ain't a miracle worker. Anyway, incineration is next at fifty one percent. At just under fifty is piercing with a wooden instrument. Sometimes it's a wooden stake through the heart, sometimes the neck, eyes, or abdomen. I couldn't really say if it's the wood that does the trick, or if it's stabbing in a certain place."

"Aren't vampires supposed to only get around at night?" Enzo asked.

"I found that there's a ninety two percent probability that they are primarily night dwellers, but only a forty one percent chance that sunlight will injure or kill them."

"Shouldn't those two things mesh?" Enzo asked.

The Wiz shrugged. "Beats me. I'm not claiming to be a vampire expert."

Sophie grinned. "Where's Van Helsing when you need him?"

"There's no Van Helsing," Enzo said. "It's just us."

"What about garlic?" Andrews asked. "Garlic is supposed to ward off vampires."

"Garlic is used against vampires in Germany, Greece and Romania. There's a twenty three percent chance that garlic will be useful against them. Poppy seeds, which are said to put vampires to sleep, have a higher probability."

Enzo shrugged. "Maybe we'll have our people carry both. It can't hurt."

"We should recruit a priest or rabbi," Sophie suggested.

"There's little evidence that suggests a religious person or relic has any effect," the Wiz said.

"I don't want to get anyone else involved in this madness, anyway," Enzo said.

"I agree," Andrews said. "We need to operate in secrecy. The last thing we need is people thinking Alexei is a real vampire."

"There's about twenty other things on the list, like boiling their heads in vinegar, putting a nail through their navel, cutting out their hearts, and so on," the Wiz said.

Enzo pressed his lips against his folded hands. "I think we have some good ideas. We need to know how to identify vampires in case there are more like him."

The Wiz turned around and began typing. A few seconds later the whirring of the printer sounded. He handed them additional pages. "All right, this was tricky since there was less data to work with. People were more interested in killing them or preventing them from attacking rather than figuring out who they were. Maybe they could easily identify vampires back then. A lot of stuff on the list isn't practical. There's a forty six point three percent chance that vampires don't have a reflection in the mirror. The next best thing is that there's a thirty six percent chance that an animal, most likely a horse or a dog, would have an extreme negative reaction to their presence. Once again, pretty impractical. The other thing that comes up is that if you put a female virgin in the middle of a cemetery, they'll flock to her. Good luck finding a virgin around here."

Andrews put his hand to his forehead. "I'm getting a headache thinking about this."

Enzo studied the Wiz's results, ignoring the chatter. After a few minutes he looked up. "The problem with this list is that it's derived from olden times. Beheading was fine when people carried swords, but we use guns. Why the hell won't bullets work?"

"Maybe it has something to do with the materials they used," Sophie said. "I'm just thinking out loud. Maybe it's the metal of the sword or the type of wood used for the stake. If poppy seeds or garlic are effective, then something about their chemical reaction harms vampires. Same with the sunlight."

"I don't really give a shit about vampire theory. I want to know how to kill the bastards. We can't go around the city carrying stakes or swords. We know guns with conventional bullets don't work." Andrews paced around the room. "What if we shoot him with something that could harm him?" He turned toward Sophie. "If your theory about the wood is accurate, then maybe we could use that."

"Wooden bullets?" Enzo asked.

Andrews shrugged. "Why not?"

"Never heard of them," Enzo said.

"Neither have I. We could use a wood bullet with less gunpowder than a conventional bullet, creating a high-speed wooden projectile."

"How in the hell are we going to get wooden bullets?" Enzo asked. "I'm guessing they don't sell them in gun stores."

"I can get the boys at Quantico to work on it. If it's possible to make them, they can do it."

"It can't hurt," Sophie said. "Maybe we should also get stakes. Hey, a shotgun with wooden pellets might be interesting."

"Sure," Enzo said. "I have a guy who owns a lumber yard."

The Wiz returned from the kitchen with a bottle of Mountain Dew. "What about the whole beheading thing? That's got a higher percentage."

Andrews scowled. "Don't you have something else to do?"

"You have a bad attitude. Are the rest of the Feds like you?"

"Enough already," Enzo said. "Don't worry about the swords. I know a guy who can get us samurai swords, ninja swords, the medieval kind, whatever we need."

"Do you have a guy for everything?" Andrews asked.

Enzo shrugged.

"What about bows?" the Wiz asked. "We can use the same wooden material from the bullets and make arrows out of them."

"Not a bad idea," Andrews said. "We'll stockpile weapons. This way, the next time we find him, we'll be ready."

Sophie asked, "We know what Alexei looks like, but what about other vampires?"

"First, we need to find out where he lives," Enzo said. "If we can track him down, then we can find others of his kind."

"Where would a vampire live?" Sophie asked. "Would he live in a house? Or maybe a cave or something like that?"

They all turned to the Wiz, who had become the resident vampire expert. "I didn't find out about that, but if he's roaming around Philadelphia, I doubt he'd live in a cave."

"We have to find Alexei and follow him," Andrews said. "That way we can get him when he's least expecting it, and we can get his friends while we're at it."

"We have to wait until he gets out of his little rat hole," Enzo said. "If he doesn't leave willingly, then we're going to have to smoke him out."

Chapter XXV

The Goat coughed uncontrollably when he entered the Russian's house. It stank of mildew and old people. Still feeling like death from yet another bender last night, he ran to the bathroom, fell to his knees and vomited his breakfast of bacon and scrambled eggs. As he lifted his head, he realized he should have eaten something less abrasive.

Vladimir stood outside of the bathroom. "You okay?"

The Goat braced himself on the toilet. "No. How do you fucking live here?"

Vladimir spoke in Russian to Ksenya. She nodded and walked away.

"Where's she going?" The Goat asked.

"She get grandfather," Vladimir replied.

The Goat experienced several unsteady moments and nearly vomited again.

Fortunately, Ksenya returned soon after with the old Russian. The sooner he talked to him, the sooner he could leave. The man reeked of cigarette smoke and vodka. His speech was slurred and his movements shaky. If he wasn't able to tell them anything, and The Goat came to this shit hole for no reason, he was going to be pissed.

The old man began a long narrative. Ksenya translated as Vladimir made coffee.

The tale began in Georgia eighty years ago. As a young boy, an evil had terrorized Vasilly's village. Something mysteriously killed farm animals and drained their blood. His father, Dimitri, and neighboring farmers stood guard at night, armed with rifles. After a week, the villagers became the target of these attacks. On several occasions, the men spotted a shadowy figure moving so fast they could barely see it.

One night, a loud shriek came from the house next to Dimitri's farm. He grabbed his rifle and ran toward the sound. He circled the house and found a vourdelak with long, dark hair kneeling over his neighbor's wife, sucking blood from her neck.

He shot her, but to his astonishment, it had no effect on her. The blood drinker approached him with a crazed look, like a rabid animal. Blood and flesh hung from her mouth. Her narrow eyes shifted. She appeared to have little intelligence.

He reloaded his rifle and shot her, causing her to fall backward. Just when he thought she was dead, she rose to her feet.

Dimitri offered a prayer, thinking for sure she would kill him. When the other villagers came in mass, the vourdelak fled.

They chased the vourdelak for several miles down a valley and backed her into a cave. Before they opened fire, she charged at them with inhuman fury.

In a flurry of action, the vourdelak grabbed a man's head and tore it off with inhuman strength. His head fell to the ground and rolled past Dimitri. She grabbed another villager by his left arm and swung him around several times before releasing him. He flew through the air and smashed into a stone wall. Dimitri continued to shoot, but never came close to hitting her. Other villagers shot her, but it only slowed her down.

Dimitri yelled for his neighbors to escape while they still could. He fled and did not dare look back.

Vasilly stopped his narrative and asked for a bottle of vodka. Ksenya retrieved it for him. He topped off his half-filled cup of coffee with vodka.

"Go easy, old man," The Goat said.

Vasilly grunted.

The Goat nodded. "That's some fucking story. Is any of it true?"

Ksenya's face tightened. "It is all true."

After drinking his coffee-vodka mixture, Vasilly resumed his narrative.

The vourdelak continued her night attacks. A week later, the villagers went to the elders for advice, there were stories of these creatures of the night invading the area before. The elders had conflicting opinions on how to deal with them.

Dimitri and Vasilly rode by donkey thirty miles to see an old woman who was known as a seer. When they arrived at her house, the old woman's great-granddaughter would not let them talk to her. She was in deep meditation and would not take visitors. They waited for hours, and the great-granddaughter made them dinner. When the seer emerged, Vasilly had fallen asleep. He woke up staring at the oldest woman he had ever seen. Her wrinkled skin sagged. Her mouth was withered and narrow. She was so hunched over that she only reached his chest.

Her great-granddaughter handed the seer a steaming cup of tea. As the old woman sipped it, Dimitri told her about the vourdelak.

She appeared to doze during the tale. Vasilly's head snapped back when she spoke in a clear voice. "To kill the vourdelak, you must penetrate its black heart with a stake from an ash tree."

Numerous ash trees grew a few miles down the road, but it was late at night, so they slept in a stable behind the house, barely protected from the biting wind. The next morning, Dimitri and his son chopped down a tree and carved stakes.

Later, Dimitri met with men from the village. They decided to attack and not retreat until they killed the vourdelak.

Dimitri forbade his son to accompany them. If he died,

Vasilly had to take over the farm and care for his mother and two sisters. Vasilly was adamant that he help fight the vourdelak, but his father would not hear of it. With tears streaming down his eyes, he watched his father leave.

Vasilly made the decision to disobey his father. His father would beat him with a rawhide strap, but he was willing to face the consequences. He left shortly thereafter, taking an ash stake. He maintained a distance as he followed, hiding behind bushes and trees when possible. The men were intent on their task and did not notice him.

They walked for over a mile and scaled a tall hill, lighting the night sky with their torches. At the top of the hill, they approached a large cave. After brief deliberation, three men entered the cave. Dimitri was not among them. Overcome by curiosity, Vasilly crept up the hill, no longer concerned about being noticed.

Vasilly dropped his stake when shrieks followed by the heavy sound of running came from the cave. The vourdelak emerged with unnatural skin that looked like porcelain. With her massive fangs, she tore into the back of a man's neck. She gulped his blood before ripping the shoulder out of the socket of another fleeing man.

Vasilly watched in terror as the men made a futile attempt to fight. She spun and fought like a demon. Despite her quickness, they inflicted wounds on her. Still, one by one, they fell. It was an abominable scene of gore, but Vasilly could not stop watching.

Dimitri charged the vourdelak with his stake raised at shoulder level. With little effort, she sidestepped him. He stumbled over a rock that jutted out of the ground and landed with a thud. Another farmer ran after her. In a fluid motion, she turned and raked her nails across his throat. Blood spurted from gaping wounds in his neck.

Dimitri rose to his feet. He hurled his stake at the vourdelak like a spear. She leaned back in time for it to miss its mark and land uselessly to the ground.

Like a tiger, she pounced on Dimitri. She snarled and smashed his face, causing his eyes to roll to the back of his head.

Desperate to save his father, Vasilly left his hiding spot. If he didn't do something, his father would die. Without thinking, he picked up his stake and ran. He began to cry as she was about to plunge her fangs into his father's neck.

With both hands, he rammed the stake into the vourdelak's back below her shoulder blades. She released a head splitting roar and writhed on the ground. Vasilly jumped over her body and went to his father, but Dimitri pushed him aside. He crawled over and leaned on top of the spear, further driving it into the vourdelak's back. Once more she let out a shrill scream.

Dimitri fell back, and Vasilly hugged his father. His father had always been so big and strong, but now he seemed like a feeble old man. They both watched the vourdelak moan and convulse, not taking their eyes off her until she was no longer moving.

After many minutes had passed, with his father in and out of consciousness, Vasilly mustered enough courage to approach her. He held onto the stake that stuck out of her back and used it to turn her over. Her vacant eyes indicated she was dead.

Hours later, Vasilly and his father exited the cave. They were the only survivors. Before they left, Vasilly removed the stake from the vourdelak and brought it home.

"Holy shit," The Goat muttered. "That's fucking amazing. I can't believe you actually killed that vampire."

Vladimir took a deep drag from his cigarette. He had been wide-eyed during the entire story.

"You never heard this before?" The Goat asked Vladimir.

"This is first time. I never believe in vourdelak, but now … "

"Believe me. They're as fucking real as you or me. I went face to face with one and he almost killed me."

"You speak of vampire killer in news?" Vladimir asked.

"That's the one." The Goat turned to Ksenya. "Translate this for me." The Goat recapped his encounter with Alexei and everything that had transpired since then.

Vasilly appeared alert, with no sign of his normal drunken stupor.

"My grandfather has something for you."

They followed Vasilly down a set of creaky old steps. The basement smelled of urine and stagnant water. The Goat tried to minimize his breathing to avoid the stench.

Vasilly took out a key and opened a wooden cage. He reached inside for a brass case. He opened it and reverently lifted a brittle piece of wood.

Ksenya translated, "He like you to have this."

The Goat looked in awe first at Vasilly and then at the piece of wood. "Is this the stake he used to kill the vampire?"

"Yes."

The Goat took the stake, and although it had no magical power, nobody could have convinced him otherwise.

Chapter XXVI

Alexei sat across from Nora Brooks. She was intoxicated on wine. He was intoxicated by the scent of her blood. This was their second outing this week. Previously, he declined, wanting to keep a low profile. This time he readily accepted her offer. Magnus was driving him out of his skull.

Alexei wore a dashing tuxedo. Men wearing suits and women in evening gowns surrounded them. Alexei had become a popular figure in the city's social circles. Friends frequently visited their table. He politely spoke to them, but could hardly keep his eyes off Nora.

Nora had reserved a room at the hotel. Her husband was home, so they could not go to her place.

"Hey, why don't we make ourselves scarce," Nora suggested.

A wide grin spread across his face as he followed her to her hotel room. They spent the next hour there, indulging in every pleasure of the flesh. As they got dressed, Nora started the conversation Alexei had been hoping to avoid.

"I want you to do it. I'm ready."

Alexei put on his pants. "Ready for what?"

"You know what. I want you to make me one of you."

"Nora, you don't know what you speak of. Do you understand the finality of it?"

Nora turned away from him, her arms folded beneath her chest. "I'm sick and tired of this pathetic life. I can't take my fake marriage, fake friends, and parties with people I can't stand. Can't you see, Alexei. You're the only one who matters to me, and I know you can't hold out much longer. You want this as much as I do."

"You would be missed too much."

Nora sighed as she put on her diamond necklace. "I don't want to get old and fade away. In a few years, my career might be over. Then what?" She grabbed Alexei by the waist and ran her fingers across his chest.

Alexei leaned his head back and closed his eyes. It would be so easy for him to do as Nora suggested. Right here and now. His temptation was so great, it became tangible. "Now is not a good time. I'm a marked man."

Nora released him, the hurt evident on her face. "Why do you reject me? Don't you love me?"

"Oh, Nora, there's nothing more I would rather do than pierce your lovely neck and drink your sweet blood. But now is not the time."

"When will the time be right?" she asked, pouting.

"Soon, but not now."

They returned to the hotel bar where the party was still raging. He separated from Nora and worked the floor.

He did not stay long. He grew tired of the same conversations. Before leaving, he said goodbye to Nora. She would not let him leave until he agreed to see her again that weekend. He wondered what lies she told her husband, the trial attorney. He didn't like lawyers. They were the bottom feeders, ruining what people worked for with their greed.

As he walked to his vintage Mercedes convertible, his thoughts were clouded with doubt. Nora's offer plagued his mind. He had been thinking about taking her from the moment they first met. At first he had held back as a matter of self-discipline. He wanted to prove to himself that he could control his urges. He had told the others in the brood that he would use discretion. If he tried to feed on her, she would probably wind up dead. Converting her to a creature of the night would be one big headache. If she wound up missing, they would know he was the perpetrator, and that would set off another brawl with Magnus. He still ached from their last fight. If Gabriella had not intervened, he would have defeated the sanctimonious bastard.

Nora was a diva, a vixen. She was one of the beautiful people, and they were always the tastiest. When it was all over with the police and FBI, he would give Nora what she wanted.

Then, he would settle the score with Magnus and see who was superior. He feared no one. He had lived over a thousand years, and would live a thousand more.

The cool breeze coming from the Delaware River invigorated him. He looked at his watch. It was too late to feed. Perhaps tomorrow. He could select a random victim, but that wasn't his style. He liked to get to know them.

Alexei rode home with the top down on his convertible, his long, flowing hair fluttering in the wind. He blasted the radio. He had eclectic taste in music varying from opera to hard rock. Tonight he was in the mood for rock.

When he arrived in Wyncotte, he exited the car with the distinct feeling someone was watching him. He abruptly turned, but didn't see anybody. He looked up and down the block and frowned. Perhaps Magnus or another member of the brood was lurking, keeping a tab on him. He scowled. They had no right to follow him. He told them he would tow the line and he meant it. Gritting his teeth, Alexei walked to the mansion. If someone was keeping tabs on him, he was going to find out who it was.

Tony Scrambolgni sat at the table counting the money. He looked up at his associate Charlie Senerchia. "You're a thousand short. What the fuck's going on here?"

Senerchia shrugged. "We took a beating on the Taylor fight. When he got knocked out, we got our clocks cleaned."

Tony grabbed him by the shirt collar. "What do I look like, a fucking chump? What kind of bullshit excuse is that?"

Senerchia's underling, Mike Reed, sank back into his seat.

"Boss, what am I supposed to do when I take a loss like that?" Senerchia asked.

Tony went nose to nose with him. "Am I supposed to feel sorry for you? What kind of shit are you trying to pull?"

"I'm not trying to pull nothing." Senerchia tried to back away, but Tony kept him close. "It's like I said, I had a tough week. I'll pull it together next week."

Tony dragged him to his side of the table by his mustache, and Senerchia screamed. "You're damn right you're going to pull it together. You know why? Because I gotta pay my bosses, and they don't accept anything less than paying them everything I owe. So how am I gonna pay up if pieces of shit like you don't give me my money? I don't want to hear you had a bad week. That don't mean shit to me. You're going to pay me in full every week. You understand me?" Tony pulled him up and down by his mustache, so it looked like he was nodding.

"Yeah, boss," Senerchia mumbled. His partner's face was completely white.

"So this is what's going to happen. Look at me, punk." Tony let go long enough for Senerchia to look at him. "Next week you're going to give me two G's extra."

Senerchia groaned.

"And you're never gonna come up short again. You got it?"

"I got it, boss."

When the waitress returned to their table with the check, Tony passed it off to Charlie Senerchia, who passed it off to Mike Reed.

"Sometimes you gotta learn the hard way." Tony pulled out a comb and straightened his hair. "Do you have the leather jackets? The answer better be yes."

Mike nodded. "We got 'em. They're in my car."

"Will wonders never cease. Good thing, 'cause I'm meeting buyers tomorrow."

They walked to Mike's car. Mike popped open his trunk. Inside were biker, soft leather, and suede jackets, dozens in all. Tony inspected them and nodded in approval.

"I'll pull up with my car, and you guys can load it up," Tony said.

Senerchia's mouth hung open as if he had seen a ghost.

"What's your fucking problem now?" Tony asked.

"Boss, turn around slowly," Senerchia replied, his voice barely above a whisper.

Not far away was the tall, blond, unmistakable figure of Alexei, the Vampire Killer.

"Is that him?" Senerchia asked.

Tony didn't say a word. He only nodded.

"What do we do now?" Senerchia's voice wavered.

Mike pulled out his gun.

Tony motioned for him to put away the gun.

Mike Reed frowned. "Aren't we going to take out that SOB?"

In a low voice, Tony said, "We're gonna do no such thing. We're gonna follow him to his little nest."

Senerchia smiled and then laughed. "Yeah, that's a good idea. We'll find out where he lives. That's what we'll do."

Tony grabbed Senerchia's arm. "Keep your voice down. Get a hold of yourself. If you don't got the stones to do this job, then stay behind."

"I can do this."

"All right." Tony turned to Reed. "You ever tail someone?"

Reed nodded.

"Good. That's what we're gonna do. Keep a distance and be inconspicuous."

"Sure thing." Reed said.

They got in the car and trailed Alexei as he walked to his Mercedes convertible. Reed double-parked as Alexei started his car. They waited until he started driving.

They rode briefly before taking an exit and entering an expensive Main Line neighborhood. Reed followed at a good distance, but close enough that they would not lose him. Tony thought there would be problems since Reed was green.

Alexei's Mercedes slowed. He appeared to be looking for a parking spot.

"Pull into a spot and kill the lights," Tony said.

There were no open spots, so Reed pulled in front of a driveway.

Tony smiled as Alexei exited the car. "Let's see where you're going, big boy." Alexei walked fifteen feet. "You guys stay put."

"You got it, boss," Senerchia said.

When Alexei turned his back, Tony exited. He hid behind a tree in front of a large house. He held his breath as Alexei stopped and abruptly turned. For a second, he thought Alexei spotted him. What would he do if Alexei spotted him? He was impervious to bullets and had superhuman strength and agility. Fortunately, Alexei resumed walking.

When he walked a bit further, Tony took a chance and followed him. The block was long, but sparsely filled with houses. Each was spacious, lavishly decorated, and surrounded by a large plot of land. At the end of the block, Alexei entered a house.

Tony returned to the car.

Senerchia bit his bottom lip. "What are we going to do now, boss?"

"We're going to wait. This son of a bitch is a vampire, right?"

Senerchia and Reed nodded.

"He's only supposed to be out at night. That means we're going to wait 'til dawn to see if he comes out."

Chapter XXVII

Enzo loaded four bullets into the chamber of his .357 Magnum and aimed at the target. He was no marksmen. He had shot and killed before, but always at close range.

He and Andrews were testing prototype bullets developed at Quantico. When Enzo asked Andrews how he explained the need for these bullets, the FBI agent shrugged and said his contact owed him a huge favor and was doing it with no questions asked. Enzo had not pursued the matter any further. It was not his business.

Since it wouldn't be prudent to bring a reputed mobster to an agency shooting range, Enzo picked one. He had a guy who owned a shooting range in Upper Darby.

Enzo squeezed the trigger, aiming for the chest. Despite missing the mark by nearly a foot, he pumped his fist. He removed his ear covers and pulled up the target.

Andrews took a closer look. "Your aim stinks."

"The important thing is that the bullet shot." He picked up the casing. "If a stake works, then this should too."

"We don't know for sure."

Enzo reached into his jacket and frowned when he found no cigarettes.

Andrews grinned. "You're better off. If Alexei doesn't kill you, those things will."

Enzo shrugged. "We have to take a leap of faith, just like when you finally believed Alexei's a vampire. I feel good about this. Like I told Sophie, vampires have to be vulnerable, otherwise they'd be the dominate species."

"Speaking of Sophie, how did a classy gal like that ever get involved with your organization? No offense."

Enzo rolled his eyes. "You think you're so much better than me, don't you?"

"Not at all. You're very intelligent. That's why I haven't arrested you yet. It was child's play nailing your predecessors."

"That sounds like a back handed compliment. To answer your question, Sophie realized the corporate world wasn't meant for her. Busting your nuts and kissing ass, and where does it get you? Nowhere. You got to make your own rules."

"Fair enough. Let me try a couple shots."

Enzo handed him the gun. Andrews shot with considerable more accuracy, hitting the target with three head shots.

Andrews closed a bullet in his hand. "I'm going to get my contacts at Quantico to make more so I can give them to my agents."

"I'd like to get as many of these bullets as possible. I own a gun shop through one of my subsidiary companies. If you can get me the prototype, I can get them made and supplied to my guys."

After more target practice, they went to Enzo's Escalade in the back lot. He opened the trunk and pulled out a large briefcase. Inside were dozens of wooden stakes. "Take these. I have more at my office. I don't know what we'll do with them. It's impractical to walk around the city carrying stakes."

Andrews took one out of the case. "I wish I could tell you this is a nice weapon, but I have no way of knowing."

"It's sharp and made out of wood," Enzo said. "It should do the trick."

Enzo closed his trunk, and they walked to Andrews' car.

"I'm going to meet Agents Morrow and Sheridan back at my office. I'll let you know what's been happening at the house."

"Good. Two of my guys are on night shift. That's when we'll get more info."

Andrews stepped into his car. They did not shake hands. It was mutually understood that this was a temporary relationship borne out of necessity.

When Enzo arrived at his office, Tony Scrambolgni and Pat Adesso were waiting with anxious looks on their faces.

Enzo poured a cup of coffee. He had barely slept last night. "Come inside."

The Wop and The Goat followed him. Enzo sat behind his desk.

"Before you guys tell me what's on your mind, I want to thank you, Tony. You found the vampire hiding place before the Feds did. I know we're in this together, but I enjoy beating them at their job. Good work."

Tony nodded. "I just hope we can nail these bastards."

Since Tony and his two cohorts tailed Alexei back to the brood's mansion in Wynwood two nights ago, they had set up around the clock surveillance. Thus far, they had seen six presumed vampires come and leave the house. Through the public records office, Andrews discovered that an M.G. Alfredson had purchased the house less than a year ago. He found no further information on this individual.

"So tell me what's happening," Enzo said.

"Seeds and Big Mac followed three of them coming out of the house last night. One was a short woman with red hair. Another was a tall guy, brown hair with a muscular build. The third was an incredibly hot babe with long blond hair. They went to the Ritz Theater on Walnut Street, then the Art Museum, then they lost them."

Enzo frowned. "Lost them?"

Tony shrugged. "What are you going to do? They're fucking vampires. I gave 'em heat for it. The good news is we got pictures." Tony handed Enzo an envelope.

Enzo smiled. "I'm going to scan these and email them to Andrews. Then I'll print some copies so you can distribute."

"Charlie Senerchia and Mike Reed will be at the house tonight. I don't know who the Feds are sending. I need their cell numbers so we can be in contact."

Enzo nodded. "I'll get them for you when I talk to Andrews this afternoon." He scanned the photos. "What about you, Pat?"

Tony shook his head. "The Goat has some crazy, lame-brain story to tell you."

"He first alerted us to Alexei. He showed guts and spunk by telling me what happened. A lot of other people would have turned tail and run. He's earned respect."

The Goat's eyes opened wide. For a second he looked startled, like a rabbit caught in an electric fence. "Um, that means a lot coming from you, Mr. Salerno. I gotta tell you about what happened yesterday with this old man I met. This is fucking incredible."

The Goat relayed Vasilly's story. After he finished, he produced the stake that killed the vourdelak. "This is the real deal. No bullshit."

"How can you be sure?" Tony asked. "You said the old bastard's a drunk."

The Goat narrowed his eyes. "That don't mean what he said ain't true."

Enzo gazed at the city skyline as they bickered about the merits of Vasilly's tale. After a few minutes he turned and raised his hand. Immediately they stopped arguing. "I can't say whether or not he's reputable, but if what he said is valid, then there's one important thing to note. You said that when the villagers attacked the vampire, they used a variety of weapons that didn't work, including stakes. But Vasilly's stake killed the fucking thing, right?"

The Goat nodded.

"Then it can only mean that the type of wood used for the

stake made the difference. You said it's made out of ash?"

"It sure is."

"If that's true, then the stakes we have won't work." Enzo twirled a pen with his fingers. "I'm going to contact my guy at the lumber yard. We discussed the possibility that a chemical reaction harmed the vampire, but we didn't have any information about a specific wood for the stakes. I told him to make it out of whatever. Maybe you got something here, maybe you don't, but it can't hurt to try."

"If you heard this dude, you'd agree. Um, do you mind giving me back the stake? If I ever go up against Alexei again, I want to have it with me."

Enzo stifled a chuckle and handed it back. The Goat was hanging on to a thread of belief. In many ways, they all were.

Chapter XXVIII

Alexei's anger had been simmering over the past few days. The others were watching him, he was sure of it. It wasn't overt, but he was tired of it. He would not be a slave in his own house. They would treat him with respect.

He went out the previous evening to unwind, but kept looking over his shoulder, convinced someone had followed him the last time he went out with Nora.

He gritted his teeth as he walked down the stairs of the mansion. They were watching a German movie on the enormous plasma television. He grabbed the remote control and turned it off. "I know what you have been doing and I'm sick of it. I demand it stop. If anyone has a problem with me, then say something now."

Sasha raised his left eyebrow and crossed his arms. "What are you talking about? Speak some sense, man."

"I don't know who's responsible, but I know you've been watching me. I told you I would be cautious. This is no way to treat someone of my stature."

Heinrich put his hand on Alexei's shoulder. "I have a good grasp of what happens in the house. If someone was tracking you, I would know about it. You have known me for a long time. You can trust me."

Alexei pursed his lips. He wasn't sure he could trust anybody.

Magdalena curled herself into his arms and ran her fingers across his chest. "You've been too stressed. I can feel your tension. You need to relax."

Alexei released himself from Magdalena. He stared at the others and found pity in their eyes. How dare they pity him! He was more powerful than any of them. His anger rose at the sight of Magnus' smug face. The brood leader was enjoying his consternation.

"I'm not paranoid. Perhaps those of you without my heightened senses are incapable of comprehending this, but I know when I'm being followed."

Magnus remained seated. "If you're going to make accusations, then back it with proof. If this was true, I would know about it."

Alexei laughed. "And I should trust you?"

Magnus' voice remained steady. "Think what you want. If you choose to let paranoia consume you, then there is nothing I can do about it."

Gabriella, who had been standing in the back of the room, stepped forward. "I think there might be something to your claims, Alexei."

All eyes were on Gabriella. Magnus' brow furrowed.

Alexei put his index finger in the air. "Ah, I knew it."

Gabriella said, "Your suspicions may be valid, but your anger is directed at the wrong target. On several occasions, I have noticed people driving by or sitting in their vehicles. I had never noticed them before in the neighborhood."

Magnus' face tightened. "I don't like this. People can't learn the truth about us."

Heinrich frowned. "We'll investigate. If there's a problem, we'll deal with it."

"Oh, I'll deal with it," Alexei said.

Gabriella shook her head. "That would be a bad idea. You're too hot right now."

Alexei exhaled. His body was one big bundle of tension.

"I'll find out if there is anyone watching us and I'll deal with them." Magnus said.

"I'll join you," Heinrich said.

Alexei folded his arms across his chest. "I would like to be there. For all I know, you'll do nothing and tell me the situation has been settled."

Gabriella grabbed his hand. "Alexei, you must trust us. We're family."

Alexei sat on one of the comfortable chairs. Magnus shouldn't be in charge. He was probably the one spying on him.

He brooded in silence after Heinrich and Magnus left. The others resumed watching their German movie. Alexei had little interest in it. His mind was filled with conspiracies and distrust.

Charlie Senerchia kicked aside the beer cans that littered Mike Reed's living room. "What the fuck? You been drinking all afternoon?"

"Sure have," Reed said. "You want a beer?"

"No, I don't want a fucking beer." Charlie kicked a can of Coors. "What the fuck are you thinking? You know we're staking out the vampire house."

"That's why I've been drinking. How did we get stuck with this job, anyway?"

"Because Tony said so. He's the boss, and if he says go to the vampire house, then we go. After coming up short with the cash, the last thing I want is to piss him off."

"I don't want to go," Reed said.

"Well, you don't have any choice, 'cause Tony expects us there. What's the matter with you? You scared?"

"You're damn right I'm scared. You should be too after what happened with Johnny Gunns, then Mike, Tony and Vinny? They went down against one vampire. We're going into their nest."

"We're just scoping the place out. If we see anything, we call Tony. This is an easy job." Charlie pulled him to his feet.

"Let's get the hell out of here."

They drove to Wynwood. When they arrived, Charlie dialed Agent Maples.

"What took you so long?" Maples asked. "You shoulda been here an hour ago."

"We had some issues," Charlie said.

In the background, Reed let out a loud belch.

"This is ridiculous." Maples paused. "If you see anything, call me."

"You got it."

Maples clicked off the phone.

"Asshole," Charlie muttered.

Reed chuckled. "Of course he's an asshole. He's a Fed. They live to bust our balls."

Charlie changed the station on the satellite radio and sunk back into his seat.

A half-hour after they arrived, dusk settled into the placid evening. Reed looked around frantically. "This is when they come out, you know. We're fucked now. They're going to get us."

Charlie glared at his partner. "Just chill." He reached into his glove compartment and pulled out a packet containing Valium. "Here. Take a few of these."

Reed swallowed the pills.

He was quiet for a while. Just when Charlie thought he was going to have a peaceful evening, Reed started up again. "Man, I'm hungry. I can't hold out all night."

Charlie shook his head. "What the fuck's with you? You were drinking all day. Shouldn't you be filled with liquid or something?"

Reed shrugged. "All I know is I'm hungry."

"Tough shit. It's not like we can order a pizza and have it delivered to the car. And we can't leave, so you're stuck."

Reed grumbled, causing Charlie to turn the volume higher. Because of the radio's volume, Charlie barely heard his phone ring.

"What are you doing over there?" Maples asked. "Jerking off?"

Charlie gritted his teeth. "I had the radio on."

"Well turn it down," Maples said. "You're supposed to be paying attention."

"I am paying attention!"

"We just saw three of them leave the house. We're going to follow. I'll have Andrews send back up. Got it?"

"Yeah I got it."

"Good." Maples hung up the phone.

"Those assholes should treat us with respect. Hey, we found out about this place."

"What are we going to do?" Reed's voice sounded frantic. "We're all alone."

"Chill, dude. Some new Feds are coming."

"I don't like it."

"Tough shit," Charlie said. "We're not going anywhere."

"This is the last time I get involved with this shit. Next time I'm telling Tony to ... "

"You're not telling Tony anything unless you want to eat your meals out of a straw."

Reed grumbled something, and then complained again that he was hungry, so Charlie turned up the volume on the radio.

Reed started again. "Dude, I have to go to the bathroom."

Charlie shook his head. "You're like a little kid. Go outside."

"But this is a classy neighborhood."

"I don't give a fuck. There's plenty of trees."

"Can't we go to a pizza joint or something?" Reed asked.

"Just go outside."

Reed froze. "We got trouble."

Charlie's eyes went wide when two figures approached the car. One was tall, about six two, with short blond hair and icy blue eyes. His face was smooth and he was powerfully built. The second had brown hair and a mustache. He was shorter and stockier, but no less imposing.

"They're, um, vampires, aren't they?"

Charlie nodded. "Yeah, I think so."

"Now what?"

Charlie's heart pounded. His throat constricted. He never thought they would actually encounter any vampires.

"We need to think of something, quick," Reed said.

"All right. My girlfriend's cheating on me, so we're spying on her."

"Okay."

The blond vampire approached the driver's side, and his companion went to the other side. He motioned for Charlie to lower his window.

Charlie complied.

The vampire smiled. "I don't believe you're from this neighborhood, and it appears you've spent an inordinate amount of time parked here. Several neighbors expressed concern. I like to be hospitable, but my neighbors are concerned about burglars. Would you be so kind as to state your business?"

Reed fidgeted, which didn't help Charlie's nerves. For a while he said nothing. He took a deep breath. "My girlfriend lives down the block, and, um, I think she's cheating on me. I'm trying to find out if she is, you know."

The blond vampire frowned. "That doesn't sound legal. I can't imagine the police would appreciate a stalker in this exclusive neighborhood, so I suggest you leave."

"Yeah, I was just going to," Charlie said.

Before he started the car, the second vampire spoke in a foreign language.

The blond's face darkened. "Please step out of the car."

"Just drive out of here," Charlie said.

"No fucking way." Reed had a wild look on his face as he reached underneath his seat and pulled out a stake.

In German, Heinrich said, "Be careful. They have a stake in the car."

Judging by the driver's lack of intelligence, he thought they were Mafia and not law enforcement. Regardless, he would have to deal with them.

Magnus scanned the surrounding area. "Step out of the car."

He heard the driver's heart beat quicken. Sweat beaded down the other's forehead.

The passenger yelled, "No fucking way!" He reached underneath his seat and pulled out a wooden stake.

So these two want a fight. They just sealed their fates.

Magnus yanked the driver out of the car. He lifted him high in the air and slammed him onto the concrete sidewalk.

He glanced at the other side. The driver's companion lunged at Heinrich with his stake. With one hand, Heinrich gripped the man's wrist. With his other hand, he clutched the man's neck and squeezed. The stake fell harmlessly to the asphalt.

Magnus glanced at the driver. He was unconscious and did not look like he would wake anytime soon.

Heinrich covered the man's mouth and sunk his fangs into the side of his neck.

Magnus dragged the driver to Heinrich.

"We need to remove this car," Magnus said.

Heinrich glanced at him. "Let's put them in the back seat. Is that one still alive?"

"Yes."

"Good. Perhaps we could get information from him."

Magnus put the driver in the back. After Heinrich finished feeding, he put his victim's body there as well. Heinrich then entered the car, turned on the engine and drove to the other end of the block.

Magnus brought the driver into the house.

When he returned, Heinrich said, "I'll take care of the car and the body."

Magnus clasped his hand. "Be careful, my friend. It appears that our friend Alexei may not have been paranoid after all. Unfortunately this situation has taken a drastic turn for the worse."

Chapter XXIX

Bleary-eyed, Enzo ran his fingers through his hair. His face was wrought with tension. It was four in the morning, and he had yet to sleep. "We have to do something."

"You can't be sure they didn't take off," Mark Andrews said. "Agent Maples told me that Senerchia was belligerent and uncooperative."

"What the fuck difference does that make?" Tony Scrambolgni said. "Those fucking vampires took them. I'd stake any amount of money on it."

Rick Carroll finished eating his cheeseburger. "Maybe we should try their cell again. They might have turned it off or gone out of range."

"Come on, Carroll," Enzo said. "They're not going to answer. We've called them a hundred times. The vampires know we're on to them. They're either going to lash back or blow out of here."

Sophie emerged from her bedroom with a change of clothes, and entered her living room where the men congregated.

It wouldn't make sense for Enzo to go to the FBI offices, or for the Feds to go to Enzo's home or office, so she suggested they meet at her house in Media. It was the closest place she could think of as neutral territory.

The two parties had been in phone contact throughout the evening. She, Tony and Enzo arrived before midnight. Andrews and Carroll arrived a half hour later.

Enzo said, "Mark, look at the situation logically. Agent Maples left at 8:32. Winfield and Barnes arrived at 8:45. Why would Charlie and Mike choose to leave during those thirteen minutes without telling anyone? The logical conclusion is that once your agents left, the vampires attacked. You've already alerted the police in Pennsylvania, New Jersey, Delaware, Maryland and New York, and there's been no ID on their car. They haven't shown up at their homes. We've contacted their family and friends, as well as establishments they frequent. Unless they drove into the Schuylkill ... "

Mark paced, his arms folded. "So what do we do now? We have about a half dozen ash stakes. We've got, I don't know, thirty or forty wooden bullets, none made of ash. We need more time."

"We don't know that the other stakes won't work," Enzo said.

"The last time we talked, you seemed convinced they had to be made out of ash."

"If they flee, then what do we do?" Enzo asked. "It ain't enough to let them leave. My guys need payback."

"Damn straight," Tony said. "Five of our boys are dead. We can't let that shit go unpaid."

"This isn't about revenge," Carroll said. "This is about saving lives."

Enzo folded his arms. "Fine. If they leave, then they'll kill people somewhere else. Don't tell me you're okay with that."

"Of course not," Carroll said. "We can keep them under surveillance. If they take off, we'll follow them."

Enzo glared at him. "We're talking about vampires. They could probably fly or walk in shadows or something, and we'd never know they left."

Mark lowered his voice. "How soon can your guy get more stakes?"

Enzo took a deep breath. "I don't know. He's got a shipment of trees coming in from Vermont. Maybe he'll have them ready tomorrow."

"Let's wait another day. We should have more bullets by then."

"They're a flight risk," Enzo said. "That's a chance I don't want to take."

"If we're going to do this, then let's do it right," Carroll said. "We haven't slept all night. We don't have our weapons ready. It would be a big mistake."

Both sides had reached a stalemate. As the voice of reason, Sophie felt she had to bring them together. She put her hand on Enzo's shoulder. "Carroll makes a good point. I don't know about you, but I'm exhausted. I doubt you can physically or mentally handle a confrontation right now. Let's rest up, meet later, and come up with a plan."

Enzo tilted his head and sighed. "I can't lose any more of my guys without striking back. What kind of boss am I if I can't protect my people?"

Tony said. "Nobody's blaming you for any of this, boss. I mean, we're talking vampires here. The guys have faith that you'll take care of it."

"You're right; we will take care of it." Enzo ran his fingers through his hair. "We can wait a day, but we can't let them out of our sight. We need better surveillance. We need to commandeer a house or something. You guys are the experts at that shit."

"Don't worry, we have it covered," Mark said. "If I thought there was a chance they were going to sniff us out, we would have been more cautious. Maybe Senerchia and Reed will show up some time today."

"Yeah, and I might grow wings," Tony said. "It ain't happening. They're either dead or captured. God only knows what those motherfuckers did to them."

Nobody spoke for a while. Sophie felt tension and distrust. It was going to take effort to make this partnership work. "So we're in agreement. We'll reconvene at my house at two in the afternoon. We can sleep, and get our stuff together in the mean time."

There were nods and assents of agreement. Carroll and Andrews left.

"This is fucked up, Enzo," Tony said. "It's bad enough we have to fight the undead, but we have to do it with them. I don't like it."

"Believe me, I wish we didn't have to. Sometimes I want to throttle Andrews, but, the truth is, we can use their help. There are certain things they can do that we can't. Rest assured, if they're not willing to act, we will. We're not going to lose this war."

Sophie sighed. "When you raid the vampire house, don't go guns blazing. I have a feeling Charlie and Mike are alive inside the house. We need to get them out."

Tony made the sign of the cross. "If they are, then God help them. I'll see you later. It's going to be a long fucking day."

Sophie walked Tony to the door. When she returned, Enzo sat staring at the ceiling.

"Can I get you something to drink?"

Enzo shook his head. "No, I should leave."

"You can stay. I have a guest room. I'm sure I can find clothes that fit."

Enzo eyed her warily. "You just happen to keep men's clothing lying around?"

"Ah, you know. People come and go. Sometimes they leave stuff behind.

"This is killing me, Sophie. I always told myself that I have to be cold. People are going to die. It's the nature of our business. Most of my predecessors and their associates are dead and buried, and not from old age, but this tears me up. I'm responsible for these men. They have mothers and fathers, wives and children whose lives have been shattered. They look at me like I'm to blame. Maybe I should have just said forget about it when we discovered Alexei was a vampire."

Sophie sat next to him. She leaned her head on his

shoulder, fighting a sudden urge to take him in her arms.

"If you didn't do something about Johnny's murder, you'd have lost respect. Now we're in too deep. We have to finish this thing, and rescue Charlie and Mike."

"I think they're dead. I think the vampires figured out who they were and didn't let them out alive. They have to know we're after them."

Sophie sighed. "Maybe they'll just leave."

Enzo shook his head. "No way. I want retribution, damn it."

"At what cost? And don't tell me at any cost. You're too smart for that type of thinking. If they figure out who we are and start attacking us, then things can get dicey."

"You think I don't know that? We have to stay the course, even if it gets tough."

Sophie frowned. She had been pondering the wisdom of this course of action even before Charlie and Mike disappeared.

Enzo yawned. "I really need to go."

He got up, but Sophie grabbed his hand. "Sure you don't want to stay? It really wouldn't be a big deal." For a moment, she thought he would accept her invitation.

"Thanks for the offer, but I need to take care of things at home. I'll see you later."

Sophie followed him to the door. She watched as he turned the corner and walked to his car. She sighed, feeling a pang of regret.

Chapter XXX

Magnus sat at the piano playing a melody. He could not concentrate. The notes sounded all wrong. Instead of relaxing him, playing the piano was making him more irritable. He turned, startled to find Gabriella standing behind him. She had an uncanny ability to sneak behind him despite his preternatural senses.

"How's our *friend* doing?" Magnus asked with a wry smile.

"Still unconscious. I imagine he'll be out for a bit longer. You hit him good."

"I didn't intend on doing serious damage. I just wanted to immobilize him."

"You certainly did that. You almost put him out for good."

"So what do we know about him?" Magnus asked.

Gabriella tossed his wallet, and Magnus caught it. "His name is Charles Senerchia. He lives on Catherine Street in Philadelphia. I'm going to check my source at the DMV to get more info."

"Good." Magnus fished through the wallet. He counted over three thousand dollars. "He carries quite a large sum of cash."

"Because he's a gangster?" Gabriella giggled.

"Probably not a good one. Who do these fools think they're dealing with? Don't they know this can only end in their deaths?"

"Perhaps they don't know who we are."

Magnus frowned. "After Alexei's display outside the nightclub, I doubt it. When Mr. Senerchia recovers, we'll find out what he knows."

"How will this end?"

"I don't know. They have linked Alexei to the people he killed. We must move with caution." Magnus drew Gabriella toward him. She leaned in, and his lips met hers. "We haven't survived this long by accident. If we have to kill these meddlers, then so be it."

"We should go somewhere secluded where we'll be less conspicuous."

"We've tried that before. After a year or so, we start to draw attention, not to mention there's a limited food supply. Plus, I'd miss the culture and entertainment you get in a big city. We should be more selective with whom we travel. Possibly splinter this group."

Gabriella closed her eyes. "It isn't easy to let go of those you love."

"I know. Tell me if Mr. Senerchia wakes up. I need to chat with the young man."

When Gabriella left, Magnus began pacing the living room. In need of fresh air, he put on a pair of shoes and was about to leave when Heinrich walked through the door.

"How did it go?" Magnus asked.

"As well as could be expected," Heinrich replied. "I cremated the body and abandoned the car in an unsavory section of the city. It'll be stripped down by tomorrow. How about his friend?"

"Still out."

"That's unfortunate," Heinrich said. "How's Alexei?"

"I don't know. I haven't spoken to him since I returned. After his tirade about us following him, he's kept himself scarce. What a fool."

"He's been under stress lately."

"Stress he created. He's acted like an idiot, hardly becoming of an elder vampire."

Heinrich said nothing.

Magnus sighed. "But he is one of ours, I suppose, and therefore we must accept his flaws."

"Well said. I'll check on our guest."

Magnus left the mansion to clear his head, hoping to sort out the recent developments.

A couple hours before dawn, Magnus sat in a chair in the basement, which had five finished rooms. Its living space was larger than most houses. In front of him, Charlie Senerchia slept on a futon. He began to stir.

Magnus waited patiently.

Charlie opened his eyes. They darted across the room. He attempted to rise and let out a low moan.

When Magnus approached, Charlie shrank away, his body trembling.

"No need to be afraid," Magnus said.

Charlie scanned the room. "Where am I? What are you doing here?"

"You're a guest in my house. Welcome."

Charlie attempted to rise, wavered slightly, and then vomited.

Magnus handed him a handkerchief, and Charlie used it to wipe his mouth.

"How did I get here? What happened? Where's Mike?"

"I'll answer your questions one at a time. I brought you here. We had a scrap, and you came on the short end of it. Your friend is no longer with us."

"You-you're a fucking vampire!" Charlie shouted. "Get the fuck away from me."

"Well, I guess there's no need for pretenses. I am what you would call a vampire, but you need not fear me."

"What do you want with me?" Charlie's eyes held a wild look of desperation.

"Cooperation." Magnus smiled. "You know more than you should. How did you obtain this information and who else knows? Work with us, and you can go free."

"You fucking killed Mike! Why should I believe you?"

"Believe what you want. You're hardly in a position to dictate terms. You're alive because I let you live. If your survival is important, then calm down and cooperate."

Magnus turned his back to Charlie. He reached into a box and pulled out a stake that had been in the car. He tossed it to Charlie, who caught it in mid-air.

"I assume you meant to harm us with that trinket. That, my friend, was a mistake. Fortunately for you, not a fatal one. What an unfriendly way of introducing yourself."

"Fuck off." Spit flew from Charlie's mouth.

Magnus circled around Charlie. "Don't be so crude. It's not an accident that you had those pieces of wood in your vehicle. How did you find where we live?"

Charlie chuckled. "I don't have to answer anything without my lawyer present."

Magnus gripped Charlie's neck, not enough for him to suffocate, only enough for him to gasp for air. "Do you think this is a game? Your life hangs in the balance. Don't tilt it."

Magnus released his grip and paced around the room. He didn't expect resistance. He figured Charlie would just be glad to be alive.

A rustle came from behind him. He turned in a split second, in time to intercept Charlie as he raced crossed the room in an attempt to plunge the stake into him. He grabbed the stake, ripped it from Charlie's hand and tossed it aside. He punched Charlie in the gut. Charlie doubled over. With one hand, he lifted him in the air.

Charlie groaned and fell to his knees after Magnus released him. He coughed blood.

Magnus put his foot on Charlie's back, making him lie flat on the floor. "I won't hold that against you. You underestimated me. Don't do it again. Are you ready to cooperate?" Magnus took his foot off Charlie's back.

"I ain't saying nothing," Charlie said.

"A defiant one. I have ways of making you talk." Magnus chuckled. "I think I heard that line in a movie. For now, ponder the situation."

Alexei rose from the dining room table, shaking his head. "I'll make him babble about anything that's ever happened in his miserable, worthless life."

Magnus rolled his eyes, not looking at Alexei. "Don't you think I know how to get information from people? This one is tough. He has a strong sense of loyalty and stubbornness, which overshadows his fear. Don't worry. I'll break him."

"Let me at him," Alexei said. "I'll give him a lesson in fear."

"You'll only torture or kill him," Magnus said. "That won't be productive."

Kristoff asked, "Why don't we just kill him and be done with it? If we have to, we'll leave. It won't be the first time."

"Coordinating such a move with so many takes planning, especially with young ones like yourself."

Kristoff propped his chin on his fist. Ursula put her arm around his shoulder and leaned his head against her chest.

"I'm with Alexei," Heinrich said. "We need to use all means at our disposal to get him to talk. Let me do it."

Gabriella shook her head. "Torture is overrated. The information you get is unreliable. Usually, they will say anything just to stop the pain."

Heinrich's brows furrowed.

"I've read quite a bit on the subject," Gabriella said.

Magdalena, who had been standing at the corner of the room, stepped forward. She extended her bare leg against the table. "You men are all alike. You think you can solve all the world's problems with brute force. There are better ways of getting what you want. Give me time with the young man, and I'll find out everything."

Alexei grinned. "How can you be so sure he'll give in to you?"

Magdalena batted her eyelashes. "He's a red-blooded male. None have ever refused me."

Magnus leaned back. "Magdalena, work your magic on him."

Charlie was searching for a way out while fighting a severe headache and nausea. He already tried to bust through the door leading out of the basement to no avail.

Charlie entered a game room. It had two large couches, a pool table, a foosball game and a Bose stereo. A third room housed six coffins, along with numerous paintings lining the wall. He had no idea if they had any value.

After Magnus left, other vampires visited. One was a creepy, dark haired vampire named Sasha who looked liked he could have been a stunt double for Dracula. Sasha brought him a pitcher of lemonade. After pouring a glass and handing it to Charlie, he put the pitcher inside a refrigerator. Then a blond vampire named Jurgen brought him a bag of Doritos and a soft pretzel.

"When the hell are you gonna let me go?" Charlie asked.

Jurgen smiled. "Magnus will decide what to do with you. Until then, relax."

"How the hell am I supposed to relax? You fucking vampires make me nervous."

"Then I'll leave." Jurgen walked up the steps.

Charlie would have attacked him from behind, except it hadn't worked so well when he tried it on Magnus.

After exhausting all possible avenues of escape, he shot some pool to distract himself. They killed Mike. They weren't going to let him live. Oddly enough, he was no longer afraid, just filled with anger and despair.

After clearing the pool table twice, footsteps sounded from upstairs. He did not bother looking at his new visitor. He concentrated on his next shot, hoping his false confidence would help get him out of there.

He pulled back his stick and tapped the cue ball, knocking the seven ball into the side pocket. He looked up, dropped his stick, closed his eyes and quickly opened them. He had to be hallucinating, because if he wasn't, then he was staring at the most drop-dead gorgeous woman he had ever seen.

"Hello, Charlie." She glided across the room.

She was a goddess. Still, she was one of them, regardless of how beautiful or sexy she looked. She was not human. She drank blood and only came out at night.

She tilted her head and her wild, auburn hair fell past her shoulders. "You don't speak much, do you?"

"Um, hello." Charlie could only imagine how stupid he sounded.

She circled around him.

He shifted his eyes to catch her movement. He wanted to touch her to make sure she was real, but didn't dare. If she wasn't, he didn't want to dispel the illusion.

She put her arms around his neck. "Charlie, you're too tense."

Charlie pulled back. "I need to get out of here."

"In time. Until then, enjoy your stay. I can help."

Charlie gulped. "You can?"

"It would be my pleasure."

With her hands behind his neck, she pulled him closer until his lips met hers. That was when he knew it was over. No matter how hard he tried, no matter how much will he thought he had, he could not resist her. It was unlike anything he had ever felt before.

An hour before dawn, Magdalena emerged from the

basement, locking the door just to be sure her new toy wouldn't run away. Magnus and Heinrich waited in the kitchen. She sat next to Magnus and wrapped her arms around his shoulders.

"And you said he would be difficult to crack." Magdalena laughed. "He was putty in my hands."

"What did you find out?" Magnus asked.

"He's a mobster. Ooh, scary." Magdalena gave a fake shudder. "He works for a man named Tony Scrambolgni, also known as The Wop."

"The Wop? Using an ethnic slur as a nickname?" Heinrich shook his head. "I don't think I'll ever understand these people."

"What else did you learn?" Magnus asked.

"Scrambolgni works for a man named Enzo Salerno, who controls the city's crime. Salerno gave the order for Charlie to patrol our house."

Magnus stroked his chin. "I have to find out more about this Salerno. What else?"

"That's all for now," Magdalena replied.

Magnus arched an eyebrow.

"It's early yet. I have to establish his trust. By dawn tomorrow, I will tell you all you need to know."

Magnus grinned. "Very well. I'll wait until then."

Magnus knocked on Alexei's door.

Alexei, who had been reading a book, looked up before returning to his book. "Can I help you?"

"Close your book. I have something important to discuss with you."

Alexei obliged. "You have my full attention."

"I realize that you and I don't get along, but we face a significant danger. The major crime syndicate in the city knows where we live and will likely strike. They will come during the day. We are the only two in the house capable of functioning in daytime. Therefore we must work together to protect the others. Neither of us can stay awake all day or we would lose our strength. Therefore, I propose we work in shifts. I'll take the first one, and you can take the second one."

"That's fine with me."

Magnus raised his brow, expecting an argument. "If anyone gets in, wake me immediately."

"I can fight them off," Alexei said.

"Regardless, get me first. We'll be more effective as a unit. I, in turn, will wake you at the first sign of someone breaking in."

"As you wish."

Magnus lingered, still not knowing what to make of Alexei's cooperation.

"Will that be all?" Alexei asked.

Magnus nodded. He slowly backed out of the room, not sure if he should feel reassurance or dread at Alexei's sudden willingness to cooperate.

Chapter XXXI

Enzo looked out the window of Sophie's living room. A government van followed two unmarked government cars. Mark Andrews and Rick Carroll filed out of the lead car. Four additional FBI agents emerged from the other vehicles. *Good. The fewer Feds, the less chance of this becoming a snafu.*

"How do you think I should hold this, Enzo?" Tony Scrambolgni asked.

He took the ash stake from Tony and gripped it with both hands at the top of the stake. "Lift it head high and plunge. That should do the trick."

Although it was only a couple feet in length, The Goat hoisted Vasilly's stake like a spear. "I'm going to throw this right into their black hearts."

The Wop smacked him in the back of the head. "What the fuck are you thinking? You ever use a spear before?"

The Goat scowled. "No."

"Then why would you throw it like a spear? You'll miss the fucking vampire and lose your stake. Wait 'til you get close and then use it."

"What if I'm far away?"

"That's why we got guns. Hey, Enzo, you sure these wooden bullets'll work?"

Enzo nodded. "They'll work. I tried them the other day at a shooting range. I just hope Andrews was able to get some ash bullets."

"About that whole ash thing. I don't believe the old

Russian bastard."

"He had an encounter with a vampire," Enzo said. "You and I haven't. Besides, it feels right. Sometimes you have to go with your gut."

"Well, I trust your judgment, Boss."

When the door bell rang, Sophie answered.

For this job, Enzo wanted men who were tough, experienced and loyal. He made an exception for The Goat and Mike Tarracone. They earned their spots because they had survived against Alexei. He chose Fat Paulie despite his portly physique because he knew how to handle himself in dangerous situations. Mad Sal Demonte was psychotic, and it was always helpful to have someone like that.

Sophie led the contingent of FBI agents inside her house. Enzo looked at his watch. It was 2PM. As always, Andrews was punctual.

"Any luck with those bullets?" Enzo asked.

Andrews nodded. "I got a case."

Enzo shrugged. "It ain't much, but it's better than nothing."

"Let's split them up." Andrews handed him a packet of bullets. "We got enough non-ash wooden bullets to go around."

Tony Scrambolgni and Fat Paulie opened two briefcases.

"We got these last night," Enzo said. "Genuine ash stakes."

Special Agent Carroll picked up a stake. "I can only hope these things work."

Sophie folded her arms, her face a mask of worry. "Aren't you guys nervous? We're talking vampires, something a couple of weeks ago I would have dismissed as the stuff of legend."

Enzo said, "For better or worse, they crossed our paths. We can't ignore them."

Sophie lit a cigarette. "I wish we could."

"Don't worry," Andrews said. "They should be sleeping

during the day, plus, we have the element of surprise."

"It didn't work for Charlie and Mike," Sophie said.

"No use fretting over it," Enzo said. "Let's roll."

As they loaded their guns and distributed stakes, Sophie paced the room, chain smoking.

"Well, that's it," Andrews said.

"Good luck," Sophie said as the men filed out of her house. She grabbed Enzo's arm before he left. "You better make it back, Enzo Salerno."

"I fully intend to," Enzo said.

As she closed the door behind him, a tear ran down her cheek.

Alexei put down his book and turned the television on to CNBC. He was not a big investor, but a high society friend had recommended a cloud computing company that was ready to explode. After three weeks, it was up twenty percent.

Normally, Alexei had to wait until the stock market closed before finding out how his company performed. Since he was guarding the mansion during the day, he could track it in real time. Unfortunately, his lack of rest did not help his surly disposition.

Yesterday's shift was uneventful. He listened for strange sounds, but the only thing he heard was the mailman.

He frowned as the CM Networks ticker scrawled across the screen. It was down eight percent.

He spread himself across the couch. Unlike yesterday, he was having a hard time staying awake. He closed his eyes.

When he heard the faint rumble of a car, followed by three more vehicles, Alexei jumped to his feet. What were the chances of four cars driving in succession on this street at ten in the morning? Slim. Very slim.

He ran upstairs and pulled back the Venetian blinds that covered the large bay window and winced. Down the street, a group of men were exiting four parked cars. Among them were the two men who survived their encounter outside the club.

"Damn." He gritted his teeth. Magnus was right. They were coming back for revenge.

He cracked his knuckles. He should get Magnus. Not that he needed his help, but he could only imagine Magnus' reaction if he found out that these thugs invaded the mansion and Alexei hadn't notified him.

Alexei ran up the steps. He walked into Magnus' darkened room and found him lying on a king sized bed. Unlike most of their kind, he did not sleep in a coffin.

He gripped his shoulder. "Magnus. Wake."

Magnus opened his eyes. He blinked twice. "It's early, so they must be here."

"Yes," Alexei said.

"Let's defend our home against those who wish us harm." Magnus leaped to his feet and bared his fangs. "It's time to feed."

Alexei rolled his eyes. The brood leader was so melodramatic.

He exited the room, ready for a fight.

Mark stood at the side of the mansion with Enzo Salerno, Tony Scrambolgni and Rick Carroll. They had blocked both entrances to the street with their vehicles.

"All right," Mark said. "I'll lead my men inside. We'll secure the house and signal you to follow. If they ambush us, we leave. Got it?"

"We've been over this a dozen times," Enzo said.

Mark nodded. The butterflies in his stomach had finally subsided after being jittery all morning. If this operation turned into a disaster, it would sink his career, but he felt confident in his decision to trust Salerno. Even Carroll had eased on his opinion of the mobster.

Mark and five handpicked FBI agents approached the house. They were among the few at the Agency who knew about the vampires.

Agent Winfield, an expert at breaking and entering, led the way. Within a minute, he opened the door.

Silence greeted Mark as he stepped inside the house. He scanned the foyer and living room. The rooms were spacious. Expensive leather furniture, a stereo system and a large plasma television decorated the room. Paintings lined the walls, and sculptures adorned the living room. Whoever furnished this house had expensive taste.

Mark pulled out his two way radio. "We're inside. No sign yet."

On the other end, Enzo said, "We're right behind you."

Just before he entered the kitchen, Mark caught movement out of the corner of his eye. It was so quick he could hardly react. "Watch out!"

A vampire flew from the overhanging balcony and landed on top of Agent Staples.

Mark immediately recognized the face of Alexei the Vampire. He pulled out his .357 and aimed at the vampire, when an enormous force landed on top of him. He crashed to the floor, face first. Blood gushed from his nose.

The vampire grabbed him by the throat and lifted him to his feet. Gasping for breath, he reached for the stake he had strapped to his belt like a sword. His face turned deep red, and the room darkened. He was quickly losing consciousness. *Have to get it.*

A bullet whizzed past the side of his head, and the vampire released him. He landed on the floor with a thud. He tried to stand, but didn't have the strength. Instead he crawled on all fours. He looked up and found Enzo Salerno leading his mobsters inside like the cavalry.

Magnus saw the bullet coming. It was unlike any he had ever seen. He took a fraction of a second to examine it as it flew through the air. His eyes widened. It was made of wood. He dropped the FBI agent and jumped back, narrowly avoiding the bullet. Another bullet shot at him. He rolled to his side and then lunged at the shooter, ramming the FBI agent with his shoulder and knocking him to the ground.

Rick Carroll stared with his mouth open as the vampire dodged his bullet. *Impossible.* He shot again with the same result before making a futile attempt at dodging the lunging vampire.

The vampire tackled him. He couldn't breathe. All he felt was pain. Lying on the floor, he wondered what the hell they were thinking trying to fight vampires.

The vampire straddled him. He tried to fight, but was helpless as the vampire came down with his fangs.

Magnus plunged his fangs into the FBI agent's throat. He took four swallows of blood. They were badly outnumbered, so he did not have time to feed, but he needed extra strength.

"Magnus, there's more coming," Alexei shouted from across the room.

Six more stormed through the doors. These weren't law enforcement agents. They had a rougher look. Magnus licked his lips and bared his fangs.

Enzo entered the vampire house, not expecting this kind of carnage. Agent Staples was dead on the floor with a gaping hole in his chest. The vampire Alexei identified as Magnus was on top of Agent Carroll, who was also dead. Andrews stood in the middle of the room, a dazed look on his face.

"You son of a bitch." Enzo took his stake with both hands and charged at Magnus, who was looking the other way. The vampire moved, but not in time. The stake tore his shirt and pierced his tricep.

Magnus screamed.

Damn, these things actually work.

Magnus glared at him and bared his fangs. He gave Enzo a backhanded slap that made him see stars. Enzo fell and dropped the stake.

Blackness surrounded him. A loud whooshing sound came from above, like he was being sucked into a vacuum. He had to get to his feet. When the room came back into view, Magnus had his back to him, occupied by new attackers.

Enzo crawled to his stake. He reached arm over arm until he gripped it. Using the wall for leverage, he lifted himself.

Fighting the haze, he wondered why only two vampires were fighting. Perhaps, the others in the house weren't capable of fighting, which meant they were vulnerable.

He contemplated taking another shot at Magnus, but the vampire had incredible quickness and instincts. Instead, he snuck down a staircase.

He entered the closest room and smiled at the sight of two mahogany coffins. Clutching the stake, he propped open a coffin.

Alexei hadn't had this much fun in years. Standing at the top of the balcony, he targeted the FBI agent from his encounter outside of the club. Somehow the agent survived their first encounter. History would not repeat itself.

He swooped down and viciously yanked at Staples' head, tearing it off. He held it so the other invaders could see. Over the years, he found that showing people their mortality was an effective tactic.

He didn't have time to savor this kill. An agent came after him with a stake. He sidestepped and tripped the man. Another pulled out a gun and pointed it at him. He bolted to that agent and grabbed his wrist. The agent squeezed the trigger, sending a bullet into the ceiling. Alexei elbowed him to the neck twice, causing him to drop his gun. Before he finished the agent off, more armed men entered the house.

He shouted to alert Magnus.

Suddenly a hint of desperation entered Alexei. He and Magnus had to fend off these humans, armed with guns and stakes, in the daylight. The odds were no longer in his favor, but he had not lived for over a thousand years to die so easily.

A bullet from a new intruder shot past him. If he was going to survive, he had to go on the offensive.

The Wop came in behind Enzo, his jaw dropping at the sight of the bloodbath. Instead of panicking, he gritted his teeth.

In front of him, Enzo stabbed Magnus with a stake, causing the vampire to howl. Magnus swatted Enzo like a fly.

He wasn't about to let Magnus kill his boss. "Try me on for size, asshole."

He stabbed at Magnus with the stake, but the vampire deftly avoided the blow. He had been in knife fights in the past, and that was how he wielded the stake, taking swings and trying to clip him, but Magnus was too quick.

Fat Paulie stood next to him. Tony expected Paulie to attack with his stake. Instead, he pulled out a wooden cross and held it up to the vampire. "Go back to hell where you came from."

Magnus threw his head back and laughed. He grabbed the cross and tossed it. "You shouldn't believe everything you read."

Tony took the opportunity to attack with his stake. Magnus avoided the blow, then threw a right hook that connected with Tony's jaw. His legs felt like jelly and he crumpled to the floor.

Magnus grabbed Fat Paulie by the folds in his neck and gave him a twist, causing a horrible cracking sound. Fat Paulie's eyes rolled to the back of his head and he fell backward, his ample weight knocking over a lamp.

"You fucking bastard," Tony yelled from the floor. He had known Fat Paulie his whole life. They stole their first car together when he was fourteen. Now the fat man was dead, all because of this vampire.

Tony stabbed the back of Magnus' calf. The vampire shrieked and limped around the room. He fell to all fours, trying to remove the stake.

Tony tried to pull himself to his feet, but his head felt ready to explode. The room spun, and he closed his eyes. He had to take out Magnus.

With a stake in hand, Enzo removed the lid of the coffin. Inside was a sleeping vampire with dark hair and a pointy nose. His skin was like porcelain. Enzo stabbed him in the chest.

The vampire popped up, his fangs exposed. Enzo removed the stake from his chest and stabbed him again. This time the vampire whimpered and fell back into the coffin. He closed his eyes and stopped breathing.

Enzo smiled. "One down."

He walked across the room to the silver coffin. This time he lowered his stake, confident the vampire wouldn't jump out when he opened the lid.

He paused after removing the lid. Inside was a petite brunette, pretty as hell. *She's still a vampire.*

"I suppose she is," Enzo muttered. With two hands, he plunged the stake into her abdomen. She wailed like a baby, and for a moment Enzo felt remorse. He was killing this beautiful creature, but she was a beautiful creature who would turn on him in a second.

He pushed the stake deeper into her abdomen, and she moaned.

"No mercy."

He waited until he was sure she was dead, then scanned the room for more coffins. Finding none, he opened the door and exited. "Time to go vampire hunting."

The Goat hit the ground as Mad Sal Demonte fired his gun. As if it wasn't tough enough to fight vampires, he had to worry about friendly fire.

Unfortunately, the bullet missed Alexei. The Goat couldn't believe the blond vampire's quickness. He darted around the room like a blur.

He had shot all of the bullets from his .357 already. He didn't have time to reload, but he still had Vasilly's stake in hand.

The Goat stepped in front of Alexei. "Remember me. It's time we finish our fight."

Alexei smiled. "Of course I remember you. You were lucky I didn't kill you. Are you foolish enough to tempt fate twice?"

The Goat nodded. "Hell yeah."

"As you wish."

Alexei stepped forward. The Goat swiped at him with his stake. Alexei leaned back and avoided the blow with ease. Alexei feinted once and then slapped The Goat in the back of the head. He staggered and fell to the floor as a thudding pain reverberated through his head.

"Motherfucker!" He looked up, thinking Alexei had attacked him again, but the vampire's eyes darted past him. He grabbed his shoulder and felt blood. Lodged inside was a bullet. Some asshole just shot him.

Alexei leapfrogged him and landed in front of Mad Sal Demonte. He lifted him by the throat, then slammed him to the floor, cracking the back of his skull. He knelt down and plunged his fangs into Sal's neck.

The Goat's body flooded with pain. With his good hand, he grabbed his stake. He looked up as Alexei stepped on his wrist.

Mark put his hand to his head. The operation had gone horribly wrong. He thought they would catch the vampires sleeping. *Of course they would be asleep. It's the goddamn daytime.* He figured the vampires would be easy prey. Now Rick Carroll and Ross Staples were dead. Among Enzo's men, the vampires had killed Paul Randazzo and Salvatore Demonte. The two vampires still stood fighting. How long had they been inside? Three minutes? Four minutes? Before long, all his people would be dead.

Tony Scrambolgni stood beside him. "Come on. You get him from one side, and I'll get him from the other."

Mark nodded. He gained respect for the mobster during this massacre.

They spread out so Magnus stood between them. Tony tried to stab him with the stake, but the vampire easily dodged it. Simultaneously, Mark attempted to pierce him with his stake and just missed. They tried it again. Magnus dodged Scrambolgni's shot, but Mark grazed his abdomen. If his shirt wasn't covering him, he would have made contact.

Gaining in confidence, Mark prepared for another strike. Before he could, Magnus leaped from the floor and grabbed the railing on the second floor.

Agent Winfield shot Magnus twice, missing with each shot. Mark watched in awe as Magnus soared through the air and landed on top of Winfield. Magnus bit him on the neck and tore into his flesh like it was butter.

Mark raised his stake, charged, and thrust it at the vampire. With uncanny speed, Magnus lifted Winfield, turned him around and used him as a shield. Instead of piercing the vampire, Mark stabbed his colleague. It didn't matter. Winfield was already dead.

Mark backed away. Enough was enough. They had to escape.

He grabbed Scrambolgni's arm. "Let's get the hell out of here."

"Where's Enzo?" Tony asked.

"I don't know. I'll contact him on the radio and tell him we're leaving."

As Scrambolgni gathered the others, Mark spoke on his radio. "Enzo, we're pulling out. Get the hell out of here."

On the other end Enzo said, "Not yet. I'm in the middle of something."

"Leave now. We're getting annihilated. We're not waiting."

"Then I'll catch you later."

Enzo turned off his radio. "Damn." He needed more time.

A single coffin sat in the last room. He just killed the vampire lying inside. Her screech was so loud he was sure the other vampires would hear her, but apparently when they slept, they were dead to the world.

He entered another room. Two more coffins, one white and one brown. He lifted the lid to the first coffin. This vampire looked like a teenager, but that wasn't indicative of his true age. After all, vampires were immortal.

He kept that in mind when he plunged his stake into the vampire's heart. Surprisingly, his only reaction was a soft whimper. Enzo closed the lid when the vampire's head slumped to the side and he stopped breathing.

When Mark called, there was panic in his voice, which meant things had gone horribly wrong up there. He had to bust out of here soon. If he had additional time, he would dispose of more vampires. Since he didn't want to die today, he would kill this next one and find a way out, hopefully avoiding Alexei and Magnus.

He opened the lid to the brown coffin and jumped back when a blonde vampire with pale skin opened her eyes and popped out of the coffin.

"Shit!"

The vampire drove him back. The other four had gone down easily, and he expected more of the same from this one.

She snarled and reached for his throat. Enzo turned his head to avoid her. He kicked her in the abdomen. When she tried to dive on him, he held his stake in front of him. She plunged into the stake and let out a shrill scream. She flailed at him to no avail.

Enzo slid out from under her, his heart pounding. He wrenched the stake out and thrust it into her again. "Damn it, what's it going to take?"

He remembered the Wiz telling him that beheading should be an effective tactic against vampires. With that in mind, he took out a knife with a long blade. He grabbed her by the hair and sawed through her skin, flesh and cartilage with the knife. For a moment he turned away from the gruesome sight. He continued, not stopping until he finished the job. When her head came loose, he dropped it in disbelief at what he just did.

"I gotta get out of here."

He exited the room as footsteps came from the hallway. He found a window, unlocked it, slid it up, then knocked out the screen window. He stumbled out of the window and onto the grass below. Without looking back, Enzo ran like hell.

Chapter XXXII

Charlie Senerchia paced around the room. He hadn't heard a sound for hours. Earlier on, he heard gunshots, furniture breaking, and people screaming. Enzo and the Feds must have raided the house. Why hadn't they come for him? Maybe they didn't realize he was inside, or maybe the vampires wiped them out. He yelled and banged on the door, but nobody came.

Despite this, he couldn't stop thinking about Magdalena. She was ... he didn't have the words to describe her. She was unlike anyone he had ever met. She completely captivated him. Magdalena was a goddess.

Last night was pure ecstasy. She could only see him at night since she had to rest during the day. He had been dozing off when the fighting woke him.

Afterward, he tried to shoot pool to distract himself, but his restlessness grew.

He sat on the floor holding his pool stick when footsteps sounded. He leaped to his feet. The door opened, and his heart skipped a couple beats. It was Magdalena, looking even more amazing than he remembered.

He rushed up the stairs and held her tight. "What the hell happened? You okay?"

Magdalena smiled. "I'm fine. Unfortunately they killed some of the others."

Charlie's face sagged. "No. Why would they do that?" He should want them dead, but he could no longer bear the thought.

"Your kind always wants to kill us."

"What's going to happen now?"

She ran her fingers through his hair. "I don't know yet."

He walked down the stairs holding Magdalena's hand. He could help them out by using his contacts, but once he did, there was no turning back. His old life would be over. He took a long look at Magdalena. How could he not help her?

The vampires sat at the long living room table. They would grieve later over their fallen brothers and sisters, but now Magnus had to consider practical matters.

He and Alexei let the attackers leave. They could have continued fighting, but Magnus felt weak after one of them stabbed him with a stake. They had done him a favor by escaping. The same was true for Alexei, although he would not admit it.

He and Alexei gave the invaders a severe beating, killing five and leaving the others wounded, limping out of the house. Then he found Cecilia, Carmen, Francois, Jorge, and Claudius.

He had no idea how it happened. He and Alexei repeatedly went over the details of the fight. One of the thugs stabbed Magnus with a stake. After swatting him away, that was the last Magnus saw of him. He must have been responsible for the deaths of his brood members.

Magnus cursed himself for not killing that one. With so many attacking, it was difficult to keep track of them.

Magnus stood at the head of the table. The rest of the brood remained quiet. "We can't stay. They'll be back."

Alexei had his feet up on the table. "I wouldn't be so sure, not after that ass kicking we gave them."

Magnus glared at Alexei. "These are mafia figures and members of the Federal Bureau of Investigation, not peasants in a European village. They'll be back. Probably tomorrow. I doubt they will strike again tonight, but just to be sure, we'll patrol the neighborhood."

"It's going to be difficult to move," Gabriella said.

"I'm painfully aware of it." Magnus stared at Alexei, who seemed oblivious of the implication. "But we have no other option."

"I'm willing to fight them again, if you're game," Alexei said. "It was fun."

Magnus pounded his fist on the table. "This isn't a game. Five of our own are dead."

Alexei sat straight. "I know, and it saddens me, but we can take them on again. This time, I'll make sure there are no mistakes."

Magnus clenched his fist. "We can't risk another encounter."

"Moving will be prohibitively difficult," Gabriella said. "If we're going to do this, then we better start now."

Magnus nodded. "Does anyone know where we can move, at least temporarily, until we find a permanent residence?"

The members of the brood provided suggestions, but each had problems. They debated, but Magnus saw little progress. He was not concerned for himself. He could stay anywhere. The others needed complete protection from the sunlight.

Everyone stopped talking when a mortal entered the room.

"I think our friend Charlie can help us," Magdalena said.

Magnus scowled. "How can *he* help?"

Charlie stepped forward. "The way I see it, you have two problems. First, you need a place to stay. I know people all over the city. Second, you need to transport your stuff. You have things here that are worth a lot, but you can't worry about that. They can be replaced. What you really need to do is move those coffins, right?"

Magnus nodded.

"My cousin owns a moving company. I can get a few

trucks. He owes me a favor."

Magnus folded his hands and stared at Charlie. His dreamy eyes as he stared at Magdalena convinced Magnus of his sincerity. She had snared another man. She was the most seductive creature he had ever known. The Sirens of ancient times had nothing on her.

Magnus nodded. "How quickly can you do this?"

"I need to make a few phone calls. With a little luck, maybe tonight."

They convened at Sophie's house, which had become vampire hunting headquarters. Mark Andrews broke his nose during the fight, but that was the least of his problems. Three FBI agents were dead, including his mentor, Rick Carroll.

Mark shook his head, holding ice to his face. "What a fucking disaster. It was only two of them, and they crushed us. Where the hell is Enzo anyway?"

"He's on his way," Tony Scrambolgni said. "He had to take care of a few things."

"Wonderful." Mark's head throbbed. His face felt like someone had smashed it with a sledgehammer.

"So what now?" Sophie asked.

"I have to make a full report to the Director," Mark said.

"This'll become a bigger mess if you get more agents involved," Scrambolgni said.

"What's the alternative?" Mark asked.

Sophie sat next to him. "Close your ranks. Right now, a handful of agents know the truth. Keep it that way. Your story is this was a drug bust gone bad. You were ambushed by the cartel, and three of your men got clipped."

Mark looked out the window. "I don't know if that's feasible. We're fighting a losing battle. This thing's going to break."

The doorbell rang. Sophie opened the door. A disheveled

Enzo Salerno walked inside followed by the Wiz.

Enzo put his hand on Mark's shoulder. "Tony told me what happened. I'm sorry for your loss. I know you were close to Carroll and the other men."

Mark nodded. "Thanks. I appreciate it. Like I was saying, we don't stand a chance against these vampires. They'll wipe us out if we don't change our strategy."

Salerno smirked.

Mark glared at him. "What the hell's so funny?"

"We took our hits today, but believe me, we paid them back," Salerno said.

"What are you talking about?"

"I killed five of them."

"You did what?" Sophie asked.

"While the rest of you engaged Magnus and Alexei, I snuck out. I found them sleeping in their coffins. I killed four of them with my stake. The last one put up a fight, so I cut her fucking head off. Damn, I need a cigarette."

Sophie took one from her pack and handed it to him.

Salerno gave a blow by blow account of what happened. After hearing what he had to say, the day no longer felt so bleak.

"How did you get out?" Mark asked.

"Crawled out a window," Salerno replied.

Scrambolgni slapped Salerno's shoulder. "That's what I'm talking about, boss. I knew you would take it to them."

Mark nodded. "At least we put a hurting on them. They sure hurt us."

"We can kill them," Salerno said.

Sophie lit a cigarette. "Why were Alexei and Magnus the only ones fighting? Besides that last one, you said they didn't put up a fight. Yet these two fought like hell."

"That's why I went to see the Wiz first."

The Wiz took a swig from his can of Red Bull. "We went to the library at Penn. They had this old text, and it said that a vampire's strength is directly correlated to their age. The older they are, the more powerful they are. You guys must have run into some pretty old bastards."

Mark cracked his knuckles. "So if we can neutralize those two, we can knock off these other sons of bitches. These old ones, they can still be killed, right?"

The Wiz shrugged. "As far as I know."

"I hurt Magnus when I stabbed him. They won't go easy, but we can kill them."

Scrambolgni nodded. "I got a shot on that creepy son of a bitch, too. He felt pain."

"That bodes well for us," Salerno said. "We need to formulate an effective plan."

Mark looked out the window. He should tell the Director about the vampires. What he was about to do defied every protocol and procedure, but he felt more confident dealing with the vampire problem with Salerno then by going to the Director. He turned around. "We'll go with the Cartel story for now."

"Let's get to work," Salerno said. "This fight ain't over. Not by a long shot."

Charlie hung up the phone and returned to the living room, hardly believing what he was doing. His father once told him a woman would be his downfall. Looks like the old man knew something after all.

"All right, here's the deal," Charlie said. "There's an abandoned warehouse in Camden I use to store hot merchandise. There ain't any shipments coming in, so it'll be empty for the next few days. Until you figure out where you're going, you can use that."

Magnus narrowed his eyes. "If this is true, then it could take care of our immediate shelter problem. We still have to transport our belongings."

"I got that taken care of. My cousin's got two big trucks

idle. You can use them."

Magnus glanced at Gabriella, who nodded. "Okay, make the arrangements."

Charlie just signed his death warrant. For better or worse, he was tied in with these vampires. If Enzo Salerno found out he was helping them, he was a dead man.

Chapter XXXIII

Enzo cast his eyes downward as he walked alongside Gina. His wife had been crying all morning. Fat Paulie had practically been family. It was tough telling the kids that Uncle Paulie was dead.

The wet ground near the burial site muddied his Bruno Maggli shoes. This was his third funeral this week.

The last three days had been a lesson in futility. He and Mark Andrews created teams to search for the vampires. Most of their belongings were gone from their Wyncotte mansion, and the teams had no luck so far finding them.

Sophie approached them and hugged a sobbing Gina.

"When's this going to end?" Gina asked.

"I hope soon," Sophie replied. "It's been tough on us all."

"Can't those damn vampires just leave?" Gina fought through tears.

Last night Gina had been hysterical, demanding to know what had happened. Normally, he never discussed business with his wife, but this wasn't business. Gina was friends with the wives of the deceased. She had a right to know, so he told her.

Enzo excused himself and walked away with Sophie.

"What's the latest?" Sophie asked. "I haven't heard anything since last night."

"Still nothing. We have to smoke the bastards out of their holes."

"Maybe they left town."

Enzo stood stone faced. "Until we know for sure, we have to keep looking."

Sophie shook her head. "I can't believe Paulie's dead."

Enzo nodded. "He was fiercely loyal. I can't let his death go unpunished."

For a while, they said nothing. When they reached the end of the parked cars Sophie said, "The Wiz has something to show you."

Enzo's brow furrowed. "Where is he?"

"Follow me."

Standing at the edge of the property, the Wiz stood with his hands in his pockets, wearing a shirt and tie. Enzo hadn't thought he owned any.

Enzo hugged him. "Glad you made it."

The Wiz nodded. "This sucks. I really thought, you know, you guys would have been able to take 'em out."

"It's not through a lack of trying," Enzo said.

"Yeah. A couple days ago, Sophie told me you needed to know how to spot the vampires. Well, I came up with something. From everything I've read, they don't cast a reflection in the mirror. If that's true, I got a way to identify them."

The Wiz produced a contraption consisting of two small mirrors at ninety degree angles fastened together. Attached to the mirrors was a short, leather strap.

Enzo frowned. "What the fuck is that, and how is it going to help us?"

The Wiz bent down. Enzo stepped back when the kid grabbed his Bruno Maggli shoe. He attached the leather straps to the shoe.

"Are you all right, Vito?" Enzo glared at Sophie.

"Perfectly fine."

"What's this all about?"

"Look at your shoes and tell me what you see." The Wiz walked toward Enzo.

Enzo looked down. "I see you."

"Precisely. If I was a vamp, you wouldn't see my reflection. That's how we identify them."

Enzo tilted his head. "That's fucking crazy, but it might work. I just don't know how practical this is."

"You won't even notice them. Go ahead, walk around."

Enzo walked on the muddy ground. "You're right. You don't notice them."

"I made a bunch," the Wiz said. "They're at my apartment. We can give them to the guys when they're walking around the city, going to bars, nightclubs and stuff. If they find someone without a reflection, then they've got a vampire."

"Will these things stay on?" Sophie asked.

"Sure. I used heavy duty adhesive from the chemical company my roommate works at."

Enzo patted him on the back. "I'll pick them up at your apartment. Good work, kid."

Magnus watched her walking out of the office building. She had long, muscular legs. By her firm physique and the way she carried herself, it was obvious she exercised regularly.

He had been gathering information about his foes, learning about the history of organized crime in Philadelphia including its dreadful recent history prior to Enzo Salerno's reign as mob boss. He also enlisted his contacts in law enforcement to find out about Mark Andrews and Rick Carroll of the Federal Bureau of Investigations.

After moving to the warehouse, he began working on a permanent re-location, contacting broods in San Diego and Argentina. Due to the logistics, it would be weeks before they could leave, and Magnus didn't want to roam like vagabonds. Meanwhile, his brood had to survive in Philadelphia, and he would not sit back like prey.

On the night of the attack, they loaded two large trucks with essentials, leaving behind many valuables. He could buy those things again. It was the older, irreplaceable items that he brought with him.

He had to admit that Senerchia was helpful. Of course, that was only because of his infatuation with Magdalena. He wagged his tail like a good puppy in her presence.

Seeing the effect Magdalena had on Senerchia made him think there was another way to attack this problem, so he spent the last day tailing Sophie Koch.

She went to her car. The wind blew her curly, brown hair as he darted past her.

He stood in front of her Audi TT convertible with his arms folded. Her face tightened. She hesitated and reached for her pocketbook, before moving toward her car.

A daring one. He was glad he chose Sophie as his target.

He inhaled deeply as she neared him. She was not wearing perfume, and he enjoyed her natural scent. Would she run? No, she would confront him. Perfect.

"Who are you and what are you doing near my car?"

Magnus leaned back. "You know who I am."

She pursed her lips. "I've never met you."

"Sophie, let's not play games. You know what I am. How do I know? Your pulse is racing; you're breathing heavy. Your blood is flowing with adrenaline."

Sophie stepped forward and put her hands on her hips. "You're Magnus."

He smiled and bared his fangs. "The one and only."

"You're the leader of your ... brood."

Magnus clapped his hands. "Give that girl a gold star. How do you know this?"

Sophie took another step forward. "It just turned dark. Your kind can't be out until night falls. To get here, you must have left before dusk. That means you're an elder vampire. The only two involved in the fight were you and Alexei, which means you two are the only ones capable of fighting. You're not Alexei. And you seem like the leader of the gang to me."

"You *are* something, Sophie. I see why Enzo Salerno values you so highly."

"Are you here to kill me?"

Magnus smirked. "If I wanted to do that, you'd already be dead. We're not evil. We're just trying to survive. You would do the same if you were in our shoes."

"Is that supposed to make it all better?" Sophie asked.

"Most of my kind did not choose to become creatures of the night. However, our choices are to find sustenance or die. Who would die instead of feeding?"

Sophie folded her arms. "Did you choose to become a vampire?"

"Yes. My sister, Rakel, who I cherished dearly, gave me the opportunity, and I chose to become what I am. Regardless, most of my kind try not to kill our prey. It does happen, but we do not kill for greed or malice or revenge."

"It amounts to the same thing."

Magnus circled Sophie. "I find it interesting that you would take such a moralistic tact. After all, your boss recently ordered a hit on Victor Paz.

Sophie bit her lip. She opened her mouth, then closed it.

Magnus struck a cord. "Nor do we kill for business. You may be surprised to know I have human friends. I enjoy interacting with people. If there was another way, I would choose it."

"So what are we supposed to do? Ignore the fact that you killed our people?"

Magnus felt her guard wavering. Her responses were no longer sharp and heated. "I would like to come to an understanding." He leaned toward her. "You're a beautiful woman whose looks are surpassed by your intelligence. If you care to join me, I have made reservations for two at *Le Bec Fin.*"

Sophie's brow furrowed. "You want to take me out to dinner?"

"I would enjoy nothing more."

Sophie folded her arms and walked away from her car. "I'm not dressed for it."

"You look splendid, but I understand. Go home and freshen up. Meet me at nine. If you accept my offer, I promise you an evening to remember."

Using her keyfob, Sophie unlocked her car. She walked past Magnus and slid into the driver's side. "I'll think about it." She drove off.

Normally it was next to impossible to get a last minute reservation at *Le Bec Fin*, but Magnus knew the manager. He had not lied when he said he had human friends.

In the restaurant's bathroom, Magnus fixed his tie. He looked in the mirror at his black tuxedo, then combed his long, dirty blond hair back into a pony tail.

Sophie would be waiting. He would not be here if he believed otherwise.

He emerged from the bathroom and entered the dining area. He smiled broadly when he spotted her standing near the entrance. He waved her over to his table. When she neared, he pulled a seat out for her, then signaled the waiter.

"A bottle of Dom Perignon," Magnus said.

"Yes, sir," the waiter said.

"I want to let you know this is strictly business," Sophie said.

"As you wish," Magnus said.

"I didn't think you would dress so formally."

Magnus waved his hand. "It's not every evening I have dinner with such a beautiful woman."

"What, normally you club them over the head, take them back to your place and suck their blood?"

"Touché. I don't go out often, since I've seen and done everything."

"Hmm. Exactly how old are you, Magnus?"

"Once you get into your second millennium, you stop counting the years."

Sophie raised her brows.

"Oh, yes. We aren't affected by illness and disease. We usually die at the hands of your kind."

The waiter poured champagne into their glasses and took their orders.

"Why are you here, in this city?" Sophie was trying to maintain a tough façade, but he could feel her resistance weaken. She was more than just interested in gathering information to share with her cohorts.

"Why not Philadelphia? I've lived all over the globe. As you can imagine, I can't stay in a place for too long. It looks suspicious when you don't age."

Sophie sipped her champagne. "Why are you still here? After the fight the other day, I figured you would have fled."

Magnus leaned across the table. "Why should I? I have as much right to be here as you."

"Not in the eyes of the law."

"Your laws don't govern me. We have our own laws."

"Not in the eyes of my boss."

Magnus leaned back. "Ah yes. I've learned quite a bit about Mr. Salerno and have developed a healthy respect for him. This conflict doesn't have to exist. I understand why he seeks retribution. It's unfortunate. Not all of us are discriminating in choosing those we feed upon. I don't wish to continue this blood feud, but I will if I have to. I don't wish this to be a personal matter. We know who you are. We know where you live, but we haven't attacked you because we don't wish to bring unnecessary blood and violence to the streets. Do you believe me?"

Sophie pursed her lips. "I would like to refrain from judging you right now."

"Good. I can only ask for an open mind. You know, Sophie, I like your style. I like your compassion and sense of justice. You would make an ideal creature of the night."

Chapter XXXIV

The Goat fixed the mirror contraption. At first he thought he would look like a tool, but its black straps blended in with his shoes. He had to tip his cap to the Wiz. The kid was a disrespectful know-it-all, but he had come up big.

They searched the city for the past few days with no sign of the bloodsuckers. How could they expect to find vampires if they didn't know what they looked like? At least this mirror thing gave them a fighting chance.

He turned to Tony Scrambolgni, lifting the tips of his shoes. "How do I look?"

"Like a piece of shit," Tony replied.

"You're all compliments," The Goat said. "Don't you have anything nice to say?"

"Yeah. Whack a vampire tonight and you'll be nicely rewarded."

"Killing one of those bastards is all the reward I need, believe me."

"You showed some mettle the other day in the vampire house. You got a set of brass balls. That's why I put you in charge of your team."

The Goat smiled. "Thanks, Tony. That means a lot coming from you."

Karen walked into the living room and wrapped her arms around The Goat. "Be careful, Patrick. You better come back tonight."

"Hey, I made it out alive twice against those sons of

bitches. I'm fucking bulletproof." That was all false bravado. He did his best to keep the dread he felt inside.

Karen wiped away tears. "You better not die on me before we get married. If you do, then you can't hold me to the five year rule."

"Five year rule?" Tony asked.

"Yeah, if I die, she can't even look at another guy for five years, minimum."

"Yeah, but that don't apply if we ain't married," Karen said. "So if you don't come back, I'm going to sleep with every guy in town."

The Goat's face tightened. "Like hell you are."

"The only way you can make sure that won't happen is by staying alive."

The Goat frowned. "The five year rule applies whether we're married or not."

"Uh-huh," Karen said. "You keep thinking that."

"Enough," Tony said. "Go pick up your crew."

"Right." Those words sounded sweet to his ears. He couldn't help being excited about having his own crew for the first time. Enzo Salerno had given him Fat Paulie's old territory.

They got into The Goat's Lexus and drove down Lombard Street.

"You know the drill," Scrambolgni said. "You see one, call me. Then you follow them, and don't let 'em out of your fucking sight. Got it?"

"Believe me, after the other day, I ain't stupid enough to try to take 'em on alone."

Tony was in charge of the different teams searching for the vampires, including the federal agents. The Goat was surprised Andrews had gone for this, but Andrews proved he was willing to do whatever it took to kill the vampires.

The Goat dropped Tony off at his house.

"Even if you don't see anything, check in every hour," Tony said.

"I will."

The Goat pulled out from where he double parked. Five minutes later, he was at Frankie's Steaks. He ordered a cheese steak for the road. It was going to be a long night.

"We look like a traveling freak show," Moreno said. "Here we are dressed in nice threads with these fucking mirrors on our shoes."

"I think they look pretty cool." Eddie glanced at his shoes.

The Goat led them to the front of the line at the Rock Lobster. He knew the bouncers, so they didn't have to wait like the other losers. "Just keep looking down. You find someone without a reflection, then that's them."

Inside the club, his heartbeat quickened. He planned to stay until ten. If they didn't see anything, they would go to Club Flow. Eddie suggested they go to Shampoo, but The Goat didn't think these vampires were a bunch of fags.

He shook hands with a bouncer.

"Hey, Goat, put me down for fifty on the Cards."

"No problem," The Goat said. "For you, I'll only give you five percent juice."

"My man. Step right inside and enjoy yourselves. The bouncer glanced down at his shoes. "Hey, what's the deal with the mirrors."

The Goat waved his hand. "Don't worry about it." The last thing he wanted was to be interrogated. Fortunately, the bouncer didn't pursue the matter any further.

Inside, booming music and strobe lights greeted them. This was the perfect place for vampires. Just being here gave him the creeps.

"Hey, you want something from the bar?" Eddie asked.

At first The Goat was tempted to ask for a Seven and Seven, but he needed to keep his head straight. "Get me a Coke."

"You got it." Eddie left for the bar.

The Goat walked around, looking at his mirrors. He didn't realize it would be so difficult to look for vampires in a crowded area. Twice he bumped into people. One guy told him to watch where he was going. He quietly walked away when The Goat glared at him.

He ran into Moreno.

"Any luck yet?" Moreno asked.

"You think I'd be walking around looking at my fucking shoes if I found any vamps?"

"I guess not," Moreno said.

"Keep searching."

Eddie returned. "This place is packed. We ain't going to find anything here. Maybe we should go to Club Flow."

"Let me worry about that," The Goat said. "Just do your fucking job. What's wrong with you two? They stuck me with the B Team tonight."

Moreno walked away, looking at his mirrors.

After forty five minutes with no results and a number of bruises to show for it, The Goat thought his two thick-headed cohorts might be right. It was too packed to see any vamps.

"Hey, Moreno, where's Eddie?" The Goat yelled over the deafening music.

"What?" Moreno walked toward him.

"Where's Eddie?"

"He went to the bathroom."

"Tell him we're leaving."

"Sure thing."

The Goat scanned the crowd, looking for anyone unusual. Magnus and Alexei had an aura about them. He couldn't put it into words, but he would recognize it if he saw it again.

"Shit."

A man with short brown hair and a thin mustache was speaking to a hot brunette. His skin nearly glowed in the strobe light. He had that same vampire aura.

The Goat walked toward the stranger, trying to remain cool while glancing at his shoes. Eddie waved at him.

"Hey, Eddie, we're rolling." He stared at his shoes. Still out of range, The Goat kept glancing at his shoes as he walked. He spotted the hot brunette. There was a large empty spot where the guy should be. He stifled a gasp. No reflection. He found his vampire.

Without hesitating, The Goat took out Vasilly's stake from inside his jacket. In one quick motion, he drove the stake upward, full force, and buried it into the vampire's midsection.

The vampire tilted his head and let out a skull splitting scream that reverberated over the pounding music. His fangs came out as he hissed. With both hands he grabbed the stake.

The Goat removed the stake, and the vampire howled. He was about to strike again when someone knocked into him. He lost his balance and fell face first onto the floor, still clutching his stake.

Kristoff turned his head when he heard the scream. He scanned the crowd bumping and grinding to the music. He had last seen Markus and Antoinette more than an hour ago.

Kristoff climbed on top of a guard rail to get a better view. "Damn. Where are they?"

Among the throng of people, he spotted a skirmish. He clenched his fists when he caught sight of Antoinette's jet black hair. She picked up a man and tossed him like a garbage bag.

Kristoff jumped off the rail and pushed through the crowd, clearing a path. When he reached the skirmish, many people still milled around, buzzing about what took place, but Antoinette and Markus were gone.

"He stabbed him with a piece of wood," a man with wavy, black hair said to the woman standing next to him.

"Get the fuck out of here," the woman said.

"No, I'm serious. It was a piece of wood. Sharp as hell from the looks of it."

Kristoff scowled. He had to help his friends.

After calling Tony Scrambolgni for backup, The Goat stormed out of the club followed by Eddie and Moreno. They gained ground on the vampire limping ahead of them.

"Don't let that fucker get away," The Goat yelled.

They closed the gap. After the vampire turned onto Columbus Boulevard, The Goat tackled him. He stabbed the back of his leg with Vasilly's stake. The vampire shrieked and shook out of control.

The Goat was about to stab him again when he heard a choking sound, followed by a loud crack. He turned just as a female vampire with long, black hair decapitated Eddie with her bare hands. The Goat's jaw dropped when Eddie's head rolled toward him along the cement sidewalk. Blood gushed from Eddie's empty neck where his head had been moments ago. The Goat turned and vomited.

Moreno thrust his stake at the vampire, but she swatted him with a backhand.

This was no time to get sick or feel weak. This was a fight for his life. Before he could tackle the female vampire, he had to dispose of the first one. The Goat buried his stake into the male vampire's abdomen. His shoulders slumped and his head fell to the side.

When The Goat turned around, the female vampire bit Moreno's neck.

"Holy shit!" The cement sidewalks were soaked with blood, as was the vampire's face. What was worse, she seemed to be enjoying this.

With blood dripping down her chin, she stepped toward The Goat. He gripped the stake so tightly, his knuckles turned white.

"Please help me, God." He took a deep breath.

"You killed Markus. Now I will kill you."

He was more terrified now then when he fought Alexei and Magnus. At night everything seemed creepier.

He gripped the stake tight and thrust it at her. She easily avoided the blow. On his second attempt, she side-stepped him and slapped his head, knocking him to the ground.

Getting to his feet, he held the stake like a talisman. She bared her fangs and hissed. He backed against a wall and used it as leverage to pull himself up.

He tried to stab her, but she grabbed his hand. He yelped in pain as she squeezed his wrist. "Oh, God!" He screamed and dropped the stake.

He was a dead man.

Screeching tires came from down the street. She lunged in to bite him, but before she could, her body jolted and she fell forward. He stared into her blank eyes. Slowly, he pulled away.

Mark Andrews ran in his direction with his gun in hand. "You okay?"

The Goat clutched his wrist. "I think so. Thank God you got here when you did, man, or I'd be done for."

"What's the situation?" Andrews asked.

In the background, two other cars pulled up to the curb.

"I killed one." The Goat motioned to Markus. "Two of my boys got whacked."

"Any more around?"

"Not that I've seen." The Goat breathed hard. He needed some serious pain meds.

"All right, let's take care of this mess."

Kristoff fought his way through the crowd as the throng of people tightened. He felt each agonizing second tick away as he exited the club. He scanned the streets and followed the scream, coming to a sudden stop at the sight of Markus lying motionless on the ground.

"No," Kristoff wanted to go to Markus, but he had to find Antoinette first.

Gun fire sounded. He ran to the sound of the shot, and spotted what looked like FBI agents. In the distance, Antoinette was motionless on the ground. She had been shot. He had thought his kind were impervious to bullets.

Two more cars rushed onto the scene, and five men with guns exited.

With Antoinette and Markus down, he was hopelessly outnumbered. He would wind up getting killed. The only thing left to do was to tell Magnus about what happened.

Chapter XXXV

Alexei pounded his fist on Nora's kitchen table, spilling his cappuccino. "These gangsters and FBI agents are a nuisance. I can't believe they had the temerity to strike us again. You would think after we routed them, they would stay away. If I had it my way, we would wipe them out once and for all."

Nora gently stroked his bare chest. "Then why don't you?"

"Because Magnus has been preaching restraint. Hopefully, he has seen the error of his ways. If I was in charge, none of this would have happened. I would have killed him when we fought had Gabriella not intervened."

"I know you would have. They should follow you."

Alexei nodded. "I'm more powerful and smarter than he is, but they won't see it that way. If we don't act soon, more will die. You know, sometimes I envy you mortals. You have simple problems."

"It's not that simple. In fact, I can't take it any more. You told me you would make me one of your kind." Nora grabbed a knife from the kitchen and pressed it against her wrist. "I have nothing to live for. I hate my husband and my job. You're all I have."

"Don't be hasty. You have much to live for."

Nora leaned her head back. "I want you to do it now."

"With this blood feud, now is not the time to become a creature of the night. Although you would gain great strength in time, at first you will be vulnerable. If I'm off fighting, I won't be able to protect you."

"I don't care," Nora pressed the knife into her skin.

Alexei tingled at the scent of her blood. Giving blood was tiring, and he needed his energy. Still, he found her irresistible

"If that is what you wish," Alexei said. "This is what will happen. You will experience unbelievable pleasure and pain. Don't worry about the pain. The ecstasy you feel will overwhelm all other sensation. After I finish taking your blood, you will be weak. When I give you my blood, you will feel a rush unlike anything you have ever felt before. Are you ready?"

Nora's face brightened. "Of course. I've been dreaming about this for weeks."

"Very well, my precious beauty."

Nora gasped when Alexei bit her neck. Her body quivered. Alexei closed his eyes, savoring her blood. It felt like golden nectar going down his throat. He was only vaguely aware of Nora moaning.

He opened his eyes. Her face cringed. Although he had no recollection of his own turning, he had done this enough times to know the experience in vivid detail.

Blood dripped down his chin and neck. Sometimes he got so caught in the moment that his feasts turned messy. No doubt Magnus would disapprove.

Nora's heart beat slowed. *Focus on the task.* If he let her go too far, she would die.

He pulled back and rested her motionless body on the floor. Even near death, she still radiated beauty. He certainly knew how to pick them. He only chose the exquisitely beautiful. Who had time for the plain ones?

Using his fangs, he sliced his wrist. Dark blood streamed out of it. He shoved his wrist into Nora's open mouth.

She twitched, then writhed on the floor. He used his free hand to keep her still. As the seconds ticked by, her face began to show life. She sucked greedily, like a hungry infant.

Alexei's body weakened and his head ached. It was only a

slight discomfort. He was strong enough that he could turn several mortals in a single day.

When others would have pulled away, he continued to let Nora feed. He wanted her to be as strong as possible, so she would be more independent. He didn't have the time or patience to take care of her. He was not the nurturing type. After all, the vampire who turned him abandoned him, and he had to fend for himself.

Nora perked up, looking vibrant. He had made the right choice. She would fit in well with his brood.

He gathered her in his arms and held her tight. Although it was a warm summer afternoon, she shivered. He had to take her to their temporary dwelling in Camden where the others would take care of her.

"How are you feeling, Nora?"

She tilted her head. "Tired. I want to sleep."

Alexei caressed her naked back. "It's always like this. In a few weeks, you will have strength you never imagined. Until then it will be like driving a Lamborghini that won't go past second gear."

Nora clutched him. "I feel good. Is it always like this?"

"Not always. Sometimes you don't feel like getting out of your coffin."

"Will the others ... like me?" Nora asked.

"Of course. What's there not to like? You're a splendid beauty. There's always room for more like you in our brood."

Footsteps and then a door unlocking reverberated in the room. Alexei got to his feet in the blink of an eye. "Who's that?"

"My husband."

Alexei smiled. "Good. You can have your first meal."

Magnus stared daggers at Alexei. He then glanced at Gabriella leading Nora up a set of stairs. He threw his hands in the air.

"I can't believe you. What the hell were you thinking? How can you justify turning her when we're in the middle of a ... fucking war with the mob and the FBI."

Alexei flinched. Magnus never cursed. "Don't get unruffled. It's no big thing."

Magnus crossed his arms. "You're impossible. I must have forsaken some ancient god, and now he's getting back at me by making me deal with you. Don't you think things through? You know how vulnerable she is."

Sitting on a recliner, Alexei put up his feet. "Of course. I've been around for as long as you have."

"She's a well-known model," Magnus said. "People will realize she's missing and recognize her if they see her around. She can't stay here, and right now, there's nowhere for her to go."

"The girl begged me to turn her."

"You should have refused."

"That was my intention. But she threatened suicide. What choice did I have? You're all talk, Magnus. You don't live in the real world. I did what I thought was best. Look at her, she's perfect."

"I can't deal with you. Talk to Heinrich. We're striking back."

Alexei raised his brows.

"Don't look so surprised. Get going. We have work to do."

Magnus took a flying leap and landed on the balcony of Sophie Koch's house. Anybody could enter through the front door. He preferred a more dramatic entrance.

He knocked on the sliding glass door leading to her bedroom. With his keen hearing, he listened to footsteps from inside.

This was the fourth night in a row he spent with Sophie.

She was almost his. Just a little more seduction, and he would have her.

When Sophie opened the door, a bright smile lit her face. Although her looks were not comparable to the model Alexei brought into the brood, she had substance and style. After speaking with Alexei's new girl for a few minutes, he had nothing to say to her. She was hollow.

"Magnus, I'm glad you made it."

He stepped inside. "There's no place I'd rather be."

"Can I offer you a drink?" Sophie asked.

"Wine would be nice."

Sophie smirked. "Red wine?"

"That's the only kind I drink."

As she got drinks, he slid behind her. She jumped when he put his hands on her shoulders.

"You have to stop doing that," Sophie said.

"It's fun. If you had these abilities, you would use them."

Last night, he planted in her head how great it would be for her to become a creature of the night. At first, she laughed it off, but as he kept talking about it, she seemed intrigued.

"Use or abuse? With great power comes great responsibility."

"No truer words have ever been uttered," Magnus said. "That's how these problems started between us. Unfortunately, Alexei has no concept of responsibility."

Magnus told her about Nora Brooks.

"Nora Brooks?" Sophie asked. "But people will recognize her."

"I know. To make matters worse, her husband, the prominent attorney, is now dead. Alexei's like a petulant but dangerous child."

"Why don't you get rid of him?"

Magnus leaned his head back and stared at the ceiling. "It's not so simple. A brood is like a family, and every family has their problem child."

"I understand. Our organization is like a family."

"Ah yes. La Casa Nostra. I read the Godfather and saw all three movies."

Sophie glanced down. "Fat Paulie was like a big brother to me." Sophie poured two glasses of wine.

Magnus wanted to change the subject. "Let's drink to us. To a better understanding. To an everlasting love."

They intertwined their glasses, and Magnus took a long draught. He caressed her neck with his lips. She closed her eyes and moaned softly. Tonight, in another part of the city, there would be payback, but not here.

On her bed, Sophie used Magnus' chest as a pillow. She ran her long fingernails gently against his thigh.

"So, I take it Enzo Salerno didn't think much of your proposal of a truce," Magnus said.

Sophie shook her head. "He and Andrews felt like they had to act."

"I know. We took horrible losses the other night at the club. There has been too much violence. Unfortunately, we can't sit back and let these actions go unanswered."

Sophie's head perked up. "What are you talking about?"

"I really didn't want to do this. If Salerno would meet me half way, we could have avoided this. But just like Salerno, I would have lost face if I did nothing after my people were killed."

"Damn," Sophie said. "What did you do?"

"You would have heard by now if you hadn't taken your phone off the hook and turned off your cell phone. Talk to your boss. I want this to end, but that won't happen if he retaliates."

Sophie wrapped her bed sheets around her naked body. "Leave now, Magnus."

Chapter XXXVI

Tony Scrambolgni smiled as the card game unfolded. That new guy Herman Muller was getting his clock cleaned. At least the Kraut was in good spirits. He had seen newcomers get hostile after losing so much.

With one of Andrews' guys coordinating the vampire search, Tony felt he needed a break from vampire hunting. For the past week, that's all he had been doing. They still had a business to run. Although Enzo made hunting vampires his top priority, he wouldn't be happy if the bottom line suffered.

Beans DeLuca was running the game tonight. Despite his inexperience, he was doing a good job. Muller had better be good for the money. The last thing he needed was a big talker who didn't have the scratch to back himself up, but Beans assured him this guy had money since he owned over a dozen super markets in Germany.

Beans walked to the fridge to get more beer for the players.

"Hey, Beans, you got everything under control?" Tony asked.

"Yeah, no problem," Beans replied.

"Good. I got another game in Kensington. Call if you need anything."

"Don't worry about a thing."

Tony finished his glass of wine and put it on the counter. Beans kept his place clean. He even added classy decorations. The last thing Tony wanted was for his high stakes poker games to look like they were taking place in a frat house.

When he got in his car, he called Enzo. "How's it looking tonight?"

On the other end of the phone Enzo said, "Not a peep. I guess they thought better of it after we killed a couple of them the other night."

"I've been thinking, we wiped out what, eight so far? How many can there be? If they were all in that mansion, they can't have more than twenty or thirty."

"I wish I knew. It would make our job a hell of a lot easier. Until we know they're gone, we keep hunting them."

"I hear ya," Tony said. "We'll get 'em."

For Enzo, eradicating these vampires was personal. He wanted revenge. Tony just wanted to get on with business. Until they took care of their vampire problem, business would suffer.

Heinrich smiled as he lost another hand. The guys at the table couldn't stop laughing at his jokes. They thought he was an affable German businessman who was so happy to be playing a high stakes poker game he didn't care that he was losing his shirt. Heinrich took pride in his acting skills, having performed in theater groups around the world.

"Another well played hand," he said to Big Rube, a large black man who wore enough jewelry to outfit a small village.

"Don't worry, Hermy, your luck'll change before long," Big Rube said.

"Yeah, it's a matter of time," Cisero said. His voice was barely a croak. It sounded as if he smoked three packs of cigarettes a day.

Heinrich smiled. If he played for real, he would crush these men. He had been playing poker since before they were born. "If you'll excuse me, I have to use the bathroom."

"Of course," Beans said. "Make a right at the end of the

hall."

With his acute hearing, Heinrich heard Big Rube say, "What a sucker."

When Heinrich reached the bathroom, he flipped open his cell phone and dialed a number. "The time is now." He closed the phone and waited in the bathroom, leaning against the sink and stretching his neck. He was hungry, not having fed since Charlie Senerchia's ill-fated stakeout.

He looked at his watch. After a minute passed, he exited the bathroom. The guys at the table were ready for another game, but there would be no more poker tonight.

Someone knocked on the door.

"I'll answer it," Heinrich said in his thick German accent.

"Who the hell's coming over now," Beans said. "I didn't invite no one else."

"I guess we shall see." Heinrich opened the door. "Ah, a friend of mine. You may know him."

Alexei emerged triumphantly into the room.

"What the fuck?" Beans said. He and Big Rube reached for their guns.

In tandem, Alexei and Heinrich leaped at the card players. Heinrich grabbed Big Rube's gun hand and yanked his arm back until it twisted in an unnatural manner. He head butted the big man, causing him to grunt before falling backward. At the other side of the room, Alexei shrieked with laughter as he tore into Beans' throat. Blood spurted out his neck as Alexei took a deep gulp.

"Fucking vampires," Cisero said. "I'll kill every fucking one of yous."

"Settle down, old man," Heinrich said. "You will do nothing but die, so say a prayer to your gods."

Cisero balled his hands into fists and charged. Heinrich admired the old man's futile courage. His death warrant had already been signed. Heinrich did not bother ducking or blocking his punch. He let the old man hit him, then squeezed Cisero's throat. Within seconds, Cisero's face turned blue and his eyes bulged. He threw Cisero to the floor when Big Rube's hulking figure stirred.

He lifted Big Rube by his large legs and slammed him. Big Rube's eyes were glassy as he gasped for breath. Heinrich sunk his fangs into his throat and fed, glancing back to make sure Cisero was still down. He continued to feed, extinguishing the big man's life. After nearly draining Big Rube of blood, he let go of the man.

He walked toward Cisero, who was attempting to rise. "Stay down, old man. It's done for you." He bit Cisero's throat and cringed. "Ugh." He hated the taste of old people's blood. Unlike a fine wine, age sucked the vitality out of blood. After draining Big Rube, he no longer needed to feed. Not wanting to have Cisero suffer any more, Heinrich snapped his neck, killing him quickly.

Alexei toyed with the remaining poker player. He let the man almost escape before blocking his path, making him retreat. The man gave an exasperated cry. He came after Alexei, but the vampire gave a thunderous punch to the stomach that made him double over in agony.

"Finish him," Heinrich said.

"But I'm having so much fun," Alexei said.

"Others might come tonight. Magnus wanted these strikes done quickly with no error."

Alexei rolled his eyes. "Magnus wouldn't know how to have fun in a brothel." He sunk his teeth into the man, whose chilling howl reverberated throughout the apartment. When Alexei finished feeding, he raised his head, blood dripping from his mouth.

"Well done," Heinrich said. "Hopefully this will send a message to our adversaries."

Alexei laughed. "We sent a message. Loud and clear."

"Okay, I'll stop by to check it out," Tony Scrambolgni said.

"Just don't sell the good stuff before I get a chance to look, got it?"

Tony hung up the phone. His guy in Jersey just lifted a jewelry shipment. Tony's wife had been nagging him recently because he hadn't gotten her any jewelry of late. He figured he could pick her a pearl necklace, maybe a fancy one with black pearls.

He could have sworn he just got her jewelry. Maybe he gave it to his girlfriend, Stacy. It was hard to keep track of these things. He needed a secretary, maybe a hot blonde.

Fortunately Beans' poker game had been a success. Hopefully the same held true for the one in Kensington. A few weeks ago they had problems when a group of Spics tried to crash the party. His boys took care of them, so he didn't anticipate any more problems.

Tony made a left on Allegheny as the elevated train thundered overhead. A few blocks later, he made another left and searched for a parking spot. Oddly enough he had no problem finding one. Usually he had to bust his left nut to find a spot.

He walked to the apartment, rang the bell and waited. *Quiet night.* He rang the doorbell again. Still no answer. With growing impatience, he twisted the doorknob. His brows rose when it turned. Dino Marrone wasn't sloppy enough to leave the doors open.

Tony climbed the steps and stopped suddenly. The front door to the apartment was ajar. He took out his Magnum. Something wasn't right.

He peaked inside, but couldn't see anything. He opened the door and gasped. The apartment was a slaughterhouse.

"Motherfucker," Tony said.

The poker table was on its side, and three dead bodies littered the floor. With his gun held high, he searched the kitchen and found another body.

"Son of a bitch." He ran out of the kitchen and into one of the bedrooms. All three hundred and twenty pounds of

Dino Marrone was lying dead on the mattress.

His upper lip flared. Yeah, they had gained victories against these vampires, but at what price? This shit had gotten out of hand.

For a moment, he contemplated calling Beans at the other poker game across town, but he had a feeling that also went bad. Instead he dialed Enzo's number. The boss wasn't going to like this one bit.

Chapter XXXVII

When Magnus showed up at Sophie's door earlier that evening, she asked, "How could you?"

Magnus stepped inside. She slapped him hard across the face, but he didn't flinch. She tried to slap him again, but he caught her hand.

"I want this to end. I had to send a powerful message to your boss and Mark Andrews that the path they were taking would lead to their demise. You can't fight us. There's a reason why I have been alive for over a thousand years."

Sophie turned away. He was right. If anything would deter Enzo, it was a battle he could not win. "You have some kind of nerve showing up here."

"What happened has nothing to do with us. I care about you. Nothing will change that."

Sophie glared at him. It was no use. Looking at Magnus made her lose the rational side of her mind. Seconds later, without realizing it, she found herself in his embrace. She had never felt like this before. Around Magnus, she was like a weak-kneed schoolgirl.

An hour later, Magnus slipped out of her bed. The whole time she was with Magnus, she hadn't thought about the ongoing battle on the streets of Philadelphia. Nothing else mattered when they were together.

She had to convince Enzo to end this war. The end result would be more casualties on each side, and too many had already died.

Hours after Magnus left, Enzo showed up at her door. Normally clean shaven and elegant, he looked like he had just escaped from a Turkish prison. Tony Scrambolgni wore a mean scowl, the veins on his forehead protruding. Special Agent Mark Andrews, who arrived ten minutes later, looked even more disheveled than Enzo.

Enzo sat on her couch and clenched his hand into a tight fist. "Those fucking vampires! I'm gonna kill every last one of them."

Tony Scrambolgni said. "You know, boss, I think it's time to end this. This fighting ain't getting us anywhere."

Sophie's brows rose. She thought she would be the lone voice of dissent against this blood feud. "Tony's right."

Mark Andrews folded his arms and paced around the room. "We're in too deep. I've already lost too many good men. We have to see this through."

Wonderful. The two most powerful voices wanted to continue this war. At least she had an ally in Tony.

"What, I'm supposed to forget about the guys I had to bury, and the promises I made to their families?" Enzo asked. "How could I live with myself?"

Andrews said, "Almost a dozen people have been murdered. I can't just ignore that. It's my duty to bring down these vampires."

"Believe me, I'm all for killing those sons of bitches." Tony loosened his tie. "But what if we can't win?" He eyed Special Agent Andrews. "Plus business is suffering. Our people are spooked with all this vampire shit going around."

Sophie couldn't bear seeing any more people getting killed. Even worse, what if they killed Magnus? As much as she didn't want it to happen, she had fallen deeply for the vampire. "Maybe there's a way we can end this war."

All eyes in the room stared at Sophie.

Enzo lit a cigarette. "What are you talking about?"

Sophie said nothing.

"Would you care to elaborate?" Enzo asked.

"If you got any good suggestions, we'd like to hear it," Tony said.

Andrews crossed his arms. "I'm all ears."

Sophie walked to the living room window and stared into the deep night. "We've tried hunting them. That hasn't worked. We've tried fighting them. No good either. What we haven't done is negotiate with them."

Enzo put his cigarette in an ashtray and laughed. "Now that's a good one. You want to negotiate with the fucking vampires. Are you high?"

"No," Sophie said, her voice calm. "This might be the only way out."

Tony shook his head. "You can't negotiate with fucking vampires."

"Before they became vampires, they were people, just like us. We can work this out with them."

Andrews leaned against Sophie's kitchen table. "That's going to be a tough sell, negotiating with vampires."

After Enzo finished his cigarette, he immediately lit another. "This is silly. What would we say to them? Hey, I don't think you should be killing anyone. They're vampires, for Christ's sakes. Even if we wanted to, how in the world would we get a fucking sit-down with them? It's not like I can look them up in the directory and call 'em."

Sophie took a deep breath. "I can arrange it."

The three men stared at her. No one said a word. It was as if a balloon had just been deflated.

Enzo's eyes bore into her. "What the hell are you talking about?"

"I've established contact with the vampire Magnus." She wasn't about to tell him about their affair. "Just like me, he wants to end this."

Enzo got up from the table, waving his hands. His face turned red. "Why the fuck didn't you say something before? I can't believe you've been meeting with this goddamn vampire while this shit's been going on and you haven't said anything."

"I was waiting for the right time. What good would it have done to come to you with this information a few days ago, when there was no chance in hell you would talk to them? Things have changed."

"After they massacred our people? You think I'm going to let that go?"

Tony put his hand on Enzo's shoulders. "It ain't about what happened in the past. It's about what's going to happen in the future. If we keep this up, more of us are going to get clipped, and business will go in the shitter. I'm all for a sit-down with this Magnus."

Enzo stared at Special Agent Andrews as if trying to get a life line.

Andrews sighed. "It can't hurt. If it doesn't work, we can still hunt these bastards down."

Sophie felt a rush of relief. That only left Enzo. She had never known him to be mule-stubborn despite his Italian heritage.

Enzo crushed his cigarette into the ashtray. "Fine. If everyone wants to talk to them, we'll have a sit-down with the fucking vampires." He glared at Sophie. "Since you're so chummy with Magnus, why don't you make the arrangements."

"Enzo, this is for the best."

Enzo gave her a look that showed complete disappointment in her before he left with Tony.

She started to walk after him, but stopped and watched them leave. Loyalty was so paramount to him. He had to see this as a personal stab against him. The last thing she wanted was a rift in their relationship. After they settled things with the vampires, she would work to regain his trust.

She turned around, not realizing Andrews was still there.

He sat on a chair, a sly grin on his face. "Looks like your boss isn't happy about you moonlighting with vampires."

Sophie wanted to say something, but couldn't. She felt

defeated.

"Personally, I don't care. I just want to solve this vampire problem." Andrews got up from his chair. "Well, the next couple days should be interesting. If I were you, I wouldn't be cozying up to the vampires like that. Last time I checked, they bite. Have a nice evening, Sophie." He tipped his hat and left her house.

Alexei had felt like a caged animal for the past day, stuck inside the warehouse in Camden. It was hardly the Ritz Carleton. He wanted to go out and roam the city streets. His boredom had become tangible.

He sat next to his plaything Nora Brooks. She was so weak and pathetic since he turned her into a creature of the night, always trying to cling to him like an appendage. Fortunately, others in the house were teaching her what she needed to know. Gabriella had been especially useful in mentoring Nora.

Kristoff walked across the room and gave both him and Nora an icy stare. The kid was just like Magnus.

Nora frowned, her lips pouting. "Why does Kristoff hate me?"

Alexei stroked her hair. "He doesn't hate you. He despises me and takes it out on you because of your association with me."

Nora crossed her arms. "That's not fair. Why doesn't he like you?"

Alexei waved his hand. "Who can tell with kids today? Things used to be much simpler. The modern age has complicated matters."

Charlie Senerchia entered the room followed by Magdalena. Alexei still found it unsettling that a member of the opposing team shared their quarters. If he sensed betrayal from Senerchia, he would kill him without thinking about it. To hell with the rest of them. In the mean time, Senerchia could be useful.

Senerchia waved. "Hey, Alexei, my man. I got that Sling Box you asked for in the trunk of my car."

Alexei smiled. Since relocating, Magnus' lockdown mandate necessitated that he ask Senerchia to shop for him. "Well done."

"I can also get you a sweet deal on a new Iphone," Senerchia said. "Real sweet deal."

"Good. We'll talk later."

Alexei stretched out. He thoroughly enjoyed killing those fools at the poker game the other day. He looked forward to another fight. Even Magnus couldn't deny him that.

Chapter XXXVIII

"We'll be there." Magnus smiled as he clicked off his cell phone.

Magnus jumped when he saw Gabriella standing next to him.

Gabriella's face was impassive as she stared at him.

"That was Sophie."

She sat and leaned back, her long dark hair flowing behind the chair. "I could tell by your tone of voice."

Although Magnus was fond of Sophie, she would never equal Gabriella. Nobody could. Gabriella was unique, sexy and tantalizing to his senses.

"My girl came through. She set up a meeting. Now we can settle this once and for all."

Gabriella slid closer to him. "Who will be there?"

"Salerno and Andrews will be there, so I insisted on bringing you."

Gabriella's brows rose. "Me?"

"Of course, you. Who else would I choose?"

"And what do you plan to accomplish with this summit of yours?"

"One way or the other, this has to end. These mortals have distinct advantages over us, and it will only be a matter of time before they kill us. We need a truce."

"And if they don't agree?" Gabriella asked.

"Then it will be war."

Gabriella smiled. "Even with your precious Sophie?"

"I intend on keeping her out of the crossfire. She will be the guiding voice to lead their side to the right decision."

"You're putting much faith in Sophie Koch. I hope she's everything you claim her to be, for all of our sakes."

"She is," Magnus said.

Gabriella looked unimpressed.

"Do I detect jealousy?"

"Don't you think I'm past that? If I got jealous of everyone who entered your life, I would be a wreck. I'm just concerned because the stakes are so high. We can't afford any errors in judgment."

"We won't have any. Now let's formulate our plan."

Mark sat in the passenger side of Enzo's Lexus SUV. He drank five cups of coffee today, but had eaten nothing. He doubted he could hold anything down. His stomach had been cramping since last night, and he had vomited twice.

"What if this is all a big setup to take us out?" Mark asked.

Mark couldn't stop thinking about how things went down the day they attacked the vampires. Salerno may have killed a few vampires, but Alexei and Magnus had routed them. And that had happened during the daytime.

Salerno shrugged. "Hey, I wasn't the one who wanted this. The rest of you were all gung ho about negotiating with the vampires. I got my guys waiting nearby. If something funny happens, they swarm in."

Mark nodded. "I have agents ready as well. I hope this meeting is legit. Even with backup, if they turn on us, we're dead."

Salerno nodded. "Seeing all these people die lately has reminded me about my own mortality. I don't know how this is going to turn out, but we have to finish this. I don't want my wife and kids to have this hanging over their heads."

"So far, they haven't gone after our families, but it's a

chance I don't want to take."

They drove in silence as the sun set.

"Tell me about this place?" Mark asked.

"La Spagnola's. Great Italian food. An associate of mine owns it. We'll have the entire downstairs to ourselves. There's no downstairs exit. The vampires would have to bust through the restaurant to get inside and my people have all the entrances covered."

Mark's stomach growled. "What about the wait staff? Will they be nearby?"

Salerno shook his head. "There'll be coffee and cannolis waiting for us. The waiters have been instructed not to go downstairs."

They neared their destination.

Mark took a deep breath. "God, I hope this works."

"You and me both."

Magnus walked hand in hand with Gabriella as they entered the restaurant. He carefully observed their surroundings. As far as he knew, no one had followed them.

A man with curly dark hair and a brown sweater vest greeted them. "Welcome to La Spagnola's. Would you care for smoking or non-smoking?"

Magnus smiled. "I am here to see a friend of a friend." Sophie instructed him to say that upon entering the restaurant.

The man met his smile. "Very well. Follow me."

They entered the main lobby and went down a set of stairs. The man opened the door, gave a slight bow and exited. Enzo Salerno and Mark Andrews sat at a table. Salerno was stoned faced. Andrews looked ready to combust.

Gabriella fluttered to the table. "It's a pleasure to meet you, gentlemen." She extended her hand. Magnus could tell they were taken aback that he brought her to this meeting.

No doubt they expected Alexei.

Salerno stood and shook her hand, but said nothing.

Andrews also shook her hand. "Thank you for coming."

Magnus pulled out a chair for Gabriella and then sat opposite Salerno. "You know who I am. This is Gabriella. I want to first say that I have a great deal of respect for each of you. I respect the way you run your organizations and the courage you showed when you attacked us. I wish all of this had never taken place. Things happened which caused you to react, which in turn caused us to counter, and so on and so forth. The way I see it, we are at a stalemate. This path will result in many deaths among our respective groups."

Magnus stopped talking. Neither man seemed impressed by his spiel.

Andrews spoke in a low voice. "You've broken the law. I'm here to enforce the law. You can spin it any way you want, but I have to arrest or eliminate you."

"And you just piss me off," Salerno said. "The thought of you vampires breathing the same air as I do repulses me. You should be fucking dead. Your time has passed."

Magnus let Gabriella speak since she was impossible to dislike.

"I realize you don't care for our kind," Gabriella said. "You aren't the first to hate what you don't understand. I assure you that we're not evil. Like you, we are trying to survive."

Andrews chewed his cannoli. "That's all well and good. You might have the best motives in the world, but that still doesn't change the fact that you're killing people."

Gabriella gazed into his eyes. "Unfortunately, that can happen when we feed."

Andrews shrugged. "Then we have a problem. I can't let you go around killing."

"You picked the wrong city and the wrong group of people to fuck with," Salerno said. "I don't back down from a fight. I got resources which I can use to eradicate you, no matter how long it takes."

Magnus put his hands on the table and gazed into Enzo's eyes. "That would not be wise. Even if you kill my brood, there are more of my kind from around the world who would seek retribution. This is a path to disaster. I do not want to fight you. I propose a truce. My brood will move from this area. In the meantime, we will stay invisible. You won't see or hear us."

Andrews' face tightened. "You still have to feed."

Gabriella gave a heart-warming smile. "I can assure you we will do that in the most discreet way possible. We older vampires can control our feeding habits. Unfortunately that is not often the case with our younglings. All the same, they can feed on less visible members of society."

"What?" Andrews asked. "They don't count? People are still people."

"Look, neither party will get exactly what they want," Magnus said. "I'm sure you are no stranger to negotiation. We would like to stay, but we are willing to leave to end this blood feud. In return, we still need nourishment to survive."

Salerno shook his head. "This is too much to forget about."

The mobster's tone and stance were not as rigid as they had been earlier, and Andrews' eyes suggested he wanted this to be over.

Magnus folded his hands. "Perhaps I can sweeten the pot. This is a negotiation after all. Mr. Andrews, I am offering to deliver to you dead or alive one of your most wanted criminals. Perhaps this person can be blamed for the deaths of your agents who died. Maybe a major arms or drug dealer. Someone that you can't get to, but I could. As for you, Mr. Salerno, perhaps I can eliminate a business rival of yours. Of course, this would have to be someone dealing in highly illegal activities so that Mr. Andrews does not object too strenuously."

"Think about it," Gabriella said. "This solution could

work for everyone. We will leave and you will get something of value in return."

"All right," Salerno said. "We'll think about it. Let's meet back at midnight. The restaurant will be closed, but the owner will let you in."

Enzo opened another pack of cigarettes. He wanted to quit, but with all the tension, he needed a release. He lit his cigarette and took a deep drag. "You know, the more I think about it, maybe I can live with them just going away. If they leave, we won't have to deal with those sons of bitches anymore. And it's not like we didn't take down some of their own. I can get back to business and still save face because we got rid of the vampires. Still, I have to do something to make it right for my guys that got killed."

Andrews sat back in his chair. He just polished off a rich dinner and dessert. "The offer is tempting. There are a couple of people we've been after. If Magnus could really deliver that, then it might make things better."

Enzo frowned. "I'm not so sure, considering I'm one of the people you've been after."

"Still, I don't know if I can live with it. For one thing, I'll have agents down with nothing to show for it. If they leave, they might not kill anyone in this area, but they're still going to kill people wherever they go."

Enzo waved his hand. "It won't be your problem. You can't police the whole world. Worry about what's in front of you. And you're right, they'll continue feeding, but they've been doing that for thousands of years. You just never knew about it. Unless you want to go public and declare a war against vampires, it'll continue. I'm assuming you don't want to go public."

Andrews shook his head. "People won't believe this story. We don't even have the bodies of those vampires that we killed. They friggin' disintegrated within minutes. With the vampires hiding in shadows, it will be hard to prove."

"So where does that leave you?"

Andrews gritted his teeth. "I have a duty to do something."

"Fuck your duty. We can't fix this vampire problem. We fought a good fight, but it's time to let go."

"I don't know."

Enzo waved his index finger. "I have an idea in addition to what Magnus offered that might give us payback."

On the way to La Spangnola's, Gabriella had a playful smile. "Will they bite?"

Magnus smiled. "I don't know. We're dealing with hard-headed individuals. The gangster has an unbending thirst for revenge, and the FBI man has a moral conscience that gets in the way of good decision making."

"We may be walking into a trap. You should have suggested a neutral place."

Magnus shrugged. "We might be dealing with thieves, but I sense honor among them. Plus, Sophie assured me they wouldn't try any such thing."

"Ah yes, your precious Sophie. I think she has a greater loyalty to her boss than to you."

Magnus stopped walking. "Not a chance."

"What makes you so sure?"

"I just am. Would you like to wager that she has more loyalty to me than to Salerno?"

Gabriella tilted her head. "A friendly wager?"

"Of course."

"Why not? She has to do something to prove she places you ahead of Enzo."

They walked hand in hand to the restaurant.

The owner of the restaurant waited at the entrance. With a

smile on his face, he unlocked the front door and let them inside. "Downstairs, please." He led them to their meeting spot with Salerno and Andrews.

Magnus pulled out a chair for Gabriella. "I take it you have had enough time to contemplate our proposal."

Andrews cleared his throat. "We'll accept it if a few conditions are met."

Magnus nodded. He figured they would want to negotiate terms.

"Yeah, you see, what you guys did requires payback," Salerno said. "You can't get off the hook that easy. Both of us realize that not all of your brood were responsible for this."

"But there was one vampire who started the chain of events resulting in the deaths of four FBI agents and a number of Mr. Salerno's associates," Andrews said.

"And we want him dead," Salerno said.

Magnus felt Gabriella tense next to him.

Gabriella leaned forward. "How can you expect us to give him up?"

Magnus put his hand on hers. "That's a lot to ask."

"Hey, we didn't start this clusterfuck," Salerno said.

Magnus stared into Gabriella's eyes, trying to calm her. "Is that all?"

Salerno leaned in so he was face to face with Magnus. "No. Stay the fuck away from Sophie. Whatever fucking spell you put her under, I want that shit to end."

Magnus didn't back away. "She's not under any spell. She's a rational, intelligent woman. She is more than capable of making decisions for herself."

"Back the fuck away from her."

"She can do whatever she chooses. You don't own her."

For a moment, Magnus thought Salerno was going to lunge at him. That would not have made for a productive negotiation session. Magnus stood. "We will consider your requests. Any future communications will take place through

Ms. Koch. It was good meeting you."

Chapter XXXIX

Magnus and Gabriella walked hand in hand in the warm night air.

"This decision will have significant ramifications," Magnus said.

"I know," Gabriella said.

"They're asking for a lot."

Gabriella bit her lip. "Too much. How can we give them one of our own?"

"We're in a difficult spot. If they don't agree to a truce, more will die. Before long they will find us and attack with greater numbers and firepower. They know how to kill us. Those wooden bullets are ingenious. A full out attack may decimate us."

Gabriella faced Magnus. "Don't let your feelings about Alexei influence you."

"I may not like him, but he's one of us. Regardless, we must consider this offer."

Gabriella sighed. "We should consult the others."

Magnus shook his head. "As the leader of this brood, it's my responsibility to make these decisions. We must decide our collective fate."

Gabriella looked forlorn in the moonlight. "It's not a decision I want to make."

Alexei was in the process of downloading songs onto the

iPhone Charlie Senerchia gave him when a knock on the door interrupted him. Magnus and Gabriella stood at the entranceway. This was no social call.

Nora Brooks continued to massage his back. She was like a faithful pet, always at his side. The situation had become tedious. He encouraged her to interact with the others just so he didn't have to be near her.

Alexei smiled. "How did your meeting with the society of thugs go?"

Magnus sighed. "They won't agree to a truce unless we meet their demands."

"And if we don't meet their demands, then we will be at war with them," Gabriella said. "We have no choice but to stand and fight."

Alexei tilted his head back. "Nora, please give us a moment."

She left the room.

"I could have left a while ago, but I chose to stick around because we are family. We must never forget that we are superior. In order to remain at the top of the food chain, we must work together." Alexei figured those words would sit well with Magnus. Eventually, he would either find a new home or kill the elder vampire, but for now, he had to play along with Magnus.

"We need to launch a singular decisive strike," Magnus said.

Alexei shook his head. "Impractical. There are too many of them. We must attack with surgical strikes like the other night at the poker games."

Gabriella sat in the empty chair next to Alexei. "Not necessarily. We have come across some information that may help our cause."

"I've befriended one of Enzo Salerno's closest associates, and I have learned from her that our enemies are having a strategy session. I believe they're calling it a war council. This will be our opportunity."

Alexei smiled. "Magnus, you sly devil, sleeping with the enemy. I didn't think you were that deceitful. Well, this changes things."

"There's one problem," Magnus said.

"What's that?"

"This war council is tomorrow afternoon."

Alexei put his hand on Magnus' shoulder. "So, it will be just the two of us."

"The odds will be long. We will be weaker during the day, and their numbers will be greater. However, we'll have the element of surprise."

Alexei nodded. "As I recall, the last time we routed them. The only problem was that one of their members escaped like a thief in the night and killed some of our brood. That won't happen since we will be on their turf. I'm fully capable of carrying out this mission. The only question is, are you?"

They stood face to face, Magnus' drilling holes into him with his eyes. "I will do my part. So, we're in agreement?"

Alexei nodded.

"Good. Here's the plan … "

Alexei sat in the back of the truck. He had to admit, Magnus devised a well thought out plan. Last night, Charlie Senerchia informed Enzo Salerno that the vampires had captured him, but he had managed to escape. Charlie was to meet him and tell them where the vampires were located.

Alexei listened in on the conversation. The mob boss appeared to have bought Senerchia's story, even telling him the location of the war council.

Just past noon, when all of the other vampires were sound asleep, he and Magnus got in the back of the truck, and Charlie drove. Charlie would be driving the truck inside of a large warehouse, so he and Magnus would never see the sunlight. He felt a surge of excitement. This mission would be dangerous. He might not make it out alive.

He only wished he had a better companion. Magnus had a dour look on his face. The elder vampire didn't understand what it meant to live. Sure, he survived all these years, but did he truly live?

Today, he would prove his superiority to Magnus. By the end of the day, nobody would doubt that he should lead the brood.

Alexei gazed at Magnus, who had a far away look. "How many do you expect?"

"At least thirty. As many as fifty. Most importantly, all of the top members of their organization will be there."

"Things could get dicey if they're armed."

Magnus shrugged. "If so, it will be with conventional weapons. They have no reason to think we will appear, so they shouldn't have any stakes or wooden bullets."

Alexei nodded. "Good. What about the FBI?"

Magnus shook his head. "We'll have to take them out separately. After this show of force, he may stop pursuing us. I've already made arrangements with friends in Argentina. By the end of the month, we will be gone."

Alexei smiled. "Argentina? I haven't been there since the First World War."

Magnus' radio chirped. "We're just about there," Senerchia said.

Magnus picked up the radio. "Good. Signal us when the time is ready."

"Will do."

They had gone over the plan last night. Senerchia would exit the vehicle and talk to the people. After Senerchia banged on the side of the truck, he and Magnus would jump out and wreak havoc. It would be a blood bath, one he would thoroughly relish.

The truck came to a sudden stop. Muted voices sounded from outside. Even with his acute hearing, Alexei could not decipher the conversation. As many as fifty dangerous humans, according to Magnus' intel. This would be a fight to remember.

A banging sound came from his side of the truck. Senerchia's signal.

"Are you ready, Alexei?"

"I couldn't be more ready."

"We will be inside of a building, so the sunlight won't affect us."

Alexei nodded. "I feel strong. Let's do this."

He opened the door with Magnus behind him. He jumped out of the truck ready to tear apart his victims. Enzo Salerno, Mark Andrews, and a number of others stood in front of him armed with guns and stakes. He turned back at Magnus, whose face remained impassive.

Magnus stepped out of the truck. "You nearly caused our ruination, Alexei. I wish there was another way. We must continue to survive, and therefore you must be sacrificed. In truth, I don't feel bad. You created this mess."

Alexei snarled. "You bastard."

"You must pay for your sins, Alexei."

The Goat sharpened Vasilly's stake. Today, he would get his payback. He had been looking forward to this since he and Alexei first met. Something about him changed that day. Since then, his focus had sharpened to a razor's edge. Before, he had been a small time hood without direction. Too often he was hot headed or lazy, or his drug habit interfered in his decision making. Even his relationship with Karen had been going nowhere. He took her for granted. When this whole mess was over, they would get married and start a family.

Karen stood in the corner of the living room with tears welling in her eyes as he sharpened the stake. "Patrick, you have to promise me you'll return in one piece."

He looked up at her, his face tightening. "Don't worry.

I'm indestructible. I'm fucking bullet proof."

In a way, what happened that night when he confronted Alexei had changed him for the better. Today Enzo was going to give him an opportunity to thank Alexei by extinguishing his life.

Enzo Salerno sat in quiet contemplation staring at the wooden bullet in his hand when Tony Scrambolgni's voice brought him out of his daze. "What did you say?"

"I'll be glad when this shit's finally over. Who'd a thunk we'd be tangling with vampires. Alexei picked the wrong people to fuck with; I can tell you that much."

Enzo nodded.

Unless Magnus backed out of their agreement, he was assured victory today. So why did he feel so hollow?

"We need to cover every angle. We can't let this fucker get away. It might be our only shot. You think Magnus will play ball and give up that pale assed vampire?"

Enzo closed his eyes. "Yeah."

"How can you be so sure?"

"Because it's a suicide mission otherwise. Only he and Alexei can be out during the day, and even so, they will be far from full strength. Magnus wouldn't stand a chance if he double crossed us."

Tony grunted. "Still, we should have the perimeters sealed."

"Andrews has it covered. A dozen feds will be outside just in case."

Enzo lit a cigarette. He knew what troubled him. Sophie. She had always been by his side, as faithful and trustworthy as anyone he ever knew. Her making backdoor deals with the vampire was unthinkable. He was sure she had good intentions, but it still felt like she had stabbed him in the back. In his line of work, he knew people close to him would eventually turn on him, but not Sophie. He trusted her like his wife. Even after this vampire business was resolved, things would never be the same between them.

He would worry about that later. Right now, he had a vampire to kill.

The Goat gripped Vasilly's stake at shoulder height, ready to strike.

Special Agent Mark Andrews pointed his pistol at Alexei's head. "It's over."

The Goat recoiled when Alexei bared his fangs. He couldn't stop thinking about their first confrontation. What if this time Alexei choked him lifeless? This was no time to be chicken shit. If he had a set of balls, he had to prove it now.

Alexei turned to Magnus. "You were always jealous of me. You know I'm superior to you. This is how you settle it? By betraying me? You're a coward. You have no place involving these humans in our fight."

Magnus' face remained calm. "You still don't get it. This has nothing to do with me and you. I can live with your arrogance and insolence. What you have done has endangered us. I have to look out for my brood. Even if you left, your actions would continue to endanger our kind. Your time in this world is over, Alexei."

Alexei glared at him in defiance. "I won't go down without a fight."

"I wouldn't expect you to." Magnus motioned with his fingertips for Alexei to come forward. "Let's dance."

Alexei lunged at Magnus and knocked the vampire off his feet. From the ground Magnus connected with the heel of his foot to Alexei's jaw, causing him to fly back.

Magnus jumped high in the air and landed in front of Alexei. He lifted Alexei by his throat. Gasping for breath, Alexei smashed his right arm, breaking his grip. He then kicked Magnus in the chest.

The Goat watched in awe as the two vampires went back and forth. This wasn't part of the plan. Magnus was supposed to hand the vampire over to Enzo, and they would finish him.

Magnus charged at Alexei, who met him with a barrage of punches to the face. Alexei picked him up and slammed him hard.

For a second, The Goat thought Magnus was done. He was about to attack Alexei when Enzo pulled him back. After a few seconds, Magnus got back to his feet. Didn't these vampires feel any pain?

They continued to brawl. Alexei had the momentum, displaying amazing agility, always beating Magnus to the punch, until he charged at Magnus with his head down. Magnus landed a knee to Alexei's face, and he fell to the floor with a thud. The Goat winced as Magnus pounded Alexei's head on the floor.

Magnus dragged him across the room to the door that led outside. The Goat and the others followed.

"Finish him," Magnus said.

Enzo opened the door, and Magnus tossed Alexei outside. The vampire howled, his face contorting from exposure to the sunlight. He flailed his arms and legs.

Magnus slumped to the floor and shut his eyes.

The Goat stepped outside and looked to the sky. There was not a cloud to be found.

Andrews pulled out his pistol with the ash bullets and shot Alexei in the chest.

Alexei wailed an inhuman shriek.

Enzo was about to move forward when The Goat grabbed his arm. "Let me do this."

Enzo nodded.

Tony Scrambolgni stepped on Alexei's thrashing body. The Goat felt a rush of adrenaline unlike anything he had ever experienced. He held the stake with both hands over his head. With full force, he brought it into Alexei's chest.

The vampire squealed then whimpered. The thrashing slowed until he stopped all together.

"Should I do it again?" The Goat asked.

"No," Enzo said. "He's dead."

The Goat turned toward Magnus, who was still on the ground. The vampire was completely vulnerable. This was his chance to take him out as well. He advanced on him, his stake at the ready.

Enzo grabbed his arm and pulled him back. "No. Leave him be. A deal's a deal."

The Goat glared at Enzo. He was a fucking vampire. He didn't deserve to live. He shouted at the vampire. "This ain't over between us, Magnus. Your kind don't belong in our world."

Chapter XL

The truck came to a stop, which meant they were back in Camden. A few seconds later, Senerchia opened the door. He climbed inside and pulled Magnus to his feet.

"You look like hell, boss."

Magnus closed his eyes. He didn't have enough strength to stand. "I feel worse."

Senerchia whistled. "That was a brutal fight. Man oh man. You two beat the shit out of each other. I didn't realize you hated him so much."

"It's not about hate. I had to do what was necessary."

Senerchia helped Magnus out of the truck. He didn't want to have to depend on a human to get around, but he had no other option.

"Hey, boss, I know Enzo Salerno said I can come back, but I ain't buying it. They'll put a bullet in my head before I blink."

"You're welcome to stay with us. You've proven your loyalty, and we owe you a debt of gratitude, although I'm sure your true motive lies with being near Magdalena."

"Well, there is that. I ain't sure I wanna become one of yous, but I can help you out, you know, being able to stay out in the daytime and all."

"I'm sure we can find a use for you."

Senerchia helped Magnus climb the stairs and led him to his room. Even with the escort, the exertion was almost too much to bear.

"If you need anything, I'll be around."

"Thank you," Magnus said.

Magnus opened the door to his room and stepped back when he found Gabriella waiting for him. She looked pale and weak. This was the first time she had ever been up in the daytime, and it was clearly taking a toll on her body.

"You should be sleeping," Magnus said, his voice harsher than he intended.

In a frail voice, she said, "I had to find out what happened."

Magnus sat on his bed. "It's done."

Gabriella nodded, tears streaming down her face. "Why did this have to happen? Couldn't we have avoided all of this death?" She leaned her head against Magnus' chest.

Magnus kissed her softly. "It pains me as well. I didn't want Alexei to die. But times have changed, and we must adapt to survive. We must live in shadows. Alexei wasn't willing to do that. His time on this world was limited. You know that. This was for the good of the brood. Now, we both need rest."

It was near midnight on the evening they killed Alexei. Enzo found himself in the odd position of having FBI special agent Mark Andrews in his living room. Barring a raid, he never thought that would happen.

"I'm still having a hard time wrapping my head around this blood feud we've had with the vampires. It's crazy. Real life vampires. I guess we won't see any more around here," Andrews said.

"If I never see one for the rest of my life, it will be too soon," Enzo said.

Andrews rubbed his bloodshot eyes. "I wish we could eradicate them."

"Unless you want to get law enforcement from around the

world involved, it ain't gonna happen. Forget about it. Move on with your life."

Andrews grinned. "Now that our vampire problem is over, you're top on my priority list."

Enzo raised his hands. "I'm an honest citizen. I don't know why you harass me. All I do is provide for my family and give people employment."

Andrews rolled his eyes. "Spare me the bullshit." He stood face to face with Enzo. "Make no mistake, I'm going to bring you down. You'll slip, and I'll be there to cast a net around you. We nailed your predecessors. You may be smarter and more elusive than them, but you'll go down just the same."

Enzo extended his hand. "Regardless, it was good working with you."

Andrews shook his hand before leaving.

Enzo filled his glass with cognac. He had not slept much lately, but was too wired to sleep.

After entering his office, he shut down his computer. Maybe he would watch something mindless on the dish before joining Gina in bed. He turned and stopped suddenly, his cognac flying and landing on the carpet. Sophie Koch stood in front of him.

"Holy shit. How did you get inside?" Enzo pursed his lips.

She looked different. Her skin tone was lighter. She looked radiant. She looked like a...

Enzo gritted his teeth. "Sophie, how could you? Did Magnus make you do this? That son of a bitch."

Sophie folded her arms across her chest. "He didn't make me do anything. It was hard for me to come here. I feel so vibrant and alive, but weak all the same. It's like that for us younglings. Despite that, I had to see you."

"How could you?"

"I asked Magnus to turn me."

Enzo buried his face in his palm. "Why would you want to become a fucking vampire? You have to drink people's blood. It's wrong. It's evil."

Sophie stared at him. "I was already leading a life of crime. I've ordered hits, robbed people blind, did all kinds of things I'm sure I will pay for. How is this any worse? You've hardly lived a wholesome life."

Enzo touched her ice cold arm. "Sophie, it's not the same, and you know it. That's business. What you're doing is unnatural. You're begging for eternal damnation."

Sophie shrugged. "That ship has sailed. I regret many things I've done in my life, but not this. Do you know what I regret the most?"

Enzo shook his head, trying not to stare. He couldn't take his eyes off her. She looked amazing. She might be a vampire, but that did not change the fact that she looked drop dead gorgeous.

"The thing I most regret is not telling you how I really feel about you."

Enzo stared at her cold eyes.

"I have loved you for years. I never said anything because I didn't want to ruin your marriage and our relationship. Those concerns are beyond me now. None of that matters when you have immortality on your side.

"I should have taken you up on your offer when you tried to pick me up the first time we met, but even in college, I knew you couldn't live by society's rules." Sophie laughed. "I didn't know then that I would follow in your path. It's not too late to fix past mistakes."

Enzo closed his eyes, the only way he could stop staring at her. "What are you talking about?"

"Join me, Enzo. It's exhilarating. We can be together forever. You know you love me. We were meant to be together. Now is our opportunity. Forever."

Enzo had never felt so claustrophobic. It seemed like he was trapped inside this room. Become a vampire? Sure, Sophie looked fantastic, but could he actually forge a life together with her, walking the night, feasting on blood?

She held his hands. "Let's do it. This is the life we were

meant to live. I love you. I always have. I can bring you back, and one of the others can turn you."

"When did this happen?"

"Last night when Magnus visited me. Be with me. You won't regret it."

"You expect me to abandon Gina, my kids, the empire I've built. You expect me to throw that all away and become a fucking vampire."

Sophie's face was inches from his. "Yes."

He turned away from her. He was many things, most of which weren't good. Being a religious man, he knew what he did in pursuit of building his empire was wrong. But damn it, he wasn't a cold-blooded killer. The people he killed deserved it.

He faced Sophie for the last time. "I don't want to see you ever again. And if we do, we won't be friends."

Sophie disappeared in the blink of an eye.

The Goat walked onto the cold damp earth toward the grave site of Johnny Gunns. Not normally the sentimental type, he had surprised himself by stopping at the floral shop earlier. Taking the flowers he had purchased, he laid them by Johnny's plot.

"We did it, buddy," The Goat said. "I got pay back for you. Staked that vampire right through his black heart." The Goat closed his eyes. "It's not over yet. It would desecrate your memory to let those things live in our world. I won't let your memory die. Enzo might have been satisfied, but I ain't. I'm still going after those vampires, and I'm gonna kill every last one of them."

About the Author

After graduating with a BS degree in Biomedical Engineering from Boston University and later an MBA degree from Lehigh University, Carl Alves worked in the pharmaceutical and medical devices industries.

Carl's debut novel *Two For Eternity* was released in 2011 by Weaving Dreams Publishing. His short fiction has appeared in various publications such as Sinister City, Alien Skin and Behind Locked Doors anthology.

He is a member of the Horror Writers Association and attended the Penn Writers Conference. You can visit his website at www.carlalves.com.

CPSIA information can be obtained at www.ICGtesting.com
Printed in the USA
BVOW011238181112

305795BV00003B/2/P